Inhuman Beings

"Enormously entertaining . . . Raymond Chandler meets Rod Serling."
—*San Francisco Chronicle*

"Plunges into a break-neck . . . roller-coaster ride of pulp thrills [matching] a tough, unbelievably smart and lucky private eye against alien invaders . . . a noir tale that could be called the meeting of Raymond Chandler and H. G. Wells. It has everything including a six-gun–toting president of the United States, a heroic railroad engineer and a literal bang of an ending."
—*Hartford Courant*

"A hard-boiled-private-eye take on *Invasion of the Body Snatchers.* Carroll has the Sam Spade routine down pat as he plays the lone knight against a deadly enemy. With a keen eye for San Francisco and witty dialogue, *Inhuman Beings* is a fun, fast-paced romp."
—*The Denver Post*

"Thoroughly enjoyable. [Carroll] deserves a faithful following."
—*Tampa Tribune*

continued on next page . . .

Top Dog

"A captivating romp that explores the eternal tug between good and evil."   —*Entertainment Weekly*

"If Kafka and Tolkien shared an office on Wall Street, this is the novel they might have written. [Carroll's] tight, colorful prose proves zesty and absorbing. His characters ring oddly true. And his plot has touches of the Tolkienesque irresistibility, that thing that keeps you up past bedtime turning the pages to learn what happens next."   —*San Francisco Chronicle*

"A stylish, funny combination of parable and moral tale . . . Imaginative, seductively written, and a pleasure to read, *Top Dog* is first-rate entertainment."   —Richard North Patterson

"A satirical, tongue-in-cheek, literally shaggy-dog fable."
            —*Hartford Courant*

"The Shaggy Dog meets J.R.R. Tolkien in this entertaining debut effort. The premise is wildly silly and metaphorically transparent, and has absolutely no right to succeed on any level, but Carroll—through a combination of reasonably swift pacing and gruffly funny internal monologues—pulls it off."
            —*Kirkus Reviews*

"A witty, adult, and imaginative fable."
            —Martin Cruz Smith

Dog
Eat
Dog

JERRY JAY CARROLL

ACE BOOKS, NEW YORK

DOG EAT DOG

An Ace Book / published by arrangement with
the author

PRINTING HISTORY
Ace trade paperback edition / February 1999
Ace mass-market edition / June 2000

ISBN: 0-441-00740-6

ACE®
Ace Books are published
by The Berkley Publishing Group,
a division of Penguin Putnam Inc.,
375 Hudson Street, New York, New York 10014.
ACE and the "A" design are trademarks
belonging to Penguin Putnam Inc.

PRINTED IN THE UNITED STATES OF AMERICA

10 9 8 7 6 5 4 3 2 1

To my wife Judy, without whom I'd be a rudderless skiff in the heavy seas.

The point of the football hit me behind the ear and I went down like a sack of doorknobs. It might have done serious harm if Joe Montana hadn't taken something off the ball. The game video we got afterward showed that the ponytailed president of Surveyor Software (1999 sales, $1.2 billion) also nailed me in the head with a bony knee as he jumped over.

That was when the odor hit me. It was a putrid as an arm or leg ready to fall off from gangrene. The sound of running feet chasing me. I felt the hard fear in my throat again. They were tireless and brave in their own way. Their stupidity was the only reason I had given them the slip over and over. That and luck.

"That's it for me. I don't care how worthy the cause is," Michael Brandywine said. His voice seemed to come from far off as we lay on the grass. The running sound and the sickening smell were gone as quickly as they had come. He sat up and rubbed his knee.

Montana trotted up. His big nose and famous dimpled chin hung over me, a celebrity face as familiar a decade before as the moon. "You were supposed to turn and come back to the ball," he told me. The Super Bowl ring they asked him to wear to wow us looked as big as a fruit bowl. "You all right?"

"Sure," I said. I didn't want Joe to think I was a creampuff.

I got up, waved to show it was nothing, and trotted to the sidelines to a patter of applause. The CEO of Destiny Systems ran grinning onto the field to substitute for me. There was no shortage of Silicon Valley tycoons hoping to catch a pass from the Hall of Fame quarterback for their memoirs. Half a million was in the kitty for a new multipurpose complex at the Portola Valley elementary school. That included my check for twenty-five grand.

Ben Cramer, a world-famous neurosurgeon, came up to me. "How many fingers do you see?"

"Three," I answered.

"I'm showing four. Somebody call nine-one-one."

"Very funny."

"You poor baby." Cleo Basich made a moue of sympathy.

A half dozen other peppy women in their thirties, dressed like her in perky cheerleading outfits, agreed it was too bad. They did high kicks and swished pom-poms as Brandywine limped off the field. He flashed them a brave smile.

Rich men used to avoid physical exercise and eat like horses. Look at pictures from the past and you see how they flaunted corpulence. It showed the world they could afford a French chef. Skinny meant you worked from dawn to dusk in some satanic mill to feed the family. Things got reversed in just one generation. The rich are lean, and the poor carry around big butts and potbellies, thanks to KFC and Big Macs with fries.

Cleo was the wife of a big shot who bankrolled start-up companies. She organized this flag football game we paid major bucks to play in. The old W. B. (Bogey) Ingersol, a proud throwback to the well-upholstered robber barons, would have recoiled with a sneer if invited. He is me. Or was. I have pretty much reformed myself, but I still had enough of the old Bogey that I could admire his kind of crude honesty.

I watched the shapely Cleo bounce and kick high like a teenager. I didn't really wish her ill. A pulled hamstring would be sufficient. I had been drinking coffee on the veranda when she cantered across the immaculate lawn on her glossy chestnut. Its hooves tossed divots in high arcs. I moved to Woodside, buying the Hensen estate after departing Wall Street under my famous cloud of scandal. People in New York said California was my Elba.

"Elwood Hensen used to let us play polo here," Cleo said, dismounting.

I looked at their path across the lawn. "Resodding must have run into serious money."

She took off her helmet and shook her dark curls. She wore tan corduroy jodhpurs and a blue windbreaker with her riding boots. "I smell coffee."

"You want some?"

"It's rude to force one to hint." She looked around. "You've done wonders."

"It's the new paint job."

"The Hensens let Millwood run down. They were always in Europe." She looked around. "These colors give it a kind of Mediterranean flavor."

Millwood is the name of the estate. I got it for a little over six million. I find that a place generally costs more when it comes with a name.

"We have quite a close-knit little community here," she said after Havl brought coffee and the two of us had discussed the weather long enough. She smacked a boot with her riding crop. "Everybody pitches in."

Cleo Basich had good looks to go with that nice figure. Bossy and energy to burn. She got things done. When I first moved into the neighborhood, she and her husband threw a cocktail party for me. I heard later she had to do some serious arm-twisting to get people to come.

So, to repay her, I agreed when she asked me to play flag football to raise money for the local public school. "I put you down for the limit, of course," she chirped. No good deed goes unpunished. The old me held that as an article of faith, and the new me sees no reason to disagree. A paramedic gave me ice for my goose egg.

"What happened?" Winston Byron asked. He was sixtyish and comes from the Battle Creek cereal people. He was dressed in tennis whites. Never worked a day in his life. He told you so with pride. That did not go over too well with the super-achievers who lived around here. It made him as much of an outcast as I was.

"Joe got the pass pattern wrong," I told him. Bogey never told the truth when a lie would do. Old habits die hard.

"And to think the man won four Super Bowls," Byron said.

We watched them play. It was a beautiful warm day with one or two downy clouds in a high late-summer sky. I notice details like that now. Nature didn't matter when I was a kingpin in the business world. There was no time to look up, let alone smell the roses. I plowed through life, throwing up wake. Smaller boats got swamped if they didn't take evasive action.

The committee in charge of decorating the park had put up gay red-and-yellow tents with flags and bunting. Caterers were barbecuing sides of beef and chickens marinated in a Thai sauce. A small carnival with rides kept the little kids busy as their nannies gossiped. A banjo band in straw hats and blazers began to plunk. The printed program threatened a barbershop quartet later.

Montana lived in the neighborhood, which explained his presence. He quarterbacked for both sides to keep things equal. Everyone on the field was the high-powered sort used to winning. They threw themselves into the game as if the future of their companies rode on the outcome. They hustled and dove for balls, showing Joe how much heart they had. They wore game faces and yelled, "Way to hustle!" Bogey would have been sickened.

They were all fit, that being one of the valley's ruling obsessions. Every executive worth his compensation package had a personal trainer. They walked on treadmills while doing three other things so that every moment was crammed to the fullest.

"I suppose most of these people send their children to private schools," Byron said. "It's nice they put themselves out like this, don't you think?"

He had a sly malice and resembled Dean Acheson, who was Harry Truman's secretary of state. Byron brushed up his mustache with the back of a finger. "Debonair" was the word. Cleo said he was drunk and making crank calls most nights by seven, his way of unwinding. Sometimes the police found him reeling down our quiet lanes. He sang Cole Porter in the back of the cruiser as he was driven home.

"And you, Mr. Ingersol," he said. "One has certainly read a lot about you, but I don't recall if you have family." An eyebrow as gray and distinguished as his mustache went up questioningly.

"Not so far." I was in the past, remembering the Pig Faces. Put a few together and you smelled them a mile off.

The old Bogey would not be talking to Byron. He would have cut him dead unless instinct glimpsed a possibility that the old gossip could be put to some use. In that case he would have turned on the charm. The big smile, the arm around the shoulders, the ruddy face bent close.

"Children are very ungrateful," Byron said. "You raise them, give them every advantage, and what happens? They turn against you."

"I'll remember that." I was trying to learn how to suffer fools and the other social graces, but it wasn't coming fast.

"Mine! Mine!" Seagulls shrieked as they fought over a sandwich some kid had thrown on the ground. The fight brought more of them wheeling in, fired with greed. "I want! I want!"

I kept some ability to understand their speech from when I

was a dog, but I had noticed it faded with time. Birds seldom say anything interesting anyhow.

"Someone else has gone down," Byron said, looking on the playing field. Cramer ran from the sideline and kneeled next to a man in shorts and a Harvard sweatshirt who pounded the grass with his fist. "They played horseshoes last year and no one got hurt."

The injured man was named Barlow. He owned a company that built computer workstations. Cramer waved to the paramedics. They ran with a stretcher.

"This is going to take a while," someone told the crowd as he came to the sideline. "It's a compound fracture." Cleo and the other cheerleaders gasped.

It was time for Montana to go, anyhow. He shook hands and said good-bye to people. The rest of us got a wave before he climbed into an expensive sports car and drove off. Somebody said he made a good living signing his name at autograph shows.

"I wonder if they have insurance for accidents," Byron said. "There could be a lawsuit." The possibility seemed to cheer him.

"We all signed releases," I told him.

"It looks like he's in considerable pain, poor fellow."

Bogey would have said "good." Playing flag football at his age—a broken leg served the fool right. "What an asshole," he would say. Brownnosing vice presidents would nod in agreement. Yes, they would say, served him right. I miss them sometimes. At least they were company.

It is not hard looking back to see how I got the reputation I had as a heavy. I was my own worst enemy as far as PR goes. Pictures showed that even my smile seemed predatory. That point came up often on the blue-collar radio talk shows, where I was a regular topic. Not that I cared. My slash-and-burn reputation was an advantage in the takeover game. Company directors shook in their Guccis when they learned Bogey Ingersol was quietly buying up stock. I was as welcome as cholera.

As with fellow sharks such as T. Boone Pickens and Carl Ichan, I looked for underperforming companies with lots of cash in the kitty. That was a blood-in-the-water invitation. It meant the people at the top were dozing at the switch. When I had a big enough stake, I put their companies in play.

They could pay me a fortune in greenmail to go away. Or they could stand and fight. But that was almost always the wrong choice. I didn't lose many of those proxy fights. Junk bonds were hot, and I gave stockholders an offer they couldn't refuse. When I won, I made out like a bandit by downsizing and spinning off company assets. *Mother Jones* magazine put me on a cover the year twelve thousand people lost jobs after a couple of my textbook takeovers. The headline said, "The Meanest Man on Wall Street." They put a Simon Legree mustache on me in the photo.

I laughed all the way to the bank. My shareholders voted me a ninety-three-million-dollar bonus on that deal, and Wall Street bowed down before me. When blowhards in Congress sounded off, my public relations machine planted stories in the press saying I helped keep the country competitive. "America Needs to Be Strong," the headline over one said. I was shown standing Patton-like in front of a huge American flag.

For my sins, I was turned into a dog.

That is not quite the truth. It was a mistake that happened, and I got thrown into another world or dimension, whatever you want to call it. The individual responsible for that had someone else in mind, but my fame put me in the line of fire. I cheated death a dozen times and nearly didn't make it back.

It is a long story.

The tabloids, to return to my point, made me their target during my *High Noon* of fame on Wall Street. Even now, photographers sprang from ambush with shutters clicking. They hoped to peddle a picture to the *National Enquirer* despite the fall-off in public interest. I had become yesterday's news.

"Shall we stroll to the picnic?" Byron asked. "Might as well eat lunch. I paid dearly for it, and I suppose you did, too. The Black Angus people donated the beef, so the steaks will be good."

"I don't eat much meat."

"I wouldn't have thought it."

I knew what he meant. I was strictly a red-meat guy before. There was nothing I liked better than a two-pound slab of rare roast beef on my plate with a baked potato and sour cream. A good cigar and cognac swirled in a warmed snifter afterward to release its fumes. That was living. But when you have to chase down prey, rip out its throat, and snatch a few mouthfuls of hot flesh before some more powerful carnivore shows up, believe me, you lose your taste for meat.

Byron turned to look up at me as we walked. I weighed sixty pounds more before the spell or coma, however you want to look at it. It was soft flab hidden by expensive tailoring, but the bulk made me appear more intimidating. This was an advantage entering a boardroom filled with hostile strangers at the head of my wedge of dishonest accountants and lawyers.

"That's quite a knot above your eye," Byron said. "It makes you look like a prizefighter."

I decided to pass on lunch. I politely excused myself and walked to my dusty pickup. It didn't look like it belonged with the Jaguars and Lotuses of the young crowd or the Mercedes and Lincoln Town Cars the older neighbors favored. The pickup bed carried pansies, marigolds, and petunias I bought at Orchard Hardware. Millwood was big enough to need a couple of full-time gardeners, but I also puttered around. I had a lot of time on my hands.

When I drove through the gates up the drive, the dogs came running. Thoroughbreds and mongrels, longhair and shorthair, all colors and shapes. They ran baying and barking. The high-pitched yapping was from the toy dogs. If there was a greyhound on the premises, it got there first. The lapdogs arrived last, wheezing and panting. Since my own days as a dog, I had a soft spot for them. Word of this got out, and people dropped off their unwanted pooches at night. Havl or a gardener found them tied to the front gate with notes on their collars.

Others got reprieves from the death chamber at the animal shelter. I would have been overrun with dogs if I didn't have agents offering bribes for people to take them in. Two hundred bucks usually did it in the small towns. Give a dog a choice and it will pick a small town to live in anyhow. More room to run, and the smells are better.

I stopped the pickup as they swept up like a wave. I got out and they swirled around my legs, glad the squire was back. Each thought I had ears only for him. So they all yammered at the top of their lungs.

"Where've you been, master?"

"My tail wags."

"Take me for a walk!"

"Throw me a ball!"

"Pick me up!" This from a pug used to pampering. She was indignant that the other dogs were stepping on her, and she flew at legs with needle-sharp teeth. Yelps were added to the din.

Havl walked toward me across the lawn, keeping a sharp eye for dog turds. The kennel staff was supposed to keep the grounds policed, but the supply was inexhaustible. He raised his voice over the pandemonium.

"Your former wife telephoned again. She is in Monaco. She is staying at the royal palace. She left the number."

"Throw it away."

Havl is the only member of the household staff I kept. Bogey called him his manservant. He was tall and reticent and had a gloomy, hatchet face. He was thrown out of the Czech parliament in a scandal. My memory has gaps that the doctors blame on the coma, so the details escape me.

He seemed so defeated I could not bring myself to fire him with the rest of Bogey's domestic staff. I made him my assistant and treated him as an equal, and he seemed grateful. Being called a manservant had to be tough. But his guarded watchfulness told me that he feared one day I would revert to my old self.

The mob of dogs and I reached the veranda and climbed the steps. Each arrival home was like Caesar returning in triumph from the Punic Wars. They would have carried me on their shoulders if they could. Havl and I left them at the door. The ones who had been house pets always yapped to be let in at that point, so you could hardly hear yourself think.

"Listen to that riffraff," muttered my yellow lab, Oliver. He pushed a warm nose into my hand in welcome. He had the run of the house and had a lofty attitude toward the outdoors dogs.

"Pretty high and mighty, aren't we?" I said.

Havl pretended not to notice when I talked with the dogs. He had put up with far worse from the old me.

It was Saturday, so the crowd of workmen and decorators putting Millwood into shape were gone. Felicity got most of the furniture in the divorce, and some rooms were still empty. I bought Millwood as a tax write-off for my foundation. I also needed a lot of room for the dogs.

I climbed the grand, oak staircase and went to my bedroom and lay down. Jesus, I was sore. The flashback to the Pig Faces as I lay dazed on the grass was worrying because they also had been in my dreams lately. I woke up in cold sweats. Then I didn't want to go back to sleep for fear the dreams would come again.

I wondered if someone was trying to send me a message. Either that or I was going nuts.

2

You may already know my story. I've told it often enough. I told it to doctors, nurses, psychiatrists, therapists, lab technicians, even hospital janitors with mops and pails. I was talking from the time my eyes opened from that coma the experts said would never release me. Next to hear were the lawyers, the judge, jurors, bailiffs, and the spectators at the trial. After that it was the warden and any number of prison guards and inmates. Nobody believed me except for a bunco artist I met behind bars, and he told people whatever they wanted to hear.

"His fantasy is elaborate and has a remarkable internal consistency," the psychologist testified.

The grinning prosecutor pointed out that even if every absurd story I told were true, my crime was committed before I was conjured away to where an angel struggled against a wizard with a world hanging in the balance.

"Transported, may I say," he said in a pretty good Bela Lugosi accent, "as a dog."

That was his rimshot line, used several times in the trial. The jury and spectators spotted it coming a mile off and began to titter. Then they pounded knees and wiped tears from their eyes. A couple of times the judge called a recess so he could stop laughing himself.

Bill Clancy, the famous Boston Irishman who has kept more

crooked politicians out of prison than any other lawyer in the land, objected mildly each time. He was known for an orator's voice powerful enough to call hogs home from the next county over. I asked at a recess why he almost whispered his objections.

"The appeals court will see from the transcript that this judge sustains each of my objections but doesn't stop the prosecutor from being a comedian. I'll claim his refusal to declare a mistrial was reversible error on grounds it made you a laughing-stock before the jury."

People say it is a shame there are tricky lawyers. But believe me, that is who you want at your side when you are in hot water. Clancy's strategy worked, and my conviction was overturned. But by the time I was sprung, I had spent nearly a year in the federal lockup in Lompoc. Most of the people I met there were more honest, or anyway less criminal, than those I had dealt with in the business world as the old Bogey.

Bogey got nailed for borrowing to cover a huge position in commodity futures taken on an insider's tip. There would have been less public outrage if the borrowing hadn't been from a charity that bankrolled research into childhood diseases. I was chairman of the Fund for the Little Ones at the time. I took the job when my PR people were in one of their pushes to improve my rotten public image. I was leveraged to the hilt at the time. The big Cornhill swindle I was falsely accused of masterminding had temporarily dried up my access to capital, and I was in danger of losing my shirt.

Every nickel was repaid to the Fund for the Little Ones after Bogey made his killing, by the way. I will say that in his (my) defense. Not a single research project was delayed. That didn't get mentioned at the time, and people still overlook it. It wasn't as if I was involved in peddling baby formula to Third World countries that had been ordered off the American market, to name one investment opportunity I passed on at the time. "You've got the wrong man," I told Freddie Westphal.

Bogey had a nose for that kind of risk, or what he called "downside." Westphal runs the library in a federal prison in Ohio now. He was lucky that the treaty with Guatemala let him serve his sentence in the United States. Feelings ran pretty strong down there.

It was understandable that people believed the worst of me. Bogey appeared before skeptical congressional committees and regulators investigating his complex business deals. They usually involved shell companies, interlocking directorates, and offshore banks protected by privacy laws. Clancy was always at my side to point out that, however fishy it looked, there was no proof any of these arrangements were illegal.

I was undone in the Fund for the Little Ones case by documents that were supposed to be shredded but instead fell into the hands of the *Wall Street Journal*. I had so many enemies it was impossible to know who betrayed me.

"The sneer wiped off his face and his bullying manner gone, W. B. (Bogey) Ingersol looked like a whipped cur yesterday," one newspaper article said when the verdict came in.

My last thought was wondering if weeping would help when I threw myself on the mercy of the court at my sentencing. After falling into that coma, I awoke to find myself running through a sinister forest where trees muttered to each other. It was a while before I realized that I was a huge dog. You cannot begin to imagine the horror when it sank in that this was no dream.

"And in this fairyland," the prosecutor said with one eyebrow cocked amusingly, "Mr. Ingersol maintains that a wizard named Zalzathar and an angel called Helither strove for supremacy, and that he, Mr. Ingersol—transported, may I say, as a dog [laughter]—ultimately joined the struggle, after many a thrilling adventure, on the side of Good, thereby tipping the scales against Evil."

He made it sound ridiculous, and I admit it does, but that is what happened.

• • • •

They found the real me (as opposed to the dog me) out
cold at the desk in my suite in the priciest office tower in Manhattan. When it became apparent that I wasn't going to snap
out of it, Felicity packed me off to a nursing home for human
vegetables in Florida. She was a wickedly beautiful creature
with red hair. With me out of the way, she resumed the wanton
life she had in the *haute monde* before we met.

I had married her against the advice of my accountants and
lawyers so I could rub elbows with high society. I admit part
of my motivation was trophy-wife pride, but mostly it was for
the connections she brought me. Unluckily, I fell in love with
the enchantress after the wedding. So the power in the rela-
tionship passed to her, as Felicity no doubt expected. The
woman was a siren. She had buried two husbands before me
and probably thought this was the normal course of events.
This makes her sound more cold-blooded than she actually
was, but not by much.

Havl brought me more ice for my football injuries. "How
did the game turn out?" he asked.

"Somebody won and somebody lost. I'm not sure who."

"I am trying to learn football through study. It is highly
complicated in its details. I have bought a book with diagrams.
Do you think football's minatory spirit is perhaps responsible
for American global hegemony in the modern world?"

Football was compulsory in the boarding schools where I
spent my childhood, as were all the other sports in season.
Although he enjoyed arriving late to a tackle to bite and
kidney-punch before pileups could be untangled, Bogey got his
aversion to athletics then. He never took a stroke of exercise
as an adult as a result and was sorry that sedan chairs had
passed from fashion. He could push his way through crowds
with the best of then, but the idea of being transported above

the Manhattan throngs on the shoulders of sweating porters appealed to him.

But I had an inexplicable yen for exercise after coming out of the coma, another example of how the experience had changed me. I took long runs every day, losing myself in the ecstasy of the physical. The flood of stimuli funneled to the brain by senses sharpened by my time as a canine put me in a trance. The perfume of a single flower was a distinct note in a grand symphony of odors. The whisper of the wind in the trees seemed to be a clue about the mystery of existence. Dogs are more poetic than humans, believe it or not.

I sometimes became aware on these runs of neighborhood dogs loping alongside. I guess they were drawn to the leader-of-the-pack vibes I brought back from the other world. This did nothing for my popularity with their owners. There were complaints to the humane society. It had already threatened legal action because of the number of dogs I kept at Millwood.

"You will be dining in?" Havl asked. Although he never said so, I think he was puzzled by the lack of social life for a man of my wealth and consequence.

I seldom went anywhere, quite a contrast to my life in New York with Felicity. We were out every night. Dinner parties, first nights, charity balls, the hot restaurants, courtside at the Knicks games with Spike Lee. We were in the society pages all the time. The cameras were drawn to her extraordinary beauty, but now and then I was seen at the edge of the photos, a forty-dollar Esplendido between my fingers. They weren't bad times. I had my share of fun.

Now I ate by myself on the veranda. The dogs sat in a semi-circle, silently watching. If dogs aren't eating, there is nothing they like better than watching somebody else eat. It's as involving as a good movie is for us.

"A grilled cheese sandwich with dill pickles?" Havl asked.

"How about one of your pizzas?"

Havl had taught himself to cook when I got rid of Bogey's household staff, which was loyal to Felicity. Sometimes I whipped up an omelette for the two of us. Neither of us would make the world forget Escoffier.

I didn't expect to ever get over what happened to me, but I hoped someday it would not be all I thought about. The dreams I'd been having, and now the sickening smell of Pig Faces that had hit me as I lay in the grass made that seem unlikely.

I couldn't forget Mogwert. Embodiment of Evil sums up Mogwert pretty well. And Zalzathar functioned as his CEO.

When I arrived, Mogwert had marshaled strength for the one last battle to bring Final Victory over the Two-Legs—what you and I would call humans. Two-Legs had become fat and lazy in the long years of a false peace. Even Helither, the angel who was God's deputy there, was caught napping.

Mogwert's scheme misfired because he didn't snare the man he'd really wanted for an adviser. He had aimed for Bernie Soderberg, whose way of doing business made Bogey—even then—look like a candidate for sainthood. Soderberg didn't just beat the other side, he destroyed it and then sowed the ground with salt. He was King of the Hill. Nobody else came close.

He owned movie studios and theme parks, controlled television and cable networks, had magazines, newspapers, and radio stations galore. He had big stakes in some of the hottest Silicon Valley companies and was a major player in biotech. Bernie nodded his head, and the price of a bushel of wheat went up a dime. He owned gold and diamond mines, oil wells, and more supertankers than the Greeks. He was in real estate and heavy construction. He owned satellites and trucking companies. Only the Mafia had more influence in the Teamsters. Wars didn't start or stop in some parts of the world unless Bernie gave them the okay. Then he sold arms to both sides.

In the eighteen months since I had come out of the coma, Soderberg had been expanding his holdings faster than ever. I flattered myself that Bogey's change of heart had something to do with that. People joked that he would want his own seat in the United Nations. He was American but owned palaces, castles, villas, chalets, stately homes, country estates, ranches, farms, and luxury apartments all over the world. Each had its own staff of servants. Not that Soderberg spent much time at home. He jetted around the world in his blood-red 737, making deals.

Havl brought in the evening newspaper (owned by one of Bernie's media companies), and I saw Soderberg's picture under a big headline. I glanced at the story. It said he had decided the time had come to devote his life to the betterment of mankind and was retiring from the business world.

"The woman from the humane society is outside again," Havl said. "She is counting the dogs."

I went outside to where Rita Rutaway was writing up a citation. She was a heavy woman in a brown uniform and a cap with a bill. Her Animal Protection Service shield gleamed on her breast. Her lips were compressed in disapproval. If you wanted to strike a medal to honor officious bureaucracy, Rita was the perfect model.

Her eyes were steely. "Forty-seven dogs this time, Mr. Ingersol, and I'm not sure that's an accurate count the way they're running around. You now have more dogs than are confined at the animal shelter."

"I have homes lined up for fifteen. They'll be gone by the weekend."

She did the math, making hard little dots on the pad with her pen. "Assuming you're telling the truth, that will still leave thirty-two. You may have no more than ten dogs on this property without a use permit. We've been over this many times."

Rita visited once or twice a week to count my friends. She wrote citations, and I mailed in a check to cover the fine the same day. This offended her at some deep level. Fines were meant to compel obedience. When they were shrugged off, it mocked the rule of law. The next stop was anarchy.

"These animals are unwanted and should be put to sleep," she said.

"I want them."

"You want to flout the law, Mr. Ingersol. You enjoy it."

"That's too harsh, Officer Rutaway."

She ripped the citation off the pad and handed it to me. "It is because of people like you there's a pet overpopulation crisis."

She turned her broad back to me and walked to her green truck with its built-in cages. A few dogs born to raise hell yapped at her derisively.

"Can't catch me!"

"Go 'way-'way-'way ooooo!"

"Bad fat one ya ya ya!"

I told them to knock it off and went back inside. I sat in the kitchen with Havl and we ate pizza.

Later in the day, a wind blew through the window from the ocean on the other side of the hills, meaning fog later that night. It brought the smell of the deer hiding up there. They marked time in the woods until dusk, then moseyed down to browse on everyone's expensive landscaping but mine. The smell of dogs made them give Millwood a wide berth.

"Many are up there," Oliver muttered. "And something else." His nose was better than mine.

"What is it?"

"I can't tell—there, it's gone." He snorted to clear the scent. "I want something to eat."

"You're too fat."

He waited to see if I would change my mind, as sometimes happened, and then wondered off to curl up for a nap. He took thirty or forty a day. He got up on chairs for his snoozes when no one was looking.

I telephoned Jared Snyder at his brick farmhouse home an hour out of New York. He ran funds for big investors. "I read just now that Soderberg is quitting business to make Earth a better place," I said.

"First you and now him. It must be catching," Snyder said with a chuckle. "I hope I'm spared." One of the funds he managed invested in every flier Soderberg took. Snyder argued that they were nearly as safe as Treasury notes and paid lots better. He required a minimum investment of a million dollars for this fund. I had eighty million in it. I thought of it as mad money. The rest of the cash-out I took from the sale of Bogey's investment company was socked away more conservatively.

"You want to bail out?" he asked.

"It won't be the same with Bernie gone."

"Yeah, I thought he'd go on until he owned as much as God. What's the weather like out there?"

"Nice. Anybody know why?"

"I hear he got religion of some kind."

"Bernie?"

"Hard to believe, isn't it?"

"Which religion?"

"Search me. What do you want to do with your money?"

"Park it in another fund for the time being. Icarus was doing all right the last time I looked."

"It still seems funny, a swashbuckler like you sitting back in a rocking chair while others have all the fun. Felt your pulse lately? Maybe you're dead and don't know it."

"Retirement suits me."

"Don't give me that smelling-the-roses crap again. You've still got a tiger in the tank."

Jared believed I had just been temporarily knocked off stride but would be back in the ring any day now. He was an action junkie, the jittery type, always in motion. Pacing, snapping his fingers, fiddling with things as he talked on the telephone. He couldn't sit still for a minute. He burned off as much energy as a hummingbird. But behind all the motion was a deep thinker. Nobody read the Federal Reserve Board tea leaves better. He could feel a change coming in the discount rate the way other people could with the weather. He had told the *Wall Street Journal* that Bogey was as necessary to capitalism as vultures to the natural world. Bogey took it as a compliment.

"You'll be back," he said now.

"Not me. I'm on the sidelines for good."

"Yeah, yeah. I'll talk to you Monday after the market opens. You won't be the only one repositioning with Soderberg pulling out, if he really is. Maybe he's going to lay in the weeds for a while and then suddenly buy control of Ford, Chrysler, and General Motors." He laughed.

That night, cold fog drifted in silently from the ocean. It was thicker than usual, like a London fog when they burned coal. The streetlamps that lighted Millwood's curving drive were like blurred halos. I half expected to see Holmes and Watson in a hansom cab. The watchdog breeds were restless and pacing down in the kennels. Even Oliver, who normally sleeps like somebody drugged the kibble, lifted his head from the cushion near the fireplace.

He rumbled deep in his throat. "Somethin' out there."

I asked him what.

"Dunno." He put his head back down and closed his eyes.

I wondered if I should see a psychiatrist. The lack of sleep was really bothering me. Bogey would have curled his lip. He thought people who saw head doctors were pansies and shirkers.

3

O n Monday I telephoned a professor I knew at Stanford. Ted Butler was a contender for a future Nobel Prize for economics for his work on how the commodity markets work. Maybe six other people in the world understood his theory. He was also the university's point man to get me to come through on a promise Bogey made to build a new wing for the business school.

Like everyone else, he was surprised by Soderberg's decision. "The word I get is he's going into politics."

"I thought he said he was going to makes things better for humanity."

"I'm serious. The buzz is he's locking up all the top political consultants and polling companies. He's putting them on exclusive contracts so no one else can use them. It's costing a fortune, but it's chicken feed for him."

I doubted Bernie could be elected to the sewage board without major voter fraud. "The man's more hated than I was."

"Was?" A beat. "Just kidding."

"Work on your timing and I see you in that chair next to Letterman some night." It would take a sofa. Ted was fatter than Friar Tuck. You could tell when he had gone over three hundred pounds because he ate carrot sticks for lunch.

"It's Leno or nothing." His laugh was oddly high-pitched for a man his size. "But you didn't call to talk piffle. You've decided to fund the wing, and I'm the first to know. Let me get the president on a conference call. He's still not sure he wants the Ingersol name associated with Stanford, but I think I can talk him around."

"That's not what I'm calling about."

"Prices will never be lower, and delay only drives up costs. A no-frills wing costing sixty-five million this year will be sixty-eight next year. Heed the words of your friendly neighborhood economist."

"Be serious for a minute. I need advice."

"Bandido in the third at Bay Meadows."

I wondered how many stand-up comedians wanted to be economists in their heart of hearts. "Stanford's got a pretty good school of medicine, right?" I asked.

"One of the best. But we say we have one of the best of whatever you care to name. Another hundred years and maybe we'll shake the inferiority complex we've got about Harvard."

"I've got a friend who needs to see a shrink. Can you find out who's good?"

"Is the friend you?"

"Yes, as a matter of fact."

"I'll let you know."

He called back in a couple of hours. "A psychiatrist named Alex Epperly has a very good reputation. I took the liberty of having an appointment scheduled this very afternoon. Or is that too soon?"

I told him I was impressed.

"Dr. Epperly will even come to your house, such is our regard for your welfare."

If I finance the wing, his name goes on it. Bogey expected to have his own plastered all over. Also a statue in the courtyard of him pointing toward the future in a farsighted way. A sketch was done on a napkin. This was so everybody understood there would be no abstract crap as long as W. B. Ingersol was paying the bill.

The Stanford Medical Hospital's main wing looks like waffles stacked on end. I showed up at the appointed hour and knocked on Dr. Epperly's door. A female voice said to come in.

"I was looking for Dr. Epperly." She was a beautiful woman in a pale yellow suit. She had dark hair and startlingly blue eyes. She smiled warmly and stood. She was nearly as tall as I.

"I'm Dr. Epperly." She stuck out her hand.

"You're Alex?" I had expected someone portly and bald. Perhaps a salt-and-pepper beard.

"Nobody told you I'm a woman?"

"With a name like Alex, I thought . . ." I had the feeling my surprise betrayed a belief in the innate inferiority of females.

"You should have been told." Her manner was smooth and assured. "I can refer you to a male doctor if it would be more comfortable."

"That's okay."

She invited me to sit down.

After a slight hesitation, I did. The truth was the old Bogey did think women weren't as good as men, except in those biological areas where they had the edge. "Get your biscuits in the oven and your buns in bed." The words to the song summed it up. Bogey's opinions were root balls that couldn't be changed with a snap of the fingers. It was hard work digging them out.

"The president's office called," Dr. Epperly said. "I must say I was flattered. I'm just a lowly associate professor of psychiatry."

I looked around. Nice touches made what had been a small, institutional space warm and tasteful. A patterned oriental rug was on the floor, and books filled one wall. A floor lamp and plants gave a cozy feel. Framed diplomas were on another wall. Hoover Tower across campus was visible through her window.

"Do you know who I am?" I asked.

"Oh, yes. You were very famous for a time. It seemed I saw your picture in those supermarket newspapers just about every week."

"So you must not have a very high opinion of me." If she despised me going in, it would be better to find someone else to spill my guts to.

"I admit my impression was unfavorable, but I also know the media can be unfair. You were found guilty of embezzlement, weren't you? What was the name of the charity?"

"The Fund for the Little Ones. The verdict was overturned."

"But only on a technicality. That doesn't necessarily mean innocence, does it?"

"Bogey's guilt was only technical. The money was repaid before it was missed. Bogey was no angel, but he was prosecuted because of political pressure. Left-wingers hated him, and so did the right for making capitalism look bad."

"Bogey?"

"My nickname."

She was interested by my use of the third person. It indicated megalomania usually found only in show business or the seriously deranged. "You know about the coma?" I asked.

"Your case is fairly well known in professional circles. It has even been discussed at conferences. Dr. Oliver Sacks presented a paper that I believe he called 'The Man Who Thought He Was a Dog.'"

A cottage industry had sprung up on the subject of Bogey like the one around Elvis. There were Web sites on the Internet with chat groups where I was demonized. A made-for-TV movie came out while I was in prison. Bogey was played by a German shepherd and an actor who looked like Broderick Crawford in that old *Highway Patrol* series. As I said, I used to weigh quite a bit more.

"Notoriety can't be very nice." She looked sympathetic. I guessed she was in her late thirties. Streaks in her dark hair said tennis or golf. Her skin was pale, however. People don't get tans anymore. Sunblocks make it possible to look like you live at the bottom of a mine shaft.

She leaned back and gave me a shrewd look. "Do you hear voices?"

"I'm not crazy."

"That isn't a word I use."

"I'm not any of those clinical words you people bat around that mean the same thing, either."

"Then how can I help you?" She had smile lines at the corners of her eyes.

"I'm having dreams about when I was in that other world and was a dog."

"Dreams about your dream? We have a sleep disorder clinic here. Maybe they could help."

"It was no dream. It actually happened."

"Dreams can be very real. What we call reality is in some sense a mediation by the brain of perceived physical phenomena. The brain is the seat of all dreams, therefore . . . This can get very epistemological if we're not careful."

"We want to be very careful in that case."

She laughed. "Well, at least you've kept a sense of humor."

"Bogey didn't have one and was suspicious of people who did. It meant they weren't serious."

"The Bogey you were before the coma?"

"Correct."

"And who are you now?"

"The man you see before you."

"You no longer go by the name Bogey? You are the un-Bogey, so to speak?"

"No, people still call me that. It's just a name. But I'm a changed person."

"Changed."

"Changed by what happened. I'm trying to be a better person." Nobody believed it. It was like Vlad the Impaler saying he had given up working with stakes.

"Better in what way?" She made a note on a pad. Long, graceful hands. A plain wedding band.

"Bogey had a gift for entrepreneurship. He rose from trading bonds to investment banker to one of the top takeover artists in the world."

"I'm not sure I know what that is."

"He—I—bought companies with borrowed money and sold off the assets. They were worth more that way than intact. Some were underperformers in need of a goose, but most were productive with good profit margins. When Bogey was finished with his looting, they were either saddled with junk bond debt and on life support or downsized out of existence. He picked his teeth and moved on to the next meal."

"So people lost jobs?"

"By the thousands, but Bogey didn't care. He was worth more than six hundred million at the time of the coma and had a couple of deals in the hopper that would put him in the billionaire class. But he'd still stoop to pick up a dime somebody lost."

"He sounds horrible. And you?"

"I'm setting up a foundation to give the money away."

Dr. Epperly smiled. "Well, I'm impressed. All of it?"

"I said I'm nicer, not a saint. I'm not going to live in a box under a bridge for my past deeds. But most of Bogey's ill-gotten gains will go to good causes. I haven't figured out which ones yet." After I got back, I thought I would take a vow of poverty and work with the downtrodden or something. But the more I thought about it, the less I liked the idea.

We talked some more, mostly me answering questions. She was friendly but kept a professional distance. I saw she thought I was an interesting case.

"And your wife, Felicity? What happened to her?"

"She took up with a beach boy in Rio when it looked like I would never come out of it. Since the divorce, she's gone back to hanging out in Europe with the decayed aristocracy. I hear she's in Monaco. She had Bogey wrapped around her finger. Cheap as he was, she spent money like water. He didn't get much back for it. I treat my dogs better than she did him."

"Why did you put up with it?"

"I didn't."

"Excuse me, I meant why did Bogey put up with it?"

"Love made a fool out of him."

"From what you've said, I wouldn't think he was capable of love."

"He liked having one of the most beautiful women in the world as his wife. Other men envied him, and that was the salt in the soup to him. He rubbed their noses in what they couldn't have. Also, Bogey couldn't order her around like everyone else. That made her more alluring."

"You seem to have a very good understanding of . . ." She hesitated, as if worried she might be validating my fantasy. "Of Bogey."

"I was him a long time."

"Are these dreams his you're having or your own?"

"A mixture, I guess. Shouldn't there be a couch?"

"I'm a psychiatrist, not a psychotherapist."

"What's the difference?"

"They learn Freudian analysis in addition to medical training. I can refer you to a psychotherapist if you would like. Otherwise, you have to sit in a chair." She smiled again. White teeth, very even. She seemed like a happy person.

"As long as we've started, let's see how it goes with you."

"I'll want to look at your medical records, but maybe we can spend a little time now on the dreams."

I explained that they began as fragments, unconnected scenes jerked up from memory. They were like flashes of fireworks in a dark sky. On successive nights over the past couple of weeks they had gotten longer and more detailed. The dreams were about stages of the journey Bogey made from the boundary between the worlds.

"How did he feel about that journey?"

"He assumed for a long time that he was sleeping and just having this really long dream. Then he thought maybe he had fallen and hit his head or had some other accident and was in a coma. Eventually he came to realize that in reality—the reality he found himself in—he was a dog."

"So in his dreams he believed he was in a coma?" Dr. Epperly was writing this down.

"It wasn't a dream," I said patiently.

"Sorry. This is a little slippery. Continue."

"Should I tell you the most recent dream?"

"Yes."

Bogey was being chased. Ostrichlike mammals with beaks and claws had picked up his trail hours before and crashed through the undergrowth behind him. They communicated by clicks and pops that would not be audible to a human ear but that he heard with terrible clarity. They were in a half circle behind him, spread a quarter-mile wide to see changes of direction he took to shake them. This brought warning whistles, and they all changed courses at the same time, like a flight of birds. They had gray fur and dark eyes as hard as pebbles. They were more than five feet tall. Bogey pictured their beaks and claws tearing at his flesh.

"Shit," he kept saying as he ran. "Shiiiit."

This wasn't the first time he'd had to leg it to save his hide, and he accepted his new strength and speed as a given. It was the only upside this whole business had. He would have pegged off from a coronary in his human body two minutes after the chase started.

He had stumbled across the band of hunting droliks three hours earlier in dry, windswept highlands where boulders stuck up like tombstones. They were camped in a small grove of trees that hid them from his approach. The wind was behind him, so his nose had given no warning. Bogey and the droliks stared in mutual amazement when he blundered into them.

Bogey recovered first. "Well, hi, everyone," he said with desperate gaiety.

The droliks rose to their feet. "Get him!" the leader said with a snarl.

They were coursers, used to long chases. They pursued him from the highlands down long, fertile valleys where Bogey hoped the sight of slow, fat ruminants throwing up heads in alarm would draw them off. No such luck. The droliks seemed locked on to him as the meal *du jour*.

Downcountry it was well watered. Bogey slaked his thirst as he forded streams. He yelped as devilish little pincher fish swarmed and nipped at his legs. They were half teeth and all appetite. He had learned before to find shallow crossings because of them, but there was no time for that now. One clung leechlike after he left a green stream where a hungry school of them lay in wait. He knocked it off against a tree trunk. It flipped back and forth on the ground.

"Die, you little bastard."

He smelled the sea long before he saw it. The ground started to drop off on either side, and his sharp ears picked up the far-off sound of surf pounding the shore. The droliks made a jubilant noise and Bogey's heart sank. What did they know that he didn't? The sound and smell of sea grew stronger with each stride. It was clear they were on a narrowing finger of land. He was in the cool shadow of pines that had dropped spongy layers of needles underfoot over many years. Then suddenly he was clear of them and running on a lonely white beach where huge wind-whipped combers smashed ashore. They rose so high before they broke that they looked like green mountains with snow blowing off their tops.

Bogey continued in full gallop even though he saw that he was fast running out of land. Huge black rocks getting a dunking from the sea marked the end of it. Beyond them a strait was whipped to a whitecapped chop by the wind. On the other side, a wooded island rode in the heaving sea like the dot of an exclamation mark. It was easy to see from how water moved in different directions that vicious currents swirled in the strait.

He turned to face the droliks. A score of them formed a ragged line a hundred yards behind. They had slowed, and the slow clacking of their beaks came to him over the wind. He realized they were licking their chops. He might be able to kill two or three before he was buried by the rest. He could almost feel the flesh being torn from his body.

"What happened then?" Dr. Epperly asked.

"He squeezed his eyes shut."

"Why?"

"All the time he kept hoping that when he opened them, he'd be back on Wall Street. 'This isn't really happening,' he'd say. He would put himself into a hospital and get checked out by the best specialists money could buy. Maybe he needed electroshock or something to straighten him out. But it didn't work this time, either. The droliks were closer when he opened his eyes. He trotted back and forth at the edge of the water. Which was the easier death, drowning or being torn apart by those beaks?"

"Interesting," Dr. Epperly said, writing. "Did Bogey then suffer symbolic death at the hand of these—what's the name?"

"Droliks. There would have been nothing symbolic about it. It would have been curtains. Finis. Kaput. But, no, there was a lot to come."

Bogey turned and plunged into the surf. He remembered reading that a drowning person went into a kind of dream state when he stopped struggling. He hoped it was true. But even if it wasn't, drowning still beat being eaten alive.

He struggled through the boiling surf. He hoped to swim parallel to the shore and come back where the droliks couldn't see him. Then he felt himself carried out by a powerful current. The chill water drained what was left of his strength. The sea roared in his ears, and salt water forced its way up his nose. He struggled to stay afloat. The outbound current weakened and passed him off to another. That one brought him in near the wooded island. With the last of his strength, he swam the few strokes to land before he was swept past. He hauled himself out and managed to totter a few steps before he collapsed.

Bogey lay panting and trembling on the pebbly shore. Why him? Others had done worse; he could name a dozen major Wall Street figures off the top of his head. Why not them instead? These bitter thoughts filled his mind. He got up, shook himself so the water flew, and looked around. The droliks had been too smart to follow him and were gone from the far shore. The island rose steeply from the sea and then leveled out. He crept through thick hardwood forest.

The roar of the sea fell away as he made his way inland. A silence so heavy it seemed drugged replaced it. Bogey had never been much for solitude. Silence made him pace and snap his fingers restlessly. He liked crowds and noise. His large head and bold features had become a shorthand for arrogance in political cartoons, so he was often recognized. His security detail kept the angry threats strangers yelled from being acted on. It sometimes amused him to pretend to mistake them for cheers. He circled thumb and forefinger into an O or flashed the V sign. "Bless you and keep me in your prayers," he called back. Maddened, they struggled with the bodyguards to get at him. He said, "Sorry, no time for autographs now."

The forest on the island nearly hid carved stone statues of great age that were as big as those on Easter Island. They had fat torsos and faces contorted with fury. Bogey guessed they were gods worshiped long before by an ignorant race. He had no interest in archaeology and passed on. Odd it was so quiet. It seemed as if the island slept. Bogey was thinking he would curl up for forty winks himself when someone spoke.

"Finally."

He spun around looking for the source.

"I thought I'd been completely forgotten."

The speaker sat at the foot of a towering tree. He had tangled locks and the kind of unkempt beard Bogey associated with the arty crowd Felicity liked. He stretched long, sinewy arms covered with black hair. "No need to put your tail between your legs. You don't have to be afraid."

Bogey in human form had a poker face that was valuable when it came time to hammer out a deal with a hostile board of directors. But keeping cards close to the vest was impossible with a tail. It gave everything away by wagging or drooping. Now it had curled between his legs to protect his private parts. He whined—there was also no helping that, either.

The stranger was buried to his chest by vine and creeper, as if he had been sitting there for a long time. As he began to disentangle himself, a goatish smell grew stronger.

A clock on the campus tolled the hour. "Oh, dear, so soon," Dr. Epperly said. "This is a good place to stop. I have another appointment after you." She scribbled on a prescription pad.

"This will help you get your rest. Can you come back on Wednesday? Same time?"

I said, "No problem. Quite a story, isn't it?"

"So is the way you tell it. Your detachment is striking."

"The prison psychologists mentioned that, too." They gave me batteries of tests. They scratched their heads trying to square the results with what was clearly my delusional state. "How strong is that medication you're prescribing? I tried other stuff but nothing worked."

"You shouldn't dream. It's very strong. No refills."

"Any ideas why the dreams are coming back? It's been more than a year and a half since I came out of the coma."

"It's too soon to hazard a guess."

"Post-traumatic stress disorder?" I said hopefully.

"That's a portmanteau term that holds many possibilities."

I nodded, wondering what that meant. I was saddled with Bogey's education, strong in business but otherwise full of holes. He would have demanded to know what she meant. He believed people who used big words were trying to put something over on him. "Cut the crap," he would say with a snarl. Yeah, his bum-kissers would chorus, say what you mean.

We said good-bye. I got the prescription filled at the pharmacy and walked to my pickup. I figured a couple of nights of sleep would do wonders. I drove to San Francisco to talk to the consultants I had hired to tell me how to set up my foundation. Bogey was a genius when it came to making money, but I had to admit I was a dunce when it came to giving it away. I was buried by proposals for giving, each as worthy as the next. A mail truck drove up every day with more. It seemed every cause and charity in the world had my name. And it was not only organizations making pitches with supporting documentation. Individuals wrote letters that plucked at the heartstrings. Havl sometimes wept reading them.

"I lost both my hands in an industrial accident. I, who was

once so proud . . ." I learned to stop reading any farther. I would run my finger down the rest of the letter, looking for a number. There it was, fifteen thousand dollars for prosthetics. I wrote the check and mailed it.

"My husband left me and my six babies . . ." The letter was in pencil, crudely lettered, with misspellings. She wanted a double-wide trailer house. I sent her the money. A family whose farm was washed away when the Missouri River flooded, a snake-handling evangelist paralyzed by a viper's bite. What misfortune there was in the world. Bogey never gave it a second thought. He believed people got what they deserved. But I had become sensitized to suffering the way some people get to bee stings. This also got around, and I developed a reputation for being an easy touch. My mail doubled and tripled.

People gathered at the front gate to advance their case directly. Only a few at first, but their numbers grew to a dozen and then a score. Homeless shelters, food banks, charitable foundations, environmental groups, diseases seeking cures. Their representatives elbowed for position and called out as I drove in and out.

". . . plowshares for peace . . ."

". . . the Third World unsighted community asks you . . ."

". . . The polluted Earth . . ."

When someone shouted something that caught my attention, I had a check sent out. The weakness of this approach soon became apparent. Professional bigmouths were hired, nightclub barkers and auctioneers who could say a lot of words in a short time. Signs and banners were held up. The *Journal of Philanthrophy* attacked me in an editorial. "Not since John D. Rockefeller flipped dimes to people . . ."

After I met with the consultants and crawled back in the commute jam, I pondered why a bureaucracy was necessary to give away money. They had shown me organizational charts with lines connecting boxes. Each box represented a salaried position. Their proposed mission statement had long words that described the high-sounding goals I should adopt. I had thought it would be so simple. Worthy causes could be brought to my attention, and I would write the checks. If they needed office space, they could move into Millwood. There was plenty of room. Obviously they would have to like dogs. If someone had a good idea, he could duck his head into the study, where I have my office, or maybe we would bump into each other in the kitchen.

But the consultants, Mr. Belview and Mrs. Simenon, smiled and said this was a common misconception. It was originally fostered, they thought, by *The Millionaire* on television. John Beresford Tipton stepped into lives when things were looking bad and saved the day with a check for a million bucks.

"That, of course, has no correlation to reality in the giving community," Mr. Belview said. It was naive. Even if it were true, wouldn't Mr. Tipton have needed a trained staff to identify candidates and provide needs assessment? Look at the vulgar scenes at my gate, people pushing and shoving. Had I seen the editorial in the *Journal of Philanthrophy*?

I needed a board of directors in addition to a professional staff. Community input would be desirable. Advisory committees were recommended. When Mrs. Simenon began talking about investing in arts infrastructure, I said I'd be in touch.

It was nearly dark by the time I rolled up the drive at Millwood. I heard the dogs barking in welcome and went down to the kennels to say hello. That thick, cold fog had come in again. The Doberman pinschers and Rottweilers and the other watchdog breeds were testing the wind and growling. They had to be coaxed in from the outdoor runs with rawhide chew strips, the nightly treat I handed out like John Beresford Tipton himself.

Duke, a muscular Rhodesian ridgeback, wouldn't come in.

"Something's coming this way," he said in a grumbly growl dogs used when worried.

4

Two black-and-white police cars led by an unmarked car came up the drive the next morning as the telephone rang. It was Cleo Basich calling.

"Have you heard?"

"Heard what?" I stood with the phone at the French windows, looking out. The fog had burned off, and dew sparkled on the long, descending sweep of lawn like someone had scattered sapphires overnight. But the day's bright promise was deceptive.

"Winston Byron was murdered last night."

A humane society truck followed. Rita Rutaway's substantial figure was planted so squarely behind the wheel that it looked like it would take blasting powder to dislodge her. A second dog catcher rode alongside her, a skinny man. I thought of Jack Sprat and his wife.

"It's horrible," Cleo continued. Her voice was husky, as if she had been crying. "They found him on the Morgenthalers's property. He'd been torn apart. Literally torn apart. People are saying it must be your dogs."

The cars and truck stopped, and the occupants huddled briefly before walking toward the front door. I told Cleo I would call her back.

An intense, dark-haired man in his forties who looked a little like the actor Al Pacino stepped forward from the crowd of uniforms when I opened the door.

"Mr. Ingersol?"

"Yes."

"I'm Detective John Mazzoni. May we speak with you for a moment?"

I stepped aside to let them in.

"May we have your permission to check out your dogs?"

"Go ahead."

He looked surprised, as if he expected an argument. It is nice when they are polite. In prison, you see the other side. They don't ask you nicely to bend over and spread your cheeks. Rita Rutaway, her sidekick, and three of the officers headed toward the kennel. Even the movement of her large buttocks seemed to convey official purpose.

The workmen doing the remodeling at Millwood stopped their work and stared as I led Mazzoni and the others to the morning room with the French windows. Mazzoni accepted my invitation to sit down, but the others stood.

"You know about the crime committed last night?" he asked.

"I just heard a minute ago."

"Who told you?"

"Cleo Basich called. She lives in the neighborhood."

"Mrs. Basich is a nice lady. Very active in the community. Did you know Mr. Byron?"

"I met him once."

"Did she tell you how he died?"

"She said he was torn apart."

Mazzoni looked queasy. "That describes it pretty good. Even the coroner's deputy was shocked, and those guys are pretty hardened to what you see these days."

"I almost puked," a young policeman volunteered. "Guts were scattered all over." Mazzoni gave him a warning look.

"And you think it was my dogs?" I asked.

"Did Mrs. Basich mention that?"

"They're locked in the kennel at night. A fence surrounds the grounds even if they get out."

Mazzoni nodded. "I see."

"He was on one of his walks?"

"You know about that? How he'd have too much to drink and go off?"

"I heard he was famous for it."

"His wife was always calling. We looked until we found him and drive him home. Everybody in the department's done it more than once. Anyplace else he would have been taken to the lockup, of course. Drunk in public."

He paused to see if I wanted to comment on this sympathetic treatment of a fellow property owner. When I didn't, he cleared his throat. "We're asking a lot of people questions."

"Ask away."

"Mind if I ask you informally where you were last night?"

"I took a sleeping pill at ten. Went out like a light. No dreams." I was going to compliment Dr. Epperly.

"The reason I ask is I understand you sometimes go running with dogs."

"Not at night. And those aren't my dogs. They're neighborhood pets who see me and tag along."

"Like Pied Piper."

"That was rats and kids."

He scratched his head and grinned. If he wanted me to take him for a woolly-headed rustic, he should have done something about his eyes. "So you knew the deceased?"

"I met him at the fundraiser for the school."

Havl appeared and asked if anyone wanted coffee. The officer who nearly puked said he wouldn't mind. I saw Mazzoni mentally give him another demerit.

"Before you go," he said to Havl, "do you live here also?"
Havl nodded gravely.

"So you and Mr. Ingersol didn't go out after ten?"

Havl glanced toward me. "It's okay," I said.

"No, we did not."

"A place this big, I suppose somebody could leave and the other person wouldn't know it."

"I put the alarm on at eleven. If an outside door or window opens, we know. I could show you a computer readout of activity."

"Sounds like a good system. Maybe I'll take a peek before I go. So the boss was in bed by ten, that right?"

"I looked in on him at twelve before I retired. He was sleeping soundly."

He asked a few other questions, then rubbed his hands briskly. "Well, what say we go down to the kennel and check it out?"

I led them through the house. The workmen laid down their tools again to stare. At the kennel, the dogs grinned and wagged their tails.

"Yooo yo yo yooo, master," a basset hound yodeled. "A fine day. Ooooooo." The others chipped in.

"Holy cow," Mazzoni yelled, "how many you got here?"

"Forty-eight." Rita Rutaway answered for me. "One more than yesterday."

"A mixed breed was tied up at the front gate this morning," said Alice Pepper, one of the kennel workers. She was a brassy, fortyish blond with leathery skin who was tough as a boot. She worked at the animal shelter before coming to Millwood. She hated Rita over some feud they had there. Rita did not take official notice of her glare.

"The law says there can be no more than ten dogs on these premises," she told Mazzoni. "The city attorney is preparing an abatement proceeding."

He had bigger fish to fry. "They were in their pens all night?" he asked Alice.

"Oh, yes."

"She has an apartment above the kennel," I explained.

"So you would hear any comings and goings."

"I'm a light sleeper," Alice answered.

We walked along the dog runs. Mazzoni checked the sturdy latches on each. The dogs kept up their infernal din. "These gates sure seem secure. I bet this setup cost more than my house."

"All the permits were in order," Rita said. "Zoning and building permits signed off on them. I know because I checked."

The detective gave her a blank look. I got a feeling he thought Rutaway had the potential to become a major pain in the ass.

"Nothing on the dogs?" he asked. "There was a lot of blood at the scene."

"Mr. Pinckus is checking."

"Maybe he could use some help." Rita took the hint and trudged off.

"Them dogs didn't go anywhere," Alice said firmly. "I woulda known. Bert Pinckus told me somebody was torn up by dogs? Well, it wasn't none of these here. Anyhow, that's wild-dog behavior, not domestic dog."

"There've been cases of domestic dogs going back to pack behavior. I had Sacramento look it up before we came over."

Like experts in other fields, animal welfare people don't appreciate correction from the laity. "It's very rare," Alice retorted.

It looked like Mazzoni was running a mental finger down a checklist to see if he had covered everything. He reached the bottom. "Maybe I'll take a look at that printout now."

"The dogs were restless last night," Alice said suddenly. "Nervous-like."

"I noticed that, too," I said.

"What do you mean, 'restless'?" he asked Alice.

"Pacing, whining, growling. They was smelling the wind like there was something they didn't like or were afraid of."

"Like what?" Mazzoni asked.

She shrugged and shook out a cigar with a plastic tip from a pack. "You'd have to ask them."

"It was just a feeling they had," I said without thinking. Both looked at me with surprise.

"How do you know that?" Mazzoni asked.

"A hunch," I said lamely. I didn't feel like explaining how I knew what dogs thought.

He waited to see if I had anything to add. When I didn't, he headed up to the house while I made my morning rounds greeting the guests. The athletic dogs leaped up against the fences, and the others wriggled. Alice followed me.

"I thought I had a way with animals," she said admiringly, "but it don't touch yours. It's like you and them's talkin'."

After I finished gladhanding, I walked back to the house. On the way, I smelled the flowers from the nursery I had planted to catch morning light. Each scent was as clear and distinct as John Hancock's signature. People don't know what they're missing. I found Mazzoni and Havl in the small room in the rear, where the security console was. Havl looked puzzled. "Your system says one of your doors opened and closed at one-fifteen and again at three-twenty a.m.," Mazzoni said. "Mr. Dravch here said they were locked from the inside. Anybody else live here?"

"No."

"Anyone else have keys?"

"The security company."

"I'll check with them." He paused. "The coroner's office thinks Mr. Byron was killed around two or two-thirty."

"So I'm a suspect?"

"No, no. I'm just asking a few informal questions. Do you mind if we look around the house?"

"Informally?" I smiled.

"Well, yes."

"No, I think you better get a search warrant." You pick up useful knowledge about due process from other cons in the cooler. Mazzoni left with the others, and I telephoned Bill Clancy's office in Washington, D.C. He was on a golf course.

"Christ, what is it now?" he asked cheerfully. I told him what had happened.

"You shouldn't have given them the time of day. I'll fly out as soon as I finish this round. I'm cleaning the junior senator from Idaho's clock."

"Is he in a jam?"

"This is purely social. You'd be surprised how many people make a point of staying out of trouble."

Clancy is expensive, very expensive, but service is great. He didn't waste time in airport terminals because he piloted his own business jet. Bogey used to complain that he had paid for it several times over. But he never cut corners when it came to lawyers.

I called the security company and told them to come and check out the system. "The readout shows a door opening and closing early this morning when none did."

The technician excused himself for a minute. "Yeah, we show it, too." He said he would send somebody over to find out what was wrong.

"A fine kettle of fish," I said jokingly when Havl brought in the morning's financial newspapers. He thought I was making a suggestion about dinner.

"It's a saying," I explained. "You didn't look in on me at midnight." My dog's sense of hearing would have told me. Dogs are always on guard against something sneaking up.

"I wanted to help if I could."

"You thought I needed help?"

His shrug was cynical, more French than Slav. "I know the way policemen think. Sometimes they plant suspicions in their own minds. Possibly it is different in this country."

I scanned the papers. The *Financial Times* had a front-page story about Soderberg getting out of business, also the *Wall Street Journal*. *Investor's Daily* put it inside. I read them and put them aside to think. If there wasn't a malfunction in the computer system, someone had opened and closed that door to make it look like Havl or I was outside when Bryon was attacked.

Tearing victims apart was a Pig Face trademark.

Although there was far worse in their world, they were horror enough for a lifetime of bad dreams, as I was now discovering. They were Mogwert's foot soldiers. They ran on all fours but got up on hind legs when stationary. They had small horns in addition to nasty tusks. Monkey hands and swollen purple baboon butts that stuck out. Eyes that were wells of pure evil. And, as I said, they stank to high heaven.

Nothing gave them more pleasure than gutting the creatures they caught. They did it while victims were still alive and kicking. The Pig Faces ripped them open in their never-ending search for the "secret" of life. It was as if they hoped one day to surprise life as it fluttered out like a butterfly. Bogey suspected that Mogwert encouraged a kind of crude theology around this belief, but didn't spend much time wondering about it. Everything was secondary to cutting a deal to get sent back where he belonged. Not as a dog, either.

"Tell me how we met, Havl," I said.

He was used to big gaps in my memory. "Do I like Austria?" I asked once when a fragment of memory from my life as Bogey rose to the surface.

"No, you do not like the Austrians. Any foreigner, for that matter. Or didn't. Perhaps it is different now." Havl had adapted to what he saw as my schizophrenic condition.

"I was a member of the Czech government," he said now. "You wanted a large plastics company in Prague. Approvals were necessary. You offered a great deal of money to arrange them, and I accepted. This was found out, and I was disgraced. When I approached you for assistance, you offered a position in your household."

"As a manservant."

"I was forced to accept, as I had to leave my country quickly."

"Can you go back?"

"I hope someday. But the state prosecutor has kept the case open. There is not enough evidence to justify a request for extradition, but I would surely be charged and prosecuted if I returned. Memories will dim, however."

"Why as manservant?"

He flashed a resentful look. Then the stoic mask returned. "You—he—blamed me for carelessness in allowing our arrangement to be discovered."

I pictured Bogey snapping his fingers to summon Havl. Or perhaps clapping hands like an Oriental despot. "He was an important man in his own country," he would casually explain to guests. "Been a damned good servant to me."

Havl seemed to struggle for fairness. "But you have been very good to me since your . . . awakening."

"I'm a different man," I said automatically.

I put on gardening clothes and went outside to dig in the ground where I had prepared a plot for winter vegetables. The sun was warm and birds sang. A thousand scents filled my nose. That is why dogs sometimes stand noses to the wind with thoughtful looks. It is a natural Internet where every plant and animal has a Web site.

Havl could have opened and closed the doors himself. If it was to make me look guilty, he had to know that Byron was going to be torn apart a half a mile away. Or he did it himself. But how could he know the man would be stumbling down the lane in his cups? And making it look like animals did it was too baroque. Whatever grudge he may have nursed in private, he wasn't the type for that. If anything, he was the poisoning type.

As I dug in the dirt, I realized that I was fighting against the darker possibility. I begin dreaming of the other world, a dream of a dream, as Dr. Epperly put it. Then I have that experience on the football field. And now someone is killed in classic Pig Face style. What did it add up to? Not a score the rational mind could accept. Pig Faces lived an immeasurable time and distance from me on an entirely different plane of existence.

Yet this was the thinking that held that my experience had been a fantasy and kissed me off as the Howard Hughes of the day. Just saying my name got a laugh. Before I fell off the radar screen, I was a rich source of material for stand-up comics. "So you know W. B. Ingersol, the rich guy who thought he was a dog? He shoulda met my ex-wife. They coulda started a family . . ." I was even written into a *Seinfeld* episode.

But Pig Faces could not be in my here and now, even though I had been in their there and then. That nightmare was behind me. Havl approached, and I leaned against the shovel.

"There are several newspeople at the front gate who wish to speak to you," he said. "And Detective Mazzoni is back."

"Send him to me. Tell them I've got nothing to say."

He returned to the house, and a moment later Mazzoni walked toward me with another man. He introduced him as Detective Mike McBride. He had thick red hair and freckles. We shook hands.

"There's a crowd of media vultures at the gate," McBride said.

"So I'm told."

"We can have a car sent out to keep an eye on them if you want."

"That might not be a bad idea."

Bogey was beset by the media after his indictment. Ironically, he of all people had difficulty understanding that he had become a commodity. Money and position no longer protected him. Contempt had overnight bred familiarity. Strangers with microphones asked how it felt to steal from sick little kids. Yammering mobs of reporters engulfed him at court appearances. He was a cork bobbing helplessly in a sea of vulgar media.

"We got some pictures from the crime scene," Mazzoni said. "I thought you might like to see them." He handed me a manila envelope.

"You're showing me these informally, I take it."

"Yeah, that's right." If he caught my sarcasm, he didn't show it.

Eight-by-ten colored photographs showed that Winston Byron had been spread over quite a bit of ground. "Nothing was eaten far as we can tell," McBride said.

I looked at the photos in silence. It occurred to me that the detectives hoped the pictures might trigger remorse and confession.

"Whoever did this wasn't in his right mind," Mazzoni said gently.

"He needs help," McBride agreed with a concerned look. The good cop and the good cop. I wondered who took the bad-cop role when the time came.

I put the pictures in the envelope and handed them back.

"What do you think?" Mazzoni said.

"Poor bastard."

"Nobody deserves to die like that," McBride said. "Well, Hitler, if he was still alive."

"I looked up your old case," Mazzoni said. "You thought you were a dog at one time, right? A big one."

"That's right."

"You even wrote a book. By the way, know where I can get a copy?"

"Sorry, I don't."

"But it's true, right? You thought you were a dog. You had to kill to survive."

"That's correct." We looked up at a noise. A red helicopter hovered over Millwood. White letters on the side spelled out *News Eye*.

"Channel Four," McBride said. It was joined by a blue helicopter with *News Watch* on its side in yellow letters. "Channel Five."

"Some of the crews at the gate are in Winnebagos," Mazzoni said. "They got coals going on a Weber. Looks like they mean to stay a while."

"You can have them arrested for trespass if they come over the fence," McBride said.

I had to raise my voice over the noise of the helicopters. "My lawyer told me not to answer any more questions. So if you guys will excuse me." They looked disappointed. McBride asked if I planned to travel anywhere, would I let them know?

Clancy drove a rented car from the airport three hours later. "It's like the good old days down at the gate," he said cheerfully as we shook hands. "I made a statement."

"What did you say?"

"Like all the other good people of this community, you're horrified by the death of a friend and neighbor. You trust that the responsible party or parties will be swiftly brought to justice. I asked on your behalf that they respect your privacy."

"Fat chance."

"It doesn't hurt to ask." Clancy was big and impeccably tailored, vain as a peacock. He had gray hair dramatically swept back on both sides and long in back. He called it the Senator Claghorn look. He could laugh at himself up to a point. He looked around. "Nice place. Looks like you need more furniture, though. Some pictures on the walls wouldn't hurt."

"I'm still getting it fixed up."

"I went through that once. Pain in the ass. They told me down at the gate that you have a pack of dogs."

"Nearly fifty."

"Jesus Christ, why so many?"

"I find homes for them."

"That's nuts. No wonder they're looking at you. In my father's day, they would have beaten a confession out of you by now. I guess I should ask you if you did it."

"Nope."

"Good. Given a choice, I prefer innocent clients. They're less work. But I have to admit I'd go broke if it weren't for the guilty ones."

We took drinks out to the lawn. "You ought to put in a putting green," Clancy said. "I've got a one-hole course on my land."

"I don't play golf."

"That's a selfish point of view." He lowered his bourbon. "Look at the clods they're throwing up."

Cleo Basich cantered up on a snorting horse and dismounted. I introduced her to Clancy, who looked her up and down with appreciation. He admired women enough to have married four. He was surprised that Cleo didn't recognize his name.

"Bill's a lawyer," I said. Such ignorance about who he was would not be possible inside the Beltway.

"Have the police been here?" She asked. "They're talking to everyone. People are in an uproar. Melissa and Sarah left for their Lake Tahoe houses. Three other women I know have gone to their places in the wine country."

"They've been here twice."

A thought struck her. "Is it okay to be talking to you?"

"It was still a free country last time I looked," Clancy said importantly.

"Bill called from Tokyo. He said it's on the news there." He was her husband.

"When my friend here makes the news, it generally goes global." Clancy beamed at Cleo.

"Was it your dogs?" she asked.

"They didn't go anywhere."

"Then what killed poor Winston? Poor Helen is under a doctor's care." Cleo looked from me to Clancy.

"Who is Helen?" he asked.

"His wife."

Clancy said we had every confidence the authorities would identify and apprehend the responsible party or parties responsible and that justice would be served.

"Nothing like this has ever happened here before," Cleo fretted.

"I believe a crime of this nature would be unusual for any neighborhood, ma'am." Clancy was unctuous when satisfied, as he was now. A rich client, a high-profile crime, the media at the gate doing live feeds. What more could a lawyer ask? He tinkled the ice in his glass happily.

Cleo declined my offer of a cocktail. "I never drink and ride."

Clancy told her that was a sensible policy.

"I was kind of hoping it was your dogs," Cleo admitted.

"Why?"

"It would be over."

"Open and shut." Clancy's voice throbbed with sympathy.

"And we could bury Winston and go back to our lives."

We thought about that in silence. It looked like Clancy was working up a suitable remark.

He waited too long. "It's getting dark," Cleo said with a look at the sky. "I better be going."

She mounted and cantered off. People got indoors before dark in the other world. They barred the doors and windows and hoped they held. Bogey and Felicity had gone out every night, as I said, and he hated keeping farm-dog hours. But he was scared there, too. Bad things moved in the darkness.

"That's awful hard on a lawn." Clancy watched the divots fly. "You could have taken her to small claims court. Unless," he said with a lewd wink, "there are extenuating circumstances."

He put down his glass. "Well, I'm off myself. I'm meeting an old friend for dinner." He did a Groucho Marx thing with his eyebrows to say he didn't mean some old golfing buddy, either.

I had a dim memory of a rivalry he had with Bogey. They swapped boastful claims over women they had laid. "I'm staying at Huntington, but don't call unless you really need me." The eyebrow action again. "I'll drop by your police department in the morning and have a word with the boys. Tell them to stay off your ass if they aren't going to make an arrest. In the meantime, keep your lip buttoned, okay?"

He got in his rental car and crunched off down the long drive. Alice let the dogs out, and they came running up the hill, barking happily. A fat woman stepping out of a corset doesn't feel more relief than a dog turned loose. Manure that Cleo's horse had dropped commanded respectful attention. The hounds quartered back and forth elsewhere, drawing in a day's worth of scents. "Many strangers today," one bayed. The toy breeds quarreled shrilly among themselves under my feet.

I walked the grounds, the eye of swirling canine adoration. Duke, the Rhodesian ridgeback, came up to say he didn't sense anything on the wind tonight.

Alice and Quantrel, the young man who helped her in the afternoons, put them back in their runs after a half hour. The mainstream press withdrew early in the evening, but the people from the trashy tabloids remained camped at the gate. Their partying continued long after midnight. I heard bottles breaking.

5

A midterm calm held Stanford in its grip. Dr. Epperly had called to say it was such a beautiful day, why not have our session outdoors? We strolled the arched corridors of the quad. The pale sandstone buildings seemed to hold the sun's golden light. Students were hitting the books, so the campus seemed deserted.

She wore walking shorts that showed her long legs to advantage and a blouse and vest. She breathed deeply and said, "It's a crime to be inside on a day like this." We sat on a bench, and Dr. Epperly took off her sunglasses and gave a warm, encouraging look. "Were you able to sleep with the medication?"

"I slept very well."

"No bad dreams?"

"No dreams period."

She consulted her notes. "When we left off, you had just gotten away from what you called droliks and were on an island, where you encountered something. Do you think this dream has significance? Does it speak to you?"

"Nope. It's just a memory of a bad experience I went through."

"It's important for you to understand that you didn't really have that experience." Her expression was compassionate. "It's a memory of a delusional state you were in at the time."

I grinned at her. "It really happened, doc. Honest."

"I'm sure you believe that's so. Our job is to make you see how wrong that perception is."

"What if it's the other way around? What if I convince you it really happened?"

She laughed easily. "I guess I'd have to turn in my psychiatrist's license."

"In that world, there were creatures called Pig Faces. The name was for obvious reasons. They were the infantry for the bad guys. Smelled worse than shit."

Dr. Epperly wrote. "Pig Faces," she said. "Okay."

"One of their tricks was to gut whatever they caught. Big or small, it made no difference. They'd open them up and look for life. They were too stupid to realize they were killing what they were looking for."

"Sometimes we destroy what we love."

I let that pass. "Did you hear about the murder in Woodside?"

"Yes. So awful. Why?"

"I knew the victim slightly."

"The poor man. The radio said his family started one of the big cereal companies."

"He was gutted. I saw pictures."

Dr. Epperly was shocked. "He was eviscerated?"

"A nicer word for the same thing."

"You saw pictures? How?"

"The police showed me."

"Why you?"

"I have dogs. They thought they might have gotten loose."

"Did they?"

"No. They're also interested in when I was a dog."

"That was just a delusional interlude."

I shrugged. "The point is, the victim was torn apart. The Pig Faces themselves couldn't have done a better job."

Dr. Epperly knitted her brows as if she thought this might be harder than she thought. "You're not a suspect or anything?"

"Not formally."

"Then what's your point about these so-called Pig Faces?"

"What if they followed me from there to here?"

She changed the subject. "I looked at your medical records from prison. You declined to take medication."

We were back to that again. "It was prescribed as an antipsychotic. I'm not crazy."

"It can calm anxiety."

"I'm not anxious."

"There are no such things as Pig Faces," she said firmly.

"Who killed Byron, then?"

"The police will find out. That's what they're for."

"Not if the Pig Faces did it. The cops won't believe in them either."

"Why would they follow you here?" She was going to try logic.

"They wouldn't do anything on their own. Somebody would have to send them."

"Who might that be?"

I had given that thought. "Zalzathar."

"Who is that?"

"He's who pulled me into that other world in the first place. He's a conjurer, a wizard."

"For what purpose?"

"Zalzathar was the point man for evil. There was an angel named Helither who led the other side. He was a homespun sort out to lunch until it was nearly too late. Zalzathar was at the gates of Gowyith, the capital of the Fair Lands, with an army of Pig Faces and other monsters. I was with them."

"You were evil, too?"

"This was Bogey, remember. He'd been working both sides

of the street for the best deal. He had warned Helither the bad guys were coming, but that was as far as he was willing to go before he met Elvis."

"Elvis who? Not Presley." She tried not to laugh.

"It was really the Devil. He can assume any form. He wore one of those white costumes with all those buckles and zippers the fat Elvis had at the end. Seeing the Devil scared Bogey enough to push him off the dime and to throw in with Helither. He kept Zalzathar's army from coming up from the rear and surprising Helither's outnumbered garrison. That was the key to victory. The wizard could shoot lethal bolts of blue energy from his fingers. He was inside the wall and taking aim at Helmish—he was Bogey's buddy—when Bogey threw himself at him."

"What happened then?"

"There was a flash of blue light, and I found myself in bed at the low-rent nursing home where Felicity had parked me. I awoke from my coma at the same instant Bogey sacrificed himself for the first time ever. He got what he wanted through that act."

"So you believe in black magic?" She wrote something.

"I believe in Zalzathar. The bastard made it hot for me over there."

Dr. Epperly decided this was not a promising line of questioning. "I need to know more about you," she said brightly. "What have you been doing since you came out of that coma?"

"Most of the time I was in prison. Since then, I've switched my investments from active to passive. That took a while. I moved here from New York and bought a place called Millwood. I set up my charitable foundation."

"What about friends?"

All the sycophants Bogey thought of as friends were long gone. Other people were leery. They either thought I was a criminal freed by some niggling technicality, or I was a lunatic. "I guess I don't have any."

"Is that by choice?"

"It just is."

I wondered about her. Married to another doc, probably. Kids in high school. She had her professional life. Her sports and hobbies. Dinner parties with friends. Maybe she curled up on the sofa at night and watched television with her husband. A normal life, in short. That didn't sound so bad. Felicity scorned "little women" with lives like that. She was a diva starring in her own grand opera. You would never catch her on a sofa watching television with a husband.

My time was up, and I walked Dr. Epperly back to her campus office.

"I wonder if you wouldn't be better off with another psychiatrist," she said suddenly. "I feel out of my depth. You appear able to function well, but yet . . ."

"As long as we've gone this far."

"Your condition is so unusual and I'm not familiar with the literature in the field." She smiled. "If there is any."

"Maybe this is opportunity knocking. Your passport to academic fame."

She scoffed at fame. "It doesn't interest me."

Despite her misgivings, we made another appointment. My thoughts went back to the other world as I walked toward the parking lot. Zalzathar had told Bogey it was the Final Battle between the two sides. Mogwert was throwing all it had into it. If they lost, it was all over for them. The Devil had other worlds in play. He and the Bright Giver—God—had an infinite number of contests going on. The Devil had a shot at winning any given one and wouldn't waste more time there. With plans that he had spent who knows how long perfecting down the toilet, Zalzathar was the sort who would thirst for revenge. If he could pull Bogey through the barrier separating our worlds, it stood to reason he could send Pig Faces in the other direction to get me.

When I had passed though the gate in the pickup on my way to see Dr. Epperly, the media mob assumed I was a handyman and gave me only a glance. They were standing around in knots when I came back. A blond man in a three-piece suit with the jacket unbuttoned and his tie unknotted held up a palm like a traffic cop. He looked like he belonged on a surfboard. "Hold up there, mate." A broad-voweled Australian accent. "I saw you comin' out earlier. Tom Jessup of the *National Star*, how d'ye do. You work up there, do you?"

"What do you want?" I asked. Give them an inch and next you know they are reading your mail and looking in your refrigerator.

"Just give us some idear of what's goin' on up in the big house." He dropped his voice. "Might be a little money in it, bucko. The *Star* pays well for information."

"Sorry, I'm not interested."

He gave a sarcastic bow. "A thousand apologies, in that case. But if you change your mind." The others jeered the Australian as I drove through the gate.

Clancy was practicing with a putter. "You've got the wrong kind of grass. I'll give you the name of the right seed to plant when I get back home. Lord, listen to those dogs. You'd think you'd been gone a year."

"Did you talk to the police?"

"They've got some physical evidence. They want a DNA sample. The victim had some hair in one hand. He apparently put up a struggle." He gave me a look. "Couldn't be your hair, could it?"

"I think not."

"They just need to snip a lock. I told them you didn't have a lot to spare."

Bogey had been thinking of going the hair plug route, but I decided the hell with it. Mine was thinning in the back, where I couldn't see. Out of sight, out of mind.

"I told them you'd be down sometime this afternoon. I'll go with you to hold your hand."

"It's what I pay you for."

That night I watched *Nightline*. ABC had been advertising its exclusive interview with Bernie Soderberg all day long. It had been three years since I had seen him at a charity ball in West Palm Beach that I attended with Felicity. The change was amazing. He had been a queer-looking geek. Short, rumpled, and a head shaped like the business end of an artillery shell. You noticed this all the more because he plastered a few strands of side hair over the top to try to fool the world into thinking he wasn't nearly bald. It was what got Bogey thinking about hair plugs. Soderberg had so much dandruff on his shoulders it looked like he had just come from a celebration where confetti was thrown. Eyeglasses like the bottom of Coke bottles. A real ugly little bugger, but he didn't care about looks. His brain was one of the natural wonders of the world—he supposedly had the highest IQ ever measured—and it did not descend from its Olympian heights for such minor things as appearance.

Yet here he was on *Nightline* looking like he had been the recipient of the mother of all makeovers. The thick glasses were gone, he had a reasonable head of hair, and when he smiled it was pretty apparent he had caps. Soderberg was still no matinee idol, but he looked, well, normal. He had been to see a good tailor, too. His suit was tailored to minimize the disparity between huge head and his narrow shoulders. No dandruff that I could see. He'd had voice lessons, too. Before, he sounded like a speeded-up tape. Now he spoke slowly, with more than a trace of the South. Soderberg brought up the changes himself. "Been a lotta changes in how I look at things, Paul," he told the *Nightline* host. "I never had time before to think about a wife and kids. When it comes time to look for someone you wanna spend the rest of your life with, it behooves you to look your best." Paul complimented him on the improvement.

"Wal," Soderberg replied, "I know I'm not gonna ever win any beauty contests, but I jes' hope I don't break any mirrors, either." They shared a guffaw, then Paul got him to talk about his decision to retire from business.

"Time to give somethin' back, Paul. Lordy, I had enough money. It didn't mean anythin' anymore. I wanna leave this danged old world a better place when it comes time to go. That make any sense?"

Paul said it certainly did, a whole lot. "Some say you don't rule out politics."

"Some might be right," Soderberg said with a twinkle, "but I'm not gonna say here tonight what I'm gonna do. First thing is, I don't know myself. Second is, there's a little lady who might just have somethin' to say about that question."

"May we assume from that remark"—Paul beamed—"that you have ID'd the future Mrs. Soderberg and locked on target?"

"Gracious me, you're gonna have me blushin' on national TV. But seriously, I don't think I wanna say any more on that subject right now."

Paul frowned to show he was a news pro and it was hardball time. "There've been reports you're worth as much as one hundred billion dollars. True or false?"

Everybody guessed, but nobody knew but Soderberg. I expected another evasion. but he leaned forward with an answering furrow of his own brow. "Way too high, Paul. About eighty-one billion, give or take."

"If, as some say, you intend to enter politics, doesn't a fortune that huge present problems in terms of conflict of interest?"

"I'm puttin' the whole kit and caboodle into a blind trust.

It'll be administered by a board of directors of some of the most trusted Americans there are. Would it interest you, Paul, to know your name has been mentioned?"

The *Nightline* host was flabbergasted. "I . . . I," he said, coloring.

"Didn't mean to put you on the spot," Soderberg said with a chuckle. I half expected him to shift a chaw of 'backy to his outer cheek. The telephone rang, and I muted the sound.

"Are you watching that brownnosing interview on *Nightline*?" It was Jared Snyder. "It was on earlier here."

"He just asked the talking head if he wanted to help oversee the blind trust."

"Eighty-one billion. Unbelievable. The bastard's going to run for president, mark my words. This is the opening shot. Jesus, that cornpone act makes him sound like Festus. I wonder how many shares he's got in Cap Cities/ABC to rate those powder puff questions."

"You saw the whole thing? The gloves never come off?"

"It gets even more respectful, take my word for it. You'd think it was the pope."

"I have to admit he makes a good impression."

"Good? CNN says seventy-three percent of the people in a telephone poll had a very positive opinion. That's George Bush after the Gulf War or Bill after the blow-jobs. Do you believe the change in his looks? The guy's almost handsome. President Soderberg. Might as well get used to it."

"One appearance on TV isn't going to wipe out the guy's past."

"You have a higher opinion of the voters than I do. Look at Ross Perot. He came from nowhere with only a twang and those charts he pointed at. Soderberg can spend a hundred times more and not miss it. I bet you ten grand the next stop is the Oval Office. Speaking of CNN, I saw a brief about you. Some guy was torn apart by an animal and you're supposedly involved?"

"It was a neighbor. They don't know who did it."

"It sounded from what I heard that they think you're mixed up somehow. There was a stand-up outside your gate. Talk about déjà vu."

"It's nothing."

He offered to bet me ten grand again and I said no. I watched the rest of the interview. The phone rang again. This time it was Clancy. He also had seen *Nightline* and was impressed. "I hear *Time* and *Newsweek* are tearing out their covers and rushing profiles into print."

"Unbelievable."

"Nothing's unbelievable in politics. Look at Bill Clinton, bless him. He and his administration were the best friend a lawyer ever had, at least this lawyer. But that's not what I'm calling about. Are you sitting down?"

"Why?"

"A friend in the FBI tipped me. That was your hair in the victim's hand."

I was silent.

"The DNA is a match."

Clancy said he would talk to the detectives in the morning. "They don't know I know. They use the county lab. Maybe there's been sloppy work. Problems with the chain of custody for the evidence. It happens, as we all know. But you better be prepared."

"For what?"

"There's a good chance you might be arrested for murder."

hung up and sat down. How could some of my hair be at the murder scene? I went to the window. Heavy fog was drifting in again. I could barely make out the kennels and the dogs nervously pacing in their runs. They stopped to lift noses to the wind, then resumed pacing.

Did I kill Winston Byron?

Someone had left the house, unless there was a malfunction in the security system. The technician who came to check it out had scratched his head and said it sure beat the hell out of him. That theory needed unbelievable coincidence to fly anyhow. How about this one: I walk in my sleep, come across the drunken Byron, and rip his guts out in some canine fury left over from nightmareland.

But that had problems, too. There was blood all over the murder scene. Even if I showered when I got back, my pajamas and slippers would have been soaked. Millwood had a laundry room somewhere. I saw it when I inspected the place before buying. I thought it was in the six-car garage, but it would take some hunting to find. For this theory to hold water, I had to wash my bloody stuff, run it through the dryer, put it back on, and go back to bed without being aware of anything. Anyhow, Havl had the keys to the garage.

No, it was clear I was being framed. Zalzathar must have followed Bogey back to our world to pay him back. It wasn't all that surprising, given that he was a vindictive son of a bitch. There he was, all set to rule a world in Mogwert's name until Bogey does his flip-flop. There was nothing left for him, thanks to the double cross. No wonder he thirsted for revenge.

I had a feeling in the pit of my stomach. Fear, yes, but something else. Excitement. Whatever you might say about Bogey, his life was not dull. He padded capitalism's jungle looking for prey. Companies that had lost a step drew his tigerish eye. He ruthlessly cut them from the herd and put them into play. They were spared only if directors shed their sloth, kicked out the incompetent management, and won back the confidence of the stockholders Bogey had wooed.

He made and received scores of calls each day. His sources gave him expert analyses and insider dirt. His intelligence craft was superior to any blundering government agency like the CIA. Informants ranged in a democratic arc from CEOs to shoeshine boys. Some he paid, some he tipped off so they rode the rise in price shares like balloonists. He formed alliances with other Wall Street predators and stabbed them in the back when it suited his purposes. His wits had to be sharp because he had his own investors to keep happy. A misstep and he would be prey instead of predator. He would be kicked out or their capital would move to some other freebooter.

He plotted, schemed, conspired, and strategized. He bullied and flattered, pleaded and threatened. As deplorable as he was, as base and untrustworthy, Bogey believed he was doing useful work. So what if people hated him? He rose eagerly each day and had a bounce in his step until he crawled between silk sheets at the end of it.

It was a far cry from what I did now. I found dogs new homes and dug in my garden. Whatever positives you might see in the simple life, its days did not make the pulse race. I would be giving a lot of money away at some point, but that was still in the future. And I didn't think it would bring me the same thrill Bogey got making it.

But now I was a suspect in a murder investigation, targeted for revenge by a malevolent wizard. Whose adrenaline wouldn't be pumping?

The telephone rang. "The dogs are nervous again," Alice said.

I thought of the huge house filled with its empty and half-empty rooms. There were dozens of places to hide. "Turn them loose."

"Really?" Her voice was doubtful.

"Really." If the Pig Faces were coming after me this time, they would think twice before tangling with forty-eight dogs.

"What about the neighbors?"

"Screw the neighbors. Most of them have deserted the field of battle anyhow."

"Deserted?" she said uncertainly. "Field of battle?"

"Let the bastards sue if they don't like it."

There is nothing like danger to blow off the rust. You sit up straighter and think sharper. I felt like I was back in my old skin. I was back on the bridge again, the skull and crossbones snapped smartly on the flagpole, and the decks were cleared for action. Avast, me hearties!

It was likely Pig Faces were not all Zalzathar had with him. He had a whole roster of horrors to pick from. But most would be of no use here. Their sheer hideousness would stop traffic. Even the Pig Faces would need major cosmetic work. Those yellowed tusks would have to go. A floppy hat, baggy pants to cover their stick-out baboon butts, shoes for their hind trotters, and a razor taken to their ugly, bristly boar's faces. Dunk them in vats of cheap cologne to cover their god-awful stink and maybe they could go out in public.

I went down to the kitchen and fixed coffee. I thought about

Soderberg. He was Zalzathar's kind of guy, as shown by the fact he was the first choice to be brought over there to give advice on how to outsmart the Two-Legs. The wizard told Bogey that Bernie would have been richly rewarded for his help. The same promise would be necessary on this side. But what do you give the multibillionaire who has everything? All the power he wanted. Who was the most powerful man in the world? The president of the United States.

I watched how the news handled the *Nightline* interview. It had been a dull day on the catastrophe front, so they gave the story a good ride. I was relegated to the "there are no new developments today" category and kissed off in thirty seconds. There was footage of Clancy talking to the mob of reporters camped out at the entrance to Millwood, but no sound.

The dogs were running around outside, having a fine old time. The males lifted legs to mark their territory. As soon as one did, another peed right over it.

Oliver was rumbling to himself. I asked what the problem was. "I smell cat."

"No cat would dare come near here."

"I smell cat." Oliver wasn't one to lose sleep over it, and he curled up. I closed the windows and locked the bedroom door.

The next morning, when I came down, Havl's smile was arch. "Shall I make a tray for the young lady?" he asked.

"What young lady?"

"I have spoken out of turn," he said with injured dignity. "I am sorry."

"What're you talking about?"

He hesitated before replying. "I was inspecting the doors to make sure they were locked when I saw her. It was just after three. A beautiful young woman walking down the hall toward your room."

"What'd she look like?"

He colored. "She was . . . well, she was naked."

My first thought was that Felicity had gotten in. After I came out of the coma, she tried to weasel her way back under my roof. "Can we talk?" she kept asking on the telephone. I told her no. I had settled a large sum on her beyond what the prenuptial called for and told my lawyers to tell hers I never wanted to see her again. But nobody tells Felicity what to do. "When are you going to stop sulking?" she kept asking.

"Was it my former wife?" I asked Havl.

"No. This woman's hair was as long, but it was black."

"You sure you saw someone?"

We looked at each other.

"I obviously was mistaken." It was clear Havl felt I shot him down when he tried to speak to me man to man. "I'll get the morning papers," he said stiffly.

They played the Soderberg story big as well. The coverage was admiring to the point of nausea. All the other politicians mentioned as possible presidential timber had bored everyone stiff a long time ago, but here was someone new to put under the microscope. The *New York Times* and the other heavy-weights ran their own interviews. It was clear the whole thing had been carefully orchestrated. Bernie regurgitated fine-sounding slogans whose meaning melted away when you thought about them. I remembered Ted Butler saying that the billionaire had locked up all the topflight political talent. It showed.

"I believe you saw what you said," I told Havl later. "I just didn't see her."

He let it lay. "The journalists at the gate complained that the dogs kept them awake all night."

"Gee, that's too bad."

I told him he might be seeing more strange things.

"Oh?"

"The man who was torn apart?"

"Mr. Byron."

"I think he was killed by creatures who have come after me from the other world."

Havl didn't bat an eye. "I see."

I walked through the house with Oliver, from basement to attic. There was no sign of a woman, naked or otherwise. It had been Zalzathar messing with Havl's mind. Zalzathar had great mental powers. Giving people bad dreams or making them hallucinate was child's play for him. When I got back downstairs, Havl was waiting with bags packed.

"I would like to give notice." I could see there was no arguing him out of it. It was my telling him to expect more strange things. Havl had read menace into it. He guessed the old Bogey was back.

"No hard feelings?"

"I will telephone with an address where you can send my . . . I do not know what the word is in English. The separation payment." He hesitated. "If there is to be one." I said there would be.

We shook hands and he walked out the door and down the gravel drive toward the front gate. His back was rigid, and he ignored the dogs smelling him.

"It's just you and me," I told Oliver.

He pricked his ears and looked at me intelligently. "I'm hungry." There is not much variety in a dog's conversation. Oliver's eyes said all that needed to be said. I was God and he was in heaven.

Later in the morning I drove out the gate in the pickup. The media knew who I was this time. I kept the windows up as I eased through them. They shouted questions. "Did you kill Winston Byron?" a young man in a *News Watch* blazer yelled. "Why?" I gunned the engine when I was clear. In the rearview mirror I saw them running for their cars. They didn't know the neighborhood, and I lost them by going through the little lane next to the Renslers's pasture.

I drove to El Camino Real, the business district, and headed for the Clipper Ship. That was where I got my last haircut from a barber named Tony. It was now a mass of charred wreckage, with yellow police tape around it. The guy in the flower store next door told me it had burned down the week before.

"The fire nearly spread to my place, but they got here just in time."

"How's Tony?"

"Not so good. He's wife's been sick and he had to let the fire insurance lapse."

He knew where Tony lived in Redwood City, and I drove over. I saw him through the window sitting on a sofa with his head in his bandaged hands. He looked up with a dull expression when I knocked. His face was shiny with ointment.

"Remember me?" I asked when he opened the door.

"Yeah," Tony said without interest. He was a fat Italian with a big smile. He gave off a faint smell of garlic when he cut your hair. The smile was gone now, and he was haggard and red-eyed. "You were in last week before the fire. Fact is, I think you mighta been my last customer before it broke out."

"What happened?"

"You tell me. I go into the back room and I come back there's smoke and flames. I almost didn't get out. The fire department guys said they never saw a fire spread so fast."

"Was anyone else in the shop?"

"Why do you wanna know? You one of those bastards from the insurance company? If you are, get your ass off my property. You pay for years, and when you need them, they stiff you. One lousy payment I missed. Now I'm gonna lose my house with my wife sick in the back bedroom."

"What was your loss in the fire?"

"Between fifty and sixty. Whaddya you care?"

"Let me ask you a strange question."

"What is it?"

"Was my hair still on the floor?"

"You some kind of weirdo? Get outta here."

I took my checkbook out. "Sixty on the high end?"

"What're you doin'?"

I wrote out the check and gave it to him.

"What's this?" Tony said suspiciously. He looked at it. "Sixty thousand! What's the joke?"

"From me to you. Call the bank. They'll tell you it's good."

"But . . . but why're you givin' this to me?"

"Answer the question."

"What question?"

"Was my hair still on the floor?"

He looked up at the porch ceiling to think. "Yeah, I think it was. No, I'm sure. I went to the can and when I came back I was gonna sweep up."

"Thanks," I said and walked to the pickup. Tony was still standing on the porch looking at me when I drove off.

A police car was at the gate when I came back, so the media didn't mob the pickup this time. A message from Clancy was on my voice mail.

"They're tossing a coin whether to arrest you. The DA's probably going to ask for no bail or some outrageous amount so you don't split the country like Robert Vesco."

"That hair of mine they found on Byron. Did you see it?"

"No."

"Hair pulled out in a fight would be ragged, right?"

"What do you mean 'ragged'?"

"Some short, some long."

"So what?"

"Hair cut by a barber's scissors would be even."

"Do you have a point you're making here?"

"I got a haircut last week. The barber shop burned down a short time after I left. My hair was still on the floor."

"You think we can pin this on your barber, for crissake?"

"Somebody took the hair off the barbershop floor, then burned the place down."

He was silent. "Why would somebody do that?"

"To frame me for Winston Byron's murder."

There was more silence while Clancy processed this. "Who'd do that?"

"Good question." I didn't want to say Zalzathar. Clancy was capable of getting a court order to commit me and then pat himself on the back afterward, saying at least it kept me out of jail.

"We need more than good questions, we need good answers," he said.

"Be pompous on your own dime. When you point out to the cops my hair was cut by scissors instead of torn out, they might be less eager to arrest me."

He admitted I had a point. I gave him Tony's address and hung up. I called Phil Doyle in New York. Bogey had used his big investigation agency to check out companies that looked ripe for the picking. Doyle's people tapped phones and bribed employees for a peek at secret company documents and into databases. Sometimes Bogey had the gumshoes tail Felicity to discover if she was cheating, but they never turned up anything. She was too smart for them or was innocent. Innocence was a long shot when it came to Felicity, but not impossible.

"I got a job for you," I told Doyle. He was an ex-cop with a crewcut and a look that said he had seen the worst people had to offer so nothing could ever surprise him again.

"I thought you retired," he said.

"I just unretired. How soon can you get to California?"

"If it's important, I'm on my way out the door. Oh, there's one thing."

"What is it?"

"The little matter of that ninety grand you owe my company."

I drew a blank, as often happened with the details of Bogey's past business life. "Refresh my memory."

"I sued you for not paying for work I done for you. It was an oral contract, and you won because I couldn't prove it. You mean you don't remember?"

"I'll pay you when you get here."

"I'm practically on the airplane now."

I gave directions on how to get to Millwood from the airport. "Go to the back. There's a dark green metal gate in the hedge with spikes on top. It'll be unlocked."

"I've been seeing the stuff about you on TV. Is that what this is about?" I said we would talk tomorrow.

Alice was at the door. She wore sweatpants and a baggy sweater, her usual uniform. She wanted to know if she could hire a few kids to patrol with pooper-scoopers. It was a terrific aid to digestion for the dogs to run around all night. I told her hire who she needed. She said the agents had found homes for eleven more dogs. We were staying ahead of the curve for a change.

"People aren't dropping them off because of those reporters in front," she said.

"I knew there had to be an upside."

"They find a way to keep their dogs when it's harder to get rid of them."

Toward dark I went out the gate in the hedge and walked down a lonely lane turned ghostly by fog. The tall trees on either side formed a long tunnel. They tossed restlessly in a wind, and the fog changed shape. I walked up Cleo Basich's long lawn and knocked at her front door. A fearful Mexican maid opened it after looking through a window.

Cleo came to welcome me. She wore long pants and a bulky sweater with a turtleneck under that. "What's with this fog?" she complained. "It's every night lately." I followed her into a living room big enough for basketball. A good fire crackled in the fireplace.

"I've got one burning every night. You'd think it was winter in the Orkneys. You want a drink?" I said a scotch would be fine. The maid went to get it.

I asked her when her husband would get back from Japan. "Next week, and I can hardly wait. I think you and I are the only ones left in the neighborhood, not counting domestics." Cleo's pep-squad spirits were gone. She was as spooked as the maid.

"Have you heard anything new?" Cleo asked.

"Not to speak of." A deft way to avoid the outright lie. The maid came back with my drink on a tray. I sipped it. "Your husband's a gun nut, as I recall."

"He's got enough to start a war."

"I wonder if I might borrow one."

"Borrow ten if you like." She lifted her sweater enough to show an automatic in a holster at her waist. "I don't even go out to the stable without this."

She led me to the gun room in the basement, a shrine to weaponry. There must have been a hundred handguns, rifles, semiautomatics, and shotguns on display in glass cases and handcarved racks. Track lighting and spotlights focused on the really expensive pieces. The star of the collection was a Purdy shotgun once owned by the king of England who married Wallis Simpson.

"You can't borrow any of those. My husband would have a fit. What kind do you want?" Cleo asked.

"Something easy."

"Do you know how to shoot?"

I said yes. Bogey's security advisers insisted that he learn during a company takeover that put nearly five thousand tiremakers on the street. The jobs went to China.

I chose a nine-millimeter Glock automatic. I had one before my conviction made it illegal for me to own guns. Cleo gave me a box of ammunition to go with it, and I loaded a clip as she watched. "I hope you don't have to use it, but shoot straight if you do. It's better justice than the courts." That was a side of her I hadn't seen up to now.

I promised to do my best if forced to open fire. "It's time for the news," Cleo said. I followed her into a den that looked like an Edwardian club. She turned on the TV with a remote, and we settled into green leather chairs that squeaked like new shoes.

There was the usual business with helicopter shots of familiar landmarks, snippets of footage from awful things that had happened, and a voice-over crowing about the Emmies that *News Watch* had won. Then the news anchor lifted his handsome face from a paper he was pretending to read. "*News Watch* has learned exclusively that there has been a sensational break in the Winston Byron case, called the most shocking crime of this decade."

"They've got him," Cleo said excitedly. "Yes!"

They went live to the front entrance to Millwood, where a reporter stood in a heavy parka. "Yes, Burke, we just learned moments ago that evidence at the crime scene links the notorious Wall Street swindler Bogey Ingersol to the victim." Dogs barked in the background.

"Has an arrest been made?" the anchor asked.

"Not at this time, Burke. But we're standing by for further developments." They exchanged banter about the fog, which led in to the weather guy giving the forecast.

Cleo and I sat in silence. The anchor said sports was coming. Cleo shut off the TV and slowly turned to face me.

"Is it true?" She was pale, and her eyes seemed enormous. Her hand was near her gun for a quick draw. Her husband would probably have his out and be firing by now.

"Are you asking did I kill Winston Byron?"

"No . . . well, I . . ."

"The answer is no. Somebody's trying to frame me." It sounded like a line written by a hack screenwriter in one of those 1940s detective movies.

"I better be going," I said. The look of relief on her face was almost comic. "I can find my way out." Bolts were rammed home when the door closed on me.

The fog was heavier, damp and clinging. I struck off toward where I thought the lane was. After a couple of wrong turns in the fog, one of which brought me near the stable where her horses stamped and snorted nervously, I found the lane. The streetlights overhead were like yellow smears on a dark expressionist canvas. Then they went out.

7

Then I heard running feet from behind and to the right. Many running feet. Pig Faces.

I stood stock still, panic squeezing my throat. Bogey escaped by being fleet of foot in the other world. I didn't have that four-footed advantage. I had the Glock out with the safety off, but if they came out of the fog I wouldn't nail more than two or three before the rest took me down. Then I remembered how much Bogey had wished for tree-climbing ability on the other side. He lost even more meals when prey shot up trunks than when they went to ground.

I felt my way like a blind man until I touched the rough bark of one of the trees lining the lane. I was just able to reach the lowest branch and swing up. The tree was wet from the fog, and my shoes kept slipping as I climbed higher. The running feet came closer and I froze. I heard the grunts and snuffling sounds they used to communicate. Then their smell reached me, a stink like an outhouse ripening in the summer sun. They passed below, headed for Millwood. The wind fell and there was silence except for the slow drip of fog. My heart was like a bird trying to beat its way out of my ribcage.

They realized I had given them the slip and worked their way back. I remembered that Pig Faces had poor noses but keen hearing. I stood in the tree without moving. They took a few steps and listened, then a few more. Their cunning monkey paws made them expert nest robbers. This tree would be no problem. The fog hid us from each other. I sensed them listening, waiting for sound to guide them. Time crawled as cold crept into my bones like a toothache. I was in the crotch of a limb, my back against the trunk. The wind picked up again. The leaves hissed like an audience when the villain comes on. The tree bent with a groan that seemed to rise from deep in its arboreal soul.

More time passed. I could not stay up there all night. Much longer and I'd be so numb I would fall when I tried to climb down. I had the sense that they had moved off to search elsewhere. I stuck my fingers in my mouth to warm them and then began to descend. The thing about trees is, coming down is harder than going up. I reached the last limb and dropped to the ground silently. I fumbled with the laces with numb fingers and took off my shoes to make less noise. I moved in the direction I thought the lane was. I reached it a few steps later. Keeping in contact with the curb was the only way to know I was going toward Millwood.

I crept forward for a quarter of an hour. Then the side of my stockinged feet touched an empty beer can. My notoriety had attracted a loose element, who brought litter to the neighborhood. The can rolled. You wouldn't think it would make that much noise, but the sound was like a gutter ball at a bowling alley. Off to the right, running feet again. To the left, bless them, the dogs at Millwood woofed questioningly ("Wuz 'at?"). I limped as fast as I could.

Pig Faces run on all fours, and they made up ground fast. The dogs barked furiously, adding voices as more came running to see what was up. I reached the tall, impenetrable hedge. Was the gate right or left? My life depended on the correct choice. The footsteps were louder now. I heard grunting. I headed left.

I ran with one hand brushing the hedge so I would know if I reached the gate. The keener noses recognized my scent on the other side, and the barking changed from challenge to welcome. "Master's back!"

Then came the joyous squeals Pig Faces made when they knew the end of the chase is at hand and the butchery can begin. Bogey had heard that sound many times, watching with sick horror as victims were disemboweled and their innards rifled for the secret of life.

The gate.

My hand found the cold knob. I turned it and pushed the gate open. I knew I didn't even have time to close it. I ran onto Millwood's grounds. The dogs streamed past me. Instinct told them an enemy was at hand. The fighting broke out immediately. Yammering barks, the deep voices of the watchdogs mixing with the higher-pitched terrier breeds. Snarls, grunts, yelps, and squeals. The thump of bodies being kicked by hooves. I held my fire for fear of hitting a dog. More poured past me to join the fray. Suddenly, the gate clanged shut. The Pig Faces were gone. The tension left me so fast I felt like a balloon deflating.

"What's going on down there?" Alice's worried voice came from the kennels. A flashlight stabbed the darkness.

"Mr. Ingersol, I didn't know it was you. I heard the dogs fighting."

"I came down to check."

"What happened to your shoes?"

"I didn't have time to put them on."

"What were they fighting with, raccoons?"

"I couldn't see." There was no way I could tell the truth. She would make tracks faster than Havl. The dogs came up to be praised, stiff-legged and bristling. They boasted about their valor the way dogs do.

"Did you hear him scream when I bit?"

"They won't be back, give thanks to me."

"We were losing until I got here."

I made over them, patting and stroking and telling them what fine fellows they were.

"Oh, look, it's Lola," Alice said heartbrokenly. The beam of her flashlight had found a Weimeraner who lay on the grass. Lola's back was broken. "And look at Jack." He was a mixed breed whose right front leg hung at a funny angle as he limped on the other three. Two more dogs were dead, including Duke, the Rhodesian ridgeback. Alice was crying. I bent down along-side him, stroking his warm body. His eyes were open and beginning to glaze. I gently took pig bristles from his mouth.

"No raccoons did this," Alice said in a shaking voice. "It must've been a mountain lion. They've seen tracks up near the Crystal Springs Reservoir. What's that awful smell?"

I helped her carry the bodies up to the kennels. "We'll give them heroes' burials tomorrow," I said.

Oliver stood alertly at the door when I came in. "Trouble?" his eyes asked.

"It's over now."

I was half frozen. I went upstairs and ran a hot bath to warm up. I put antiseptic on the cuts on my feet. I thought my heart rate might return to normal in a week. Oliver lay on the bathroom floor as I climbed into the tub to thaw out. I kept the Glock within reach. I had not forgotten the woman Havl saw the night before. I guessed she was a harpy from the other side. Some were toothless hags, but others gave Felicity a run for the money in the looks department. Zalzathar used them to lure Two-Legs into betrayal. When I sank into bed, I let Oliver sleep at the bottom. I awoke once to see him standing on the bed and staring at the door. His ears were cocked and he turned his head from side to side, puzzled.

"What's wrong?" I whispered.

"Thought I heard something." He snorted to clear the scent and curled up again. "I like it up here."

Alice and I were just finishing burying the dogs in the garden the next morning when Clancy strolled up, natty in a pearl gray suit and silk tie. He wore a Panama hat.

"What're you doing?" he asked. I explained.

"We think it was a mountain lion," Alice said. Her eyes were red from crying.

"Jeez, that's too bad," Clancy said. He looked at his wristwatch. "You got a minute?"

We walked back up toward the house. The workmen hammered and sawed, and power tools whined. Dry rot had been found in the south wing. The contractor was decent enough to try to hide his pleasure.

"The police agreed the hair is shaky evidence," Clancy said. "But would you tell me one thing?"

"What?"

"Why did you give the barber all that money?"

"If it weren't for me, they wouldn't have burned his shop down."

"Who's 'they'?"

"Somebody with a grudge against me," I said casually.

"Thousands match that description when you count all the poor bastards who lost jobs." He took off his Panama and turned his face to the sun. "A glorious day." He put it back on. "If we put the barber on the witness stand, the prosecution will make that money look like a bribe."

"A bribe to cut my hair so I could put it in Byron's hands?"

Clancy shook his head. "It just doesn't look good. Sixty thousand bucks. The guy wasn't even your regular barber."

"I don't have a regular barber."

"The guy would be a millionaire if you did."

"Who says I'm going on trial?"

"Those detectives were nearly on their way out the door to arrest you when I showed them the light of reason. They'd tipped off the media already."

"I know. I saw it on TV last night."

"So now they've got egg on their face."

"So they still have to find out who or what really killed Byron."

"They want to believe it was you in the worst way. A neat package with no loose strings." He paused. "What do you mean, 'or what'?"

"Was mine the only hair found at the scene?"

"I didn't ask."

"Can you find out?"

"They didn't take my last visit very kindly."

"Maybe it was the same mountain lion that attacked my dogs last night," I said. "People have also seen wild pigs up in the hills." The newspaper said they were damaging the ecology by uprooting native plants.

Clancy looked like a light had gone on over his head. "That's an idea." He thought more. "That's a damned good idea. I always wondered how he could be ripped apart like that. An animal—that's it."

After he left, Phil Doyle drove in from the airport. His pug face was wrathful, and his crewcut seemed to bristle like one of the dogs. "Those assholes at your front gate demanded to know who I was. I told them to shove it." He was not a sunny-natured man at the best of times. The red-eye flight had not improved his disposition.

"It's a crime how they treat you on the airlines," he said. "Even Greyhound was better when I was a kid in college." His disposition improved when I gave him the check for what Bogey owed him.

"I take back all those things I used to say."

We went to the kitchen and I ground beans for coffee and

ran them through the fancy German brewing machine. A cup perked him up more. "What swill they pour on the airlines," he said. "I defy the bastards who own them to drink it." He looked around hungrily. "You don't have anything to eat, do you? I'm starved."

"I think there're eggs in the refrigerator. The guy who does most of the cooking quit."

"Eggs are a good start." He peeled off his coat and hunted around. He found potatoes and onions in the pantry. He poured oil in a skillet and fried them. When they were done, he cracked half a dozen eggs and mixed them in. He filled a plate and ate. When he was finished, he gave me an up-and-down look.

"You've lost weight. Prison chow?"

"I've been doing a lot of running."

"I knew two guys who keeled over from heart attacks jogging. They both died."

"I admire a man who looks on the bright side."

"I'm a realist. So what can I do for you?"

"Did you watch Soderberg's announcement?"

"They say he's gonna run for president. You for him?"

"I haven't made up my mind."

"He's looking good, but it's way early yet."

"I want you to check him out."

"Big subject."

"Just for the past eighteen months. He's made a lot of deals."

"I read the papers. What about them?"

"Fiduciary Services, the financial holding company. The Wierker Group, German media. Peak Minerals, the big South American mining outfit. Telebourse Ltd., financial information. Two or three others. All are dominant in their field, or near it."

"And?"

"Those are an awful lot of companies to take over in that short period. Putting such deals together would make a huge demand on any organization. Nobody has that kind of talent, not even Soderberg. Or especially Soderberg. He always bragged about how lean he kept his. You'd need armies of accountants, bankers, lawyers, and specialists to pull off each one of those deals. And time. In not one case was there opposition to the sale. Where were the outraged directors and managements who used to complicate my life?"

"Maybe he paid top dollar without your flaky schemes where companies were bought with their own money. People couldn't believe how you pulled that shit off."

"Something isn't kosher, I'm sure of it. I want you to find out."

"A big job."

"You said that before."

"This isn't going to be cheap."

"Spend what you need."

He grinned. "People said you'd changed. There's the proof."

"I'm a new man." It had become a mantra.

"I guess I better get to work." He put on his coat and walked out. There wasn't a lot of unnecessary talk with Doyle.

That afternoon I drove the pickup to Stanford. The news that I would not be arrested had melted the crowd at the gate. The man who reported this on the radio sounded disappointed, but looked on the bright side. "Police say they still don't rule out the convicted Wall Street swindler as a suspect."

"I'm interested in hearing more about this Helither," Dr. Epperly said in her office. She was wearing a cardinal skirt and sweater with matching lipstick. There was a football game in the afternoon, and that was the Stanford color. Even the face of her watch was red. Her hair was in a French braid. "You described him as an angel."

"He kept an eye on things for the Bright Giver."

"The Bright Giver is God, obviously."

"That's correct. Bogey—"

She interrupted. "I'd like you to not refer to him as 'Bogey.' I want you to say 'I.' It's important. Was Helither a spirit? A voice in your head?"

"He was a gardener. A real humble guy. You wouldn't give him a second look. I met him in Gowyith when I finally got there. He knew at a glance I wasn't a dog. It shook him up that the wizard had conjured me from here to there. It told him Zalzathar had a lot more power than before."

"To refresh my memory, the Two-Legs were humans?"

"That's right. They'd been fighting Mogwert for genera-tions, though there had been a long cease-fire since the last war. Helither was a surrogate for the Bright Giver, and Mog-wert and Zalzathar were stand-ins for the Devil. Put another way, it was the struggle between good and evil. Helither told me it went on in an infinite number of universes, and the Bright Giver was creating more all the time. That's why he wasn't there for Helither the way the Devil was for Zalzathar That's why it seems evil wins more than good."

"I don't believe that's true."

"Really? Look around you. Wars, famines, and the rest. Crime, cruelty, et cetera."

"I believe there's more good than bad in the world."

"You must not read the papers."

"Goodness doesn't sell papers. It's too dull. But I don't want to get into a discussion about metaphysics."

"Fine by me."

"This dream or vision you had was Manichean."

"What's that mean?"

"Seeing things as black and white."

"I admit things were a lot simpler there. What you saw was what you got. I was used to the shades of gray here, to things not always being what they seem."

"To ambiguity and nuance."

"If you want to put it that way."

"That's why you thought you could make a deal with the Devil." She made air quotes to show that she had a secular take on Mephistopheles.

"I was a dealmaker. It's give-and-take on Wall Street. One hand washes the other. You've got to let the other guy win a little. It took a while to realize it didn't work that way there. There was no middle ground. It was one side or the other. You've heard about the shock of recognition? That's what I got when I met the Devil looking like Elvis." Behind his hip irony, I had a sense of evil beyond human comprehension. Compromise with it was impossible.

"Do you have any habits you would consider compulsive?"

"I always give beautiful women a second look. Does that qualify?"

She smiled. "I mean mannerisms or, say, rituals. Do you always brush your teeth a certain number of times? Do you avoid stepping on sidewalk cracks? Do you always do something in a certain way?"

I had gone through that with the prison psychiatrists. "No."

We talked the rest of the fifty minutes that psychiatrists call an hour. She asked questions that allowed me to ramble on about the other world. I told her how Helither talked me into leaving besieged Gowyith and pretend to throw in with the other side so I could spy. That's when I did the con job on Zalzathar that saved the city. I talked him into pinprick attacks that wasted time and squandered his strength as Helither raised armies in the outback.

"That sounds very brave of you," Dr. Epperly said.

"I was still playing both sides of the street. Each promised to send me back home if he won. I favored Helither, of course. Who wouldn't? But I wasn't going to let sentimentality get in the way. I was playing the odds until that meeting with the

Devil. It changed my mind for good." I paused. "It changed me."

She looked at her watch and sighed. "Time goes so fast talking to you. Kickoff's in forty-five minutes. We're playing USC." She laughed. "We call it the University of Spoiled Children."

"Maybe I could walk you to the stadium."

Dr. Epperly seemed to consider the wisdom of this. "I guess that would be all right."

We walked across campus, still talking about Helither. She noticed how I limped from my cut feet, and she commented. I didn't tell her how it happened.

"There's been quite an interest in angels through history." She didn't do the air quotes this time.

"I never thought about it before. I never thought about anything but business."

At other schools, tailgate parties featured beer and hamburgers from the barbecue. At Stanford, it was sophisticated wines and Julia Child food. I nodded at the guy who had clipped me on the head with his knee at the flag football game. He didn't nod back. He said something to the people in his party and they stared at me.

"You meeting your husband here or something?" I asked.

"No, just friends."

"You're the football fan in the family?"

"Thanks for walking with me." We shook hands, and she moved off with a strong stride. Maybe she hurried because she wanted to be around normal people for what was left of a fine fall afternoon. I wondered if she would say, "I just left a real doozy." I got the pickup from the parking lot and drove back to Millwood.

The contractor, Joe Edelman, was in his construction trailer looking at the blueprints. The game was on the radio and Stanford was behind already. He was a preppy-looking guy who specialized in restoring old houses. "Hi," he said.

I could move into a hotel, but I liked the idea of the dogs as a living moat between me and the Pig Faces. But there was the harpy. "How long do you think it'll take for that south wing?"

"Three weeks, maybe four."

"What if you worked around the clock?"

He stepped back in amazement. "That'd mean another crew from the hiring hall."

"I don't have a problem with that. Start them tonight."

"Night work means premium pay."

"I'll give you another advance if you need it."

"You really mean begin them tonight?"

I said I did. Carpenters and drywall men roaming around would put a damper on the movements of the harpy.

8

It was clear in the weeks that followed that Soderberg was putting together an unstoppable campaign organization. Soderberg for President committees sprang up in every one of the fifty states. They claimed they were the independent alternative to the status quo nobody liked. The junior senator from Virginia, the leading Republican candidate, unexpectedly dropped out of the race.

"He got bought off," Jared Snyder told me on the phone.

"I didn't think you could buy off a candidate for president so easily."

"Please. We're both adults, are we not? Nobody believes the bullshit about Bailey quitting because his wife asked him to. She's been a doormat his whole career. Soderberg must have given him bricks of hundred-dollar bills, a truckload. That's gotta be it. The way's clear for him now. By the time the Democrats stop fighting and get behind someone, it'll be too late to catch up."

It seemed Soderberg was on television day and night. He even showed up on shopping channels to hawk the computers one of his companies made. Competitors complained to the Federal Trade Commission that he sold way below cost. By the time it got around to upholding them, the election would be long over. The catch with the cheap computers was they came with software that once an hour showed Soderberg flashing the

V sign. Same with the screen saver. People put up with it because the price was right.

That was only a small part of the well-oiled campaign. It seemed overnight he went from someone whose fame was mostly in the business world to one of the best-known people in America. The whole country was guessing who the future Mrs. Soderberg would be. He was coy, and the media kept being fed new names to speculate about. One day it was an actress known for playing wise, mature women on the big screen and therefore was assumed to be one. The next it was a Harvard professor respected for feminist scholarship. Las Vegas gave odds on who would be the next First Lady.

When I went to the new Clipper Ship for a haircut, Tony had a calendar on the wall with a big picture of Soderberg smiling down with his capped teeth. Every barber shop and beauty salon in the country had gotten one. "He's a good man, not like them other bums. He's gonna win, you watch."

At night at Millwood, we heard a cat that sounded like it was in heat. Only it wasn't the usual annoying yowl. It was husky and inviting, almost seductively human. The men stopped their work and Oliver listened with cocked head. He and I searched but never found it.

Joe Edelman came up to me one afternoon as I was pruning Millwood's rosebushes. I was on no. 74. "Did the people from *Architectural Digest* get hold of you?" he asked.

"They left a message. I haven't called back yet."

"They want to take pictures when we're done. If it's okay with you. It would be a real feather in my cap."

I told him sure. The magazine called me a barbarian after Felicity bought the next-door estate in Long Island when I was out of the country and had an ancient grove of trees uprooted and a historic mansion torn down to improve the view from ours. Even the *New York Times* editorialized.

"That sure is a beautiful cat you have," Edelman said as he was leaving.

"I don't have a cat."

"Whose is it?"

"What does it look like?"

"Black. Yellow eyes. A couple of us saw it about dawn this morning. It was coming down the stairs, but scooted when it saw us."

"It's not mine."

"Somebody's feeding it. It looks real smooth and glossy."

A harpy could take a cat's form. I had seen it happen in the other world. "Tell everybody to stay away from it."

Edelman's pleasant, open face clouded. "Why?"

"It's dangerous."

He scoffed. "Aw, c'mon."

I couldn't push it too far. The *National Enquirer* had published an interview with Havl about my conversations with dogs. "Is He Sane?" the headline asked.

The cops said they had reached a blind alley in Byron's death, but the *Enquirer* wasn't giving up. Clancy said I might have grounds for a libel suit. "You'd have a shot at winning, but it comes to the punitive stage of a trial and a jury might decide you don't have much reputation to damage." The word was that Havl had been paid fifty thousand dollars for the interview.

"Just out of curiosity," Dr. Epperly asked, "is it true? Do you have conversations with your dogs?"

"Everyone who has a dog talks to it."

She frowned. "The article said it was more than that. It said there is the appearance of give and take."

I think she suspected by now I continued our sessions just to see her. I didn't need the complication, but there it was. Her eyes, her hair, her lips. It was like one of those love songs when they still wrote music for grown-ups. Zalzathar himself did not cast a more powerful spell. She did not speak of it, probably hoping my obvious infatuation would pass. I guessed that patients fell for her often. It had to be exasperating. I supposed there were times when she envied shrinks who were bald and had beards.

"I can't believe we're talking about a story in a tabloid."

"You're not answering the question."

"Do I have conversations with dogs?" I stalled.

"Yes."

"Sometimes."

"Sometimes?"

"All right, often."

"And you believe you understand what they say."

"I know what they say."

"But that's impossible."

"I know it is."

"So you're able to integrate these two mutually exclusive concepts?"

"It's not only dogs."

"You think you can communicate with other animals as well?"

We were in her office. As she jotted down this latest example of how mad I was, I looked past her out the window. It was bright but cold outside, one of those days that are like biting into a crisp apple. I thought about the nightly fogs just before the Pig Faces came after me. They had gone away, I had realized that they were orchestrated by Zalzathar. One of his powers in the other place had been the ability to whistle up storms to conceal his movements. A fogbank would have been easy.

I had become a C-SPAN junkie and got copies of all the videotape the networks and local stations shot of Soderberg, including outtakes. I studied the crowd scenes and thought I spotted the wizard once. He was standing with a group of Soderberg's staff at a speech he gave to the National PTA. "Education is vital to a well-rounded life," he said. So far Soderberg had not spoken a single word a reasonable person could disagree with. "We need to grow the economy to create more jobs." That was another example.

I had a still from that group shot blown up. The picture was too blurry to tell for sure if it was Zalzathar. He was clean-shaven but there was something about the eyes. I had sent it to Doyle in hopes he could get an identification from it.

"What do you say to the dogs?" Dr. Epperly asked. My mind returned to her office.

"I ask them how they are, that sort of thing."

"And?"

"They tell me. Dogs live in the present, like philosophers say we should. Their conversation is about what they see. A bird flying overhead or a sound they just heard. A smell in the air. Whenever Oliver drinks water, he says, 'That was good.' They're totally spontaneous. They'll tell you what their last meal was, or what they'd like if they had their choice. But that's as abstract as they get."

"Hmmmm." There was disappointment in the sound. Maybe she had convinced herself there had been some small progress in my case

I would have had detectives ferret out everything about her life before. There would be logs of her comings and goings and lists of people she talked to. I would know who her family and friends were. I would have a profile of spending habits from credit-card records. I would even know what cereal she ate. But the new me wouldn't invade her privacy like that. So her personal life was a mystery.

"Do you and your husband have plans for the weekend?" I blurted. The question surprised us both. Maybe it was brought on by my talk about how spontaneous dogs were.

A shadow crossed her face. "My husband died two years ago."

"Sorry."

"He fell over at his desk. But it wasn't a coma as with you. We don't think he felt a thing."

"And your family . . ."

"Two children, both in college. My husband was well insured, fortunately."

I let a small silence pass out of respect for the departed. "Maybe you'd like to come by and see Millwood? The restoration is nearly finished. Bring a friend. We'll have lunch." My meals now came courtesy of the Chipper Catering Co. Their truck fed the construction crew, too. "When I eat, everybody eats," I announced in a hoarse Mafia don's voice.

I must have looked so needy that Alex took pity. "I wouldn't normally," she said. "Friendships between therapist and patient are verboten, but I would like to see you interact with your dogs. How many did you say you have?"

"The morning count today was sixty-four." With the media gone, people were dropping dogs off at the front gate again.

Dr. Epperly drove her Jeep Cherokee up the drive for lunch a couple of days later. A heavy woman who had red hair was with her. She had a nose large enough to be on a Roman coin. Also a disapproving mouth. It was a Saturday, and both were in jeans and denim shirts. Dr. Epperly wore a baseball cap and a bouncy weekend manner. "This is Mildred Harris. She teaches at the university."

Mildred and I shook hands firmly. I had looked her up in the college catalog when Dr. Epperly told me she was bringing her. She was an economist with Marxist leanings. Her manner was chilly. She looked around as if to say, "Behold capitalism's excess!" The dogs made their welcoming racket from the kennels.

I gave the women a tour of the house. "The Hensens made their money in public power in the past century," I explained in the ballroom. We stood beneath the antlered trophy heads of animals an early Hensen had slain.

"They were cruel and rapacious," Professor Harris said.

"They flooded beautiful valleys with their dams and stole water rights from the farmers. I know their story well."

"Is that called a minstrel gallery up there?" Dr. Epperly asked smoothly.

"Yes," I said.

"Do you intend to have balls in here again?" Professor Harris asked. She reminded me of a prosecutor drawing up an indictment.

"A charitable foundation owns Millwood. I can see fundraisers being held in this room. Yes, maybe even balls."

Her look was withering. It said the rich have always danced on the bones of the proletariat. I took them up to a bedroom with a balcony with a good view of Millwood. "Those oak trees are more than a century old," I said.

"Is that a police car?" Professor Harris asked.

It came up the drive and stopped. Detective John Mazzoni got out and walked toward the front door. "Excuse me," I said.

"The place is looking nice," Mazzoni said when I opened the door. "Real nice."

"What can I do for you?"

"Do you know a Joseph Edelman?"

"He's my contractor."

"He was found dead in a motel on El Camino a couple of hours ago."

We went inside to one of the great rooms and sat down.

"What happened?" I asked.

"Sorry I gave it to you cold like that. He checked into the motel at seven this morning. A cleaning woman found the body. He was nude. It looked like he'd been having some pretty rough sex. We'll need an autopsy for the cause of death. Might be a heart attack."

"He's a happily married man with a family." Joe was a camera nut, and I had seen their pictures often enough.

"Well, you know how that goes. I'm trying to trace his movements this morning."

"He's usually on the job here by six."

"Was he here this morning?"

"I didn't see him. That doesn't mean he wasn't here. You can check with his crew." Mazzoni asked a few more questions and then went off to talk to the workers.

"What's wrong?" Dr. Epperly asked when they joined me. "You look upset."

"A man I know was found dead this morning."

"Was he murdered?" Professor Harris demanded

"Mildred!" Dr. Epperly said. She put her hand on my arm. "Were you friends?"

"I liked the guy."

Mazzoni came back. "He was here. One of the workers said he left carrying a black cat." He was stopped by the look on my face. "You know something I don't?"

"I told him to stay away from that cat."

"Was it valuable or something?"

"No. Just . . . vicious."

"Anyhow," Mazzoni said, "he left about six-thirty. He didn't call or leave a note or anything?"

I shook my head. "No."

"Did the man have a family?" Dr. Epperly asked.

"A wife and three little kids," I said.

"That's so sad."

Professor Harris wandered off to peer into a fireplace big enough to stand in. The rest of us stood around awkwardly. I asked how the Byron investigation was going, and Mazzoni looked glum. "We need a break."

He jingled the change in his pocket. As usual, he acted like if he hung around long enough, I'd get tired of the lie I was living and confess.

"Anything else I can do for you?" I said.

"No, I guess not." He walked down to his car and drove away.

"Maybe we should put off lunch for another day," Dr. Epperly said.

"I need to talk to you," I said. "Can I have somebody drive your friend home?"

She hesitated before deciding. "Let me tell her." She walked over to the fireplace to speak to Professor Harris. There was a brief argument, then the economist shrugged her heavy shoulders. Alice drove her home. The shocked construction crew packed up and silently left. A couple of guys wiped away tears. Edelman had been popular with his crew.

We sat at a table on the veranda and poked at our pasta salads. The sound of a power mower came from far off. A couple of dogs barked lazily down at the kennels. "What did you want to talk about?" Dr. Epperly asked.

"This'll sound strange."

"That will be a change."

"You heard me say I warned him to stay away from that cat."

"Yes."

"That was no cat."

She closed her eyes to steel herself. She opened them. "What was it, then?"

"Something from the other side. A harpy."

"Hmmmm."

"They can change themselves into cats."

"I see."

"Somehow I doubt that."

"The cat killed your contractor. Is that what you want me to believe?"

"No, the harpy did. She'd been hiding in the house hoping for a chance at me." The cleaners found mouse skins now and then. But no cat had eaten them. Everything was sucked out, leaving only a dry pouch. "Havl saw her once. She's very beautiful in human form."

"Havl is the man in the *National Enquirer?*"

"That's right. Edelman somehow trapped her and carried her off in his car this morning. Maybe he wanted her for his kids. Being taken away must have enraged her. She got her revenge when he took her to a motel. That's where he was found. She must have enchanted him."

"Is that what you call it?"

"I mean with a spell. Next thing he knows, they're screwing. Pardon my French. Then he's dead."

Dr. Epperly put her fork down. "Don't you see how crazy that sounds?"

"I thought you didn't use that word."

"How totally crazy?"

"There's more," I said. "You remember I told you that Zalzathar didn't really want me, he wanted Soderberg?"

"I remember."

"Now he's running for president."

"What about it?" She was wary.

"Zalzathar's behind that. He . . ."

She got up. She rummaged in her purse and yanked out her car keys.

"This isn't working out. I think you better find someone else to treat you."

"If you won't be my doctor, be my friend."

That was quick thinking, if I do say so. It made her pause, but then she stuck out her hand to be shaken. "I've got to run. Thanks for lunch." She sailed out. I went to a window and watched her drive away. At least she hadn't said no to being friends.

That night for the first time Oliver did not act like he heard strange noises in the house. I told him he was excused from sleeping on the bottom of the bed. He pretended not to hear.

"Off."

"I like this."

"Off!"

He got down grumbling and curled up on the carpet alongside the bed. Like most dogs, Oliver took what he could get. If you allowed him to sleep under the covers, next he would want to pick his side.

A courier on a motorcycle rode up the drive the next morning. I signed for a thick package and took it inside to read with my coffee. They arrived every week to ten days. Fifteen minutes later, Phil Doyle called. "Did it get there?"

"A few minutes ago." Judging from the bills he wrote out by hand for me to read and then burn, he had an army of investigators and researchers in the field. They were bribing just about everyone born of woman for information. I called him on one.

"Three million dollars?" I asked. The figure leaped off the page.

"One of my German agents has been talking to a former director of the Wierker Group. It looks like the guy got a castle on the Rhine for voting for the sale. If we want him to spill the beans even off the record, it's not gonna come cheap. He wants the money in Krugerrands and diamonds."

This latest package was an analysis of Soderberg's purchase of Fiduciary Services. There was nothing that told me why the company directors decided to sell to him. It was strongest in its field, having gobbled up the second-biggest company two years before. It was well managed and had good profitability. Logic said it should have continued aggressive growth on its own.

"The CEO was a woman, one of the few running a company that size," Doyle said. "She was on the cover of *Forbes* once. Our guys found out there's no way she'd sell the company out from under her."

"So what happened?"

"She had a breakdown. She's in a private loony bin in Connecticut. A month after she's out of the picture, her board of directors sells Fiduciary to Soderberg."

"Why'd she go around the bend?"

"Good question. She's not allowed visitors. But if I can get you in, you might find out by talking to her."

I said if she was able to talk sense, I'd like to see her. Doyle went to work on it, but it proved harder than he thought. He called two weeks later. "You might have to buy the company that contracts for security at the hospital. I'm dealing with some real hardnoses. No give to them at all."

"Buy it?"

"It's on the market for forty million. It's a good buy, what with prisons being privatized."

"I don't want back in business. I just got out."

"So, sell afterward. You might make money on the deal."

I got Lockdown Security for thirty-seven and a half million. "I think we can get it for less," the broker on the deal told me.

"I'm in a hurry."

The next day, Doyle walked in and fired the Lockdown executives who had refused to play ball. "Okay, we're ready to rock and roll," he told me. "How soon can you get back here?"

I telephoned Dr. Epperly at Stanford. "Do you still do private consulting?" I asked.

"Not in your case." She laughed. "How have you been?"

"Busy. I want you to talk to someone back East. The former CEO of a big financial services company."

"I have a day job, remember?"

"We can do it over a weekend. I pay well."

"What's the problem?"

"A woman who ran a big successful company had a breakdown."

"What kind?"

"Mental."

"That can mean a lot of things." I could tell she was interested. Maybe not having a wacko like me as a patient deprived her life of zest.

"It's good to hear your voice," she said.

That knocked me off balance so much I couldn't think of anything to say at first. "Me, too."

"I've been asking around. I got the names of a couple of specialists who might be able to help you."

"Let's talk about that afterward. Can you go this weekend?"

"Whoa. So soon?"

"I move fast."

"Let me call you back."

Before she did, Doyle telephoned. "I got a line on the man in the picture."

"How'd you find out?"

"I had a newspaper pal named Ed Broderman ask one of Soderberg's political consultants. The guy's name is William Dark. He's kind of a mystery man. Some sort of religious adviser, apparently. Nobody knows very much about him, even in Soderberg's inner circle. He apparently has a lot of clout, though. He's always whispering to Soderberg. He's the last guy the candidate sees at night and the first in the morning. People are a little afraid of him. The political pro said you don't cross him. Ed was intrigued enough that he started to do some digging for a story on Dark. He got sick, though."

"What kind of sick?"

"I don't know."

"Serious sick or the flu kind?"

"Search me."

"Can you find out?"

"Yeah. Why?"

"I'm curious."

An hour later he called back. "Funny you should ask. Broderman is totally paralyzed. They've got the poor bastard on a respirator. Came on suddenly. The doctors are being close-mouthed, but I gather the prognosis doesn't look good."

I didn't say anything for a minute. "What's his home situation?"

"A wife and five, six kids."

"Make sure he's got the best medical care money can buy."

There was silence. Doyle didn't like curve balls coming at him. "What's Ed got to do with anything?"

"Call it a whim."

I hung up. It was obvious the guy got it because he was snooping where he wasn't supposed to. Because of me. I ordered Clancy to draw up papers for a trust fund so that Broderman's family was provided for like Edelman's. Neither would ever want for money.

I would have to be careful who I got involved in this. I knew from past dealings that Doyle had caution that bordered on paranoia. He stopped just short of having food tasters, so I didn't worry about him. I had a panicky moment about Dr. Epperly, but then I figured she was safe. Alex had treated me for mental illness and still did, as far as anyone knew. Zalzathar's subtle mind would like this cloud over my credibility.

"I've never been in a private jet before." It was night, and Alex was looking out the porthole at the big jumbos taxiing for takeoff at San Francisco International.

"There was a time it felt like I spent most of my life in one," I said. "It gets old like everything else."

"But it's nice not having to stand in line to check in."

"True enough."

The Gulfstream taxied between two big jets. I whistled the "Delta is ready when you are" tune. In my old corporate raider days, the plane would have been filled with lawyers, accountants, and others who had put the target company under a microscope. We'd be talking a blue streak, war-gaming the takeover. We always hit the ground running. We were like the Visigoths swooping down on an unsuspecting village.

"I talked to your former assistant," Alex said.

"Havl?"

"I sent a letter to the *National Enquirer* and they forwarded it. He feels bad about the story they published. He said it distorted what he told them."

"It doesn't make any difference."

"Who was that woman? The one without clothes."

"It was my delusion. Or was it his?"

"Don't be sarcastic." She raised her voice over the roar of the Japan Airlines jumbo ahead of us running its engines up for takeoff.

"How do I seem to you?"

"What do you mean?"

"Do I really seem nuts? Pardon my layman's crudity."

"You seem fine now."

"Coping with the world, in touch with reality?"

"At the moment, yes."

"Good. I just wanted to make sure that point was established."

The jumbo took off and then it was our turn. The Gulfstream lifted off the runway, the lights of San Francisco ahead and the black void of the bay to the right. Then the city and its surrounding suburban sprawl were behind us. Alex settled down with a novel.

"Is that a romance?" I asked. A woman and a man in Renaissance finery were in a clinch on the cover. A stagecoach waited at the door. The anxious servants looked as if the king's men would be arriving any minute.

"Anything wrong with it?" she answered, a little defensive.

"Isn't it beneath you?"

"Not at all," she said firmly. She went back to her reading.

We headed west toward the Sierra Nevada and the vast continent beyond. I opened up my briefcase and began to read the thick file that Doyle's people had assembled on another of the companies Soderberg had taken over. This one was Total Reliance Transportation, which had begun life as a trucking company but had grown into a package delivery outfit like Federal Express. It was clearly positioned for growth and had been for years. A stumbling block was Ezrah Kleister, an eccentric investor who wore string ties and cowboy boots. He like to buy cheap and hold on to investments for the long haul. He believed a rising tide lifted all boats, particularly those that controlled costs. He did not like managements that tried to grow companies too fast. Slow, careful expansion was the ticket. Kleister put on pressure to rein in executives who thought otherwise. He would have opposed Soderberg's takeover for sure. But he died in a boating accident. He had been fishing for bass on his own lake when a freakish storm came up and swamped his dinghy. With Kleister out of the way, Soderberg made an offer the board of directors accepted. Some analysts felt he was laying the groundwork to make a run at FedEx itself.

I telephoned Doyle from somewhere over eastern Nevada. "I want to know more about Kleister's accident."

"What'dya wanna know?"

"That storm. I'd like details."

There was silence for a moment. I knew how Doyle thought. He was saying to himself, I look like a fucking meteorologist? "You're the boss," he said.

9

We landed at Kennedy at three in the morning and taxied to the business jet terminal. It was ablaze with lights but nearly deserted. I smelled snow in the air as we walked across the tarmac. Doyle waited with six men, all in dark business suits.

"Who are they?" Alex said at my side.

"Business associates."

"They're all so large."

Doyle introduced them by their first names. Each nodded as he was introduced. Their faces looked like the blank expressions never changed. "They're good men," he concluded. "The best in the field." Doyle took Alex in with a slow look, as if filing away details in case he ever had to describe her.

We left in a three-car convoy. Doyle was at the wheel of the middle car, and one of the men rode shotgun. Alex and I were in the backseat. "Be about a ninety-minute drive," Doyle said. "You want music or silence?"

We drove through the night toward Connecticut. Only a few big rigs were on the turnpike, so we made good time. "We'll get there before the day crew comes on. We attract less attention that way."

"Why don't we want to attract attention?" Alex asked brightly.

Doyle's silence left the answer up to me. "The media," I said. Blame the media for anything and people nod.

"Is this woman that famous?"

"She's very well known in her field."

We stopped for breakfast at an all-night eatery alongside the road. "It's either very early or very late, depending on how you look at it," Alex said over pancakes.

"You're cheerful," I said.

"This is an exciting switch from my dull academic routine. And you're paying me that really quite outrageous fee." She had tried to talk me down, but I stood firm.

The Pinewood Institute for Healing looked like the kind of place you would take a spinster aunt with money if she went dotty. It was out in the country and hidden from the road by shrubbery. It could have passed for a small luxury hotel in one of those wealthy enclaves where zoning keeps signs small and discreet. The lead car had arrived a couple of minutes early to tell the security people to get lost for a while. We walked through the beige and cream lobby without seeing anyone and down a pale green corridor with paintings on the wall. There were freshly cut flowers in vases on tables. Very tasteful. The nurses' station was unattended. If Alex was surprised by the freedom we had of the place, she didn't show it.

Doyle stopped at a door and fished keys from his pocket. "They tell me she might be awake." He unlocked the door and swung it open. I turned on the light.

"What do you want?" A haggard woman with dark hair hanging in her face sat in a chair by a window with bars. She wore a gown and robe and had been twisting a handkerchief in her hands. Carlotta Hamilton, the former CEO of Fiduciary Services, had a hunted look.

"I'm Doctor Epperly," Alex said cheerfully. "I'm a psychiatrist. I'd like to talk to you."

"I'm through talking to you people. It's a waste of time."

"I'm sorry you feel that way, but maybe I can help."

"Who's he?"

"This is Mr. Ingersol. He wants to help, too."

The trapped look in her eyes changed to interest. She pushed the hair from her face. "Bogey Ingersol?"

"That's me," I boomed. I thought heartiness might cheer her up.

"I recognize you now. You used to be much fatter."

"He hired me to look into your case," Alex said.

"Why?" Her stare was flat.

"I'm interested in why your company got sold to Bernie Soderberg," I said.

"My company," she said bitterly. "They took it away from me." She began crying. "But I deserved it."

"Why do you say that?" Alex asked.

"Because I'm *depraved.*"

"Will you excuse us?" Alex asked me. "I'd like to talk to Carlotta alone."

I went back to the lobby. One of Doyle's men sat behind the receptionist's desk, and another stood at the door. Doyle came in from outside after a minute and joined me.

"You've got quite a lot of security," I said.

"Things have been happening." He looked worried. "I didn't want to mention it on the phone or in front of the doc."

"What kind of things?"

"A couple of guys who should be in touch aren't. Nobody's seen them, not even their families. There was an attempted break-in at my office. Very sophisticated. They got past all but the last layer of security. A motion detector tripped them up. If it isn't on batteries, they get past that, too. A power surge like I never seen burned out all the other systems. It went through surge protectors like they weren't even there."

"Soderberg?" I asked.

"Who else would it be?" He rubbed his crewcut head with a freckled hand. "The missing guys were looking into his presidential campaign."

"What did they find out?"

"Those so-called state committees of volunteers are phony, for one thing. Every one is on the payroll, from the chairmen on down. I can't even begin to imagine what this cost. They've got some of the biggest political names in every state on board. His committee in South Dakota, just for one example, has the former Democratic and Republican state chairmen codirecting the campaign."

"He'd pay whatever it cost."

He gave me a shrewd look. "Are you telling me everything?"

"No, not everything."

His smile was cynical. Doyle was used to clients who did that. He had done work for Arab kingdoms and African tyrants and knew he never got to see all the puzzle pieces.

"You think he'd be poison for the country? That's why you're looking for something fishy about these takeovers. You want ammo to shoot him down."

"That's one layer."

"Christ, it goes deeper? Is it that guy Ed was looking into, Dark?"

"He's part of it, too." I wanted Doyle to have an inkling, but I didn't want to spook him off the case.

"Is this some foreign power trying to subvert us?" he asked. "They can't take us on straight up so they're trying the back door?"

"It's definitely a foreign power."

Doyle had been a Green Beret. His eyes flashed. "The bastards won't get away with it."

"When was the break-in and your men turn up missing?"

"Yesterday."

"You think whoever it is knows I'm the client?"

He shook his head. "I haven't told anyone, and you've got the only hard copies of the stuff. The floppies are in a safe place. Your wire transfer of money to me can't be traced from that Cayman bank. My place is swept for bugs daily, and the phone lines are secure. My lawsuit against you is still in the courts. I don't see how anybody could know."

"I've used you in the past."

"A lot of people have. You'd be surprised at some of the names, but don't bother asking."

"I know you're cautious, but you've got to be even more careful than before. Same with your people."

"I wasn't blowing smoke when I said these guys are the best in the business." He took an old wad of gum out of his mouth and put in a fresh stick. "Did the bad guys make this poor lady crazy?"

"That's what I want to find out."

He looked at his watch. "We got about an hour before we have to make tracks."

Alex opened the door after forty-five minutes. "What's the diagnosis?" I asked as I went in.

"Off the top of my head, paranoid schizophrenia."

"You said that about me."

"She's worse than you were. Or are. I haven't made up my mind about you."

"That's progress. The question is whether mine or yours."

"It's too early for drawing-room banter."

Carlotta looked like she was more with it now. I sat down. "We met years ago. It was at a stockholders' meeting in Chicago. Barlotti Industries," she said.

"I remember."

"You were very rude and arrogant."

"I've gone through some changes."

"Why did you come here?" She was a direct woman.

"I'm interested in how Soderberg got control of Fiduciary."

She looked away. "They say I'm insane. I'm not."

"Did the trouble begin after you learned Soderberg was interested in your company?"

Carlotta turned back to me. "If you think it was mental strain, you're wrong. I wasn't the least worried about beating off his challenge. My board was behind me foursquare." She reached out her hand to my arm. "Will you help me get away from this place? I'm being held against my will."

"We'll help," Alex said.

"Now? Please make it now."

Alex shook her head. "I can't sign you out without looking at your medical records and getting your doctor's permission. It wouldn't be ethical."

"How long will that take?"

"A few days."

"So," I interrupted, "Soderberg gives notice that he means to make a hostile takeover and you're committed to a mental hospital? What went on in between?"

"She'll tell you," Carlotta said. She began to cry. "I'm too ashamed."

Doyle knocked at the door and stuck his head in. "We better go."

"When will you come back?" Carlotta stood. There was panic on her face.

"Soon," Alex said soothingly.

"Take me with you."

"I told you. We can't do that without your doctor's permission."

Carlotta sat back down again with a look of defeat. "He says I have to be here a long time."

"Maybe it won't be that long," Alex said cheerfully.

"Could you be my doctor?" Carlotta said desperately. "I like you better than him."

"We'll see." Alex patted her on the back. We said good-bye.

We got in the car, and our convoy pulled away from the sanitarium. Dawn was breaking, and the first snowflakes fell.

"An earlier age would call it demonic possession," Alex said. "She believes she's visited by a creature who forces her to commit gross indecencies. Sometimes he watches, sometimes he joins in. Did you know she was arrested at a homeless encampment?"

"How would I know that?"

"I thought your detectives might've told you. She had intercourse with eleven men, and more were waiting in line when the police got there. She offered herself to the arresting officers. When they said no, she broke free and ran naked through the streets until they chased her down. She bit and scratched. She was able to hush that up, but not what happened after. She nearly caused a riot in New York's porn district when she told a crowd to watch what she could do."

"My God."

"The first vagrant that first time was only the second man ever for her. She had been very repressed up to them. My guess is her sex drive was sublimated to career ambitions."

"What happened to change her?"

"A man came to her one night. Or rather, as she put it, 'a male creature.' She woke, and he was in her bedroom. As soon as she saw him, she was aware he knew her darkest fantasies. All willpower was gone. She was his slave."

"Sounds like an incubus."

"I beg your pardon?"

I had seen one in the other world. He had a dark elegance. Thick hair and eyebrows. A good build. A sneering, knowing air. Soft hands and long eyelashes. Everybody worked like a slave in Zalzathar's army except the incubus. He was pampered and indulged, even allowed to sit at the wizard's table if Zalzathar was in a good mood, or what passed for one with him.

The incubus didn't like me, and the feeling was mutual. He could tell because my hackles were always up around him. He kicked at me if I was in range and Zalzathar was around to protect him, but I always dodged him. He turned his back on me once after doing this. I sank my teeth into his rear and gave a couple of twists. He screamed like a woman.

Alex had her look of polite doubt as I explained.

Doyle drove, and the man with him in the front spoke into a hand-held radio to the other cars. I felt tension suddenly spike between them. I paid closer attention.

"Try again," Doyle ordered.

"Bandit Two, this is Bandit One. Over." He repeated it twice.

"We can't raise the chase car," Doyle said to me. "They're supposed to be two minutes behind."

"You're doing ninety. Maybe they dropped back out of range."

"Something's happened to them. Hang on."

He hit the brakes as we neared an off-ramp and we almost went into a broadside skid. Alex gasped as the seat belts slammed us back. Her hand on my arm was like a talon. We left the turnpike and skidded to a stop behind an upholstery shop on a little service road. A minute later, we heard the scream of a high-performance engine as it shot past on the turnpike, doing way over a hundred Doyle was talking on the radio.

"Go to Ajax. Go to Ajax."

We jerked back onto the service road with tires smoking and sped to a country lane a mile off. Doyle turned right and drove east, threading his way through suburban neighborhoods and rural countryside like he had lived there all his life. Alex and I exchanged looks. She was pale and shaken. After an hour, Doyle stopped at a BP gas station and made a call from a pay phone. He was back in fewer than thirty seconds. The light snow that had started and stopped looked like it would start up again any minute.

"The guys following us never showed up," he said. "The ones ahead got off the turnpike a minute after I told them. They're gonna meet us in Boston. The plane'll pick us up."

The other man in the front seat spoke, "Good thing you knew this area."

Doyle had a funny look. "I've never been here in my life."

"C'mon. No way you were guessing at all those turns."

"I just knew." Doyle shook his head. "It was like ESP or whatever you call it."

We got on an interstate, and the highway signs that flew past started to say Boston. Doyle had the radio on an all-news station. The clouds were low and the color of pewter.

"Why were we being chased?" Alex asked.

"Who says we were being chased?"

"You're not funny."

"If I told you this back in California, you'd say it was a delusion."

"A delusion is when only one person has it. Answer my question."

"My guess is because we talked to Carlotta Hamilton."

"Why would that cause anyone to chase us? People could have been hurt."

"Let's talk on the flight back."

The thought occurred to us at the same time.

"Do you think she's safe there?" Alex asked.

I considered a snow job but didn't think I would get away with it. "I don't know."

"We should've taken her with us. I shouldn't have worried about appearances."

"Can you get her out of there?" I asked Doyle.

"I'll see what I can do after I put you on the plane."

The two men who had been in the lead car beat us to Logan International. They met us at the private terminal. The jet I had leased was on the apron. Doyle and the others walked us to the ladder.

"Be careful," I told him.

"Same to you."

Lunch was in a picnic basket on the fold-up table. I dug into the food after takeoff. "Do you like caviar?" I asked.

She shook her head. "Sorry."

"Good, it means more for me." I eased the cork out of the champagne.

"What are you celebrating?"

"Being alive." I poured the bubbly into a flute and tasted it. "Bogey used to drink quite a lot of this stuff. Sorry, I mean *I* did. Want some?"

"It's too early."

"You Californians are such health nuts."

"You said we were going to talk in the plane."

"Can you make an intellectual leap?"

"Like Wonder Woman if I have to."

"Assume everything I've told you is true." She started to say something, but I held up a hand.

"Go ahead." She unwrapped an avocado sandwich.

"Let's just say everything happened to me the way I said. And that Carlotta was telling the truth, too."

"What's the connection?"

"Soderberg. He's being used by Zalzathar."

"The evil wizard."

"Don't laugh."

"I'm smiling, not laughing."

"I'm deadly serious. So were you in the car, remember?"

"Mr. Doyle seems pretty level-headed. Are you telling me he believes this?"

"I haven't told him."

"Let me guess. Because he wouldn't have anything to do with you if you did."

"I'll tell him when the time is right. Right now, you're the only one I can confide in. Let's try it again—assume everything I say is true."

She looked out the window.

"Soderberg has been on a major expansion ever since I came out of the coma. Doyle and others have looked into every one of his deals for me."

Alex turned from the window to look at me. "And?"

"There's something fishy about each one. He went after powerful companies that no one in their right mind would sell. Carlotta is CEO of a company that more and more corporations use as an outsource instead of hiring their own bean counters. It handles everything but the petty cash drawer for them. You can imagine the inside look that would give on a company's operations. It would be like sitting in their boardrooms."

"I don't know anything about how businesses work, but wouldn't her company have to promise not to tell outsiders?"

"Absolutely. The contracts are iron-clad. And the tooth fairy leaves money under the pillow. Owning Fiduciary Services would give someone like Soderberg a huge competitive edge." I indicated the briefcase. "That stuff I was reading on the flight here is about another company Soderberg bought, a package delivery outfit. The man who would have stopped him drowned."

The look on her face changed. "It wasn't an accident?"

"They're saying it was, but I don't believe it." I took a yellow legal pad and pencil from the briefcase. "It helps to make a list. Check out these highlights. I wake up from my coma at about the same time Soderberg tells Wall Street he's beginning an expansion, the biggest in history. I bet we find out that's when a fellow by the name of Dark begins being seen."

"Who is that?"

"We'll get to him. While I'm in prison paying my debt to society, Soderberg begins picking off these plums, one after another. The financial markets are amazed at how cheaply he gets them. His brilliance gets the credit. Yet look closer, as I did, and the pattern's there to be seen. Company directors are bribed to vote for the sale, or they or their managements suffer mysterious deaths. Or, as in the case of Carlotta Hamilton, they get sick." I was numbering the points as I went. "I understand the mentality of somebody like Soderberg because I used to be like him. What he's getting with these takeovers are either payoffs or proof of someone's power. Either way, he gets all the greediest man could ever want. He is confirmed in the belief of his own superiority, and the rest of the world agrees. He moves to the top of the richest-men-in-the-world list. He's a cover boy for capitalism, mentioned in the same breath as Ford, Rockefeller, or Gates."

Alex rummaged in the picnic basket. "There's fresh fruit and carrot cake here."

"He then drops out of sight for this cosmetic makeover. He locks up the best political and polling talent in the country so nobody else can use them. The rumor mill says he's going to run for president. Sure enough, the Republican front-runner drops out, to the surprise of all. Things are looking good and there's a breather, so it's payback time A man in my neighborhood dies in a horrifying murder, just about turned inside out by whoever killed him. I become the prime suspect, thanks to evidence planted on the scene."

"What evidence?"

"Hair from the floor of a barber shop, which is then set afire. The way Byron was torn apart was the trademark of Pig Faces. They're Zalzathar's shock troops in the other world."

"According to you."

"Sorry?"

"Nobody's seen them but you, and you were unconscious at the time."

"You're supposed to be hearing me out."

"I want to keep the fantasy in perspective."

I ignored that. "After the cops make me a suspect, the media world camps out at my front door. Then the Pig Faces come after me. My dogs save me, otherwise I wouldn't be sitting here now."

"This is new," Alex said alertly. "You never mentioned it before."

"I didn't tell you."

"Because you thought it would sound unlikely?" Her irony was as dry as the Mojave.

"I was afraid you'd think I was too far gone for any help. You did anyway when I told you about the harpy."

"The naked woman," she corrected. "Isn't it easier to assume she was merely a friend of yours?"

"Edelman thought it was a friend, too. You heard Carlotta Hamilton tell what they're like. She had a succubus, the male version."

"The female version is a succubus, not a harpy. All were figments of medieval imagination. There has been some interesting feminist scholarship on the subject. Women were forced to deny their sexuality, and the succubus fantasy was one result."

"Somebody chased us back there, and two bodyguards are missing. Were those fantasies, too?"

That made her frown. People don't like facts to get in the way of theory. "I really don't understand what that was all about." She paused and frowned. "But how do I know it really happened? I heard a car pass on the turnpike going fast, and you and Mr. Doyle say two men are missing. How do I know if that's true, and if true, that there's a connection?"

"So you think this is some elaborate hoax?" I said with exasperation.

"No, I'm not saying that." But something in her voice said the thought at least had occurred to her.

The telephone on the bulkhead rang. I picked it up.

"Doyle here," the voice said. "The woman's gone from the sanitarium. Her doctor checked her out an hour after we left."

"Tell Dr. Epperly that."

I handed the phone to her. She listened for a moment and handed it back.

"Think you can find her?" I asked Doyle.

"I can try."

I put the phone back on the hook. "We should've taken her with us."

"We couldn't."

"Oh, I forgot. Ethics stood in the way."

"I don't like sarcasm." She hunted in her purse and came up with a card from the sanitarium. "Hand me the phone."

I passed it to her, and she dialed the number. "This is Dr. Epperly. I'd like to speak to Carlotta Hamilton, please." The voice on the other end said something. "When was she checked out?" When she got her answer, Alex passed the phone back to me and I hung up.

"Do you believe it now?"

"We couldn't just take her. A woman in that condition is unable to give informed consent. It would've been like kidnapping."

"You assume she's mentally ill, but I don't."

We were both annoyed now, and the silence lasted over most of Ohio. "You mentioned a man named Dark," she said suddenly.

"I'm almost certain it's Zalzathar." I had the still taken from the C-SPAN footage in the briefcase. I showed it to her.

"That's so blurry it could be anybody." She studied it some more. "There's something about him, I grant you. He's in that crowd, but it's like there's something that sets him apart."

"Or a quality?"

"A quality? I suppose you could say that."

"Would you say it's the quality of evil?"

"Oh, please." She started to hand the photo back, then took another look. "Well, there is something sort of like that about him. It's his eyes or something."

I smiled encouragingly. "Atta girl, Wonder Woman."

10

After we landed at San Francisco International, I drove Alex home in my pickup. She was silent except to excuse herself for yawning and give directions when we got off the freeway in Palo Alto. She had not said much since looking at the photo. Me, either. I was feeling odd and wondered if that caviar was a little off. Her home was a beige Spanish-style stucco with red roof tiles. It was set back from a leafy street and had a big front yard.

"As promised, the trip didn't take long," I said. My voice sounded to me as if somebody else was doing the talking. My tongue felt as thick as a rug rolled up for the moving van.

"It seems longer. I haven't been up this long since I was a resident."

"Of what?" I asked stupidly.

"A student doctor."

We turned to face each other in the cab.

"Are you all right?" she asked. "You're sweating."

"I'll be fine. I'll call you later."

She gets out with a strange look and watches me back out of the driveway. I bump down over the curb when I reach the street. I mop the sweat from my brow with my sleeve and put the car in drive. The street seems to go back and forth from big to small, accordionlike. Then, surprisingly, I'm on the freeway north. It is like a bumper-car ride, cars and trucks whizzing from all angles. My hands are fists on the steering wheel, and my ears ring. I concentrate on staying in my lane.

Drifting to the right—whoa! *Zoom.* Big Ryder truck just misses. Horn blasting, furious face in the window. "Asshole!"

Brakes behind. *Eeeeeee.* My eyes go to the blurry speedometer. Only doing thirty-five. I stomp on the gas. G-forces slam me back like on a rocket sled. Yeeee-ha!

I shoot past cars in the neighboring lanes. *Zip. Zip. Zip.* Fear-filled faces in the windows. Look out, he's crazy! My vision shifts to telescopic, able to see to distant galaxies. Beam me up, Scotty. Nae can get a fix on you, Captain—too much interference. It's those damned Klingons again. Off-ramp ahead! I tromp the brake. *Eeeeeee.*

Pinwheeling world. *Ker-thunk, ker-thunk.* The walloping giant approaches in brogans as big as boats. The truck cab collapses overhead. Silvery tinkle, a small fortune in coins flung to the pavement. Buckling sheet metal sings like the fat lady. The house lights go down. The curtain raises.

I'm running again, long four-legged bounds. Tongue out. Ears flattened. Nose filled with night smells. I'm making for the cover of a wood on the far side of this dark meadow. Flights of startled birds rise, whirring in the blackness. Something pounds behind, the concussion of horned and clawed feet jolting the ground. It is a Gutter, eyes lit with that cold, blue fire that freezes the blood. The fatigue in my muscles says this has been a long run. . . .

Five or six voices were jumbled together. Now and then they became clear, as if a radio station got tuned in from the surrounding static.

"Watch the blade, Charlie. You're real close to his arm."

"What have I got, an inch?"

"Not that much."

"I don't see any blood, but he could be bleeding internally.
"Tell them we don't smell any more gas so they can stop
with the hose."

"Look up there. We're gonna be on the news tonight."

"Pay attention."

*Wake up, Mr. Ingersol. I'm sorry I got here late, but better late than
never.*

The voice cut through the chatter like a laser. I opened my
eyes. It was immediately clear what was going on. Firemen
were using the Jaws of Life to cut me out of the cab of the
pickup. It was upside down, and so was I. The glove box was
inches from my nose.

"Hey, look! He just opened his eyes."

"Hang on, mister. We're getting you out of here."

A voice calling to others: "He's awake."

"Bring the oxygen."

"No, we're gonna need the cutting torch."

*These men will free you shortly. You're not hurt, other than a few
bumps and bruises.*

"What happened?" I asked.

"You lost control," one of the rescuers said. "An eyewitness
said your pickup was flipping like a gymnast in the Olympics."

"Was anybody hurt?" I asked.

Another voice: "Nope. It was a miracle. Just like it's a miracle
you're still living after that."

"Look out, the engine block might shift when that cable
cuts in."

"The jack underneath yet?"

"Yeah, but it might still move."

Metal shrieked like it was in pain and suddenly there was
sunlight above me. Firemen and paramedics lifted me onto a
waiting gurney. I was secured with straps so my head didn't

roll. An oxygen mask was put over my face. Heads peered down with concern as I was rolled to a waiting ambulance.

I'll ride with you. I located the voice. He was not wearing a uniform, like the others. He was in jeans and a plaid work shirt. Middle-aged, dark hair beginning to thin.

The ambulance moved, and the siren began to whoop.

"This is sure gonna screw up the commute."

"I called the wife. Told her to eat dinner in the city. It beats sittin' in traffic."

I studied the ceiling of the ambulance. Every inch was packed with wires and gadgetry. I felt the prick of a needle as an IV was hooked up.

"I got the drip going."

Minutes later, the ambulance was backing up into the hospital's emergency bay. The doors slammed open and I was rolling down a hospital corridor. A young doctor stood over me, asking questions. "Do you hurt anywhere? Does this hurt when I move this? How about this?"

I'll be back.

"No, don't try to roll your head," the doctor said.

"Where's he going?"

"Who?"

"The man in the plaid shirt."

"I don't see anyone in a plaid shirt. Does your head hurt? Is your vision blurred?"

11

I f it was me, I'd rather they found booze in my system."
Bill Clancy was looking out the window of my hospital room. Perfectly barbered and tailored as usual, he gave off his inside-the-Beltway power heat. "Pay the fine. Do the weekends in jail, whatever. Better than wondering." He paused for thought. "Except the media would jump on it. They'd be all over you again." He jingled keys in his pocket. "Even so, that would still be better than worrying that I'd had some sort of seizure behind the wheel and my days were numbered."

"They did a brain scan," I said. "There's nothing wrong upstairs." The doctors held me for twenty-four hours of observation. I felt pretty good, considering. The weird feeling was gone, and I only had a couple of bumps and bruises. Clancy had flown in from Washington. Now, as I dressed to go, there was a knock at the door. A hurried-looking man stuck his head in.

"Oh, good. I was afraid I'd missed you. I'm Dr. John Frankel from the Centers for Disease Control in Atlanta. I just flew in. Can we talk?"

"Sure," I said, buttoning my shirt. He came in and set down a heavy briefcase.

"Disease control?" Clancy said, taking charge in his usual manner. "What can we do for you, doc?"

"How are you feeling?" Dr. Frankel asked me.

"Fine."

"They told me downstairs you're lucky to be alive."

"Very," Clancy said. "His pickup was totaled. They had to cut him out of the wreckage."

"Did the doctors tell you they found something unusual in your blood?" he asked me.

"What do you mean, 'unusual'?" Clancy asked.

"There was a virus in your system," Frankel said. "There's only been one other case reported. An adult male in Baltimore."

"And?" I said, tucking my shirt in.

"It was fatal in his case. We've been very worried. Hospitals were alerted to watch for it. They faxed us the results of your blood work when they saw the markers."

My stomach did one of its flip-flops.

"He's got a virus?" Clancy said. He took a step back and gave me an accusing look.

"His immune system hung it out to dry. It seems for him it was no worse than a twenty-four-hour bug. In the other case, the man died in a couple of days. We'd like to find out how you fought it off. And where you got it. Have you traveled in a foreign country recently?"

I said no, figuring that an alternative universe isn't what he meant. "What are the symptoms?"

"The internal organs dissolve into a kind of pudding." Dr. Frankel pushed thick, dark hair back from his forehead. He had the intensity of a bright graduate student. "That's about all I can tell you. We don't want a panic."

"This victim's name wouldn't be Broderman by any chance?" I asked.

"Ah," Dr. Frankel said, as if the dots had been connected, "you knew him then." Clancy took another step back, fear on his face. His hand went to the knot of his tie as if it were a ripcord and he was considering hitting the silk.

"Never met him before," I said.

"Then how did you know that's who it is?"

"A wild guess."

"I can't stress the seriousness of this too much," Dr. Frankel said. "I'm talking about a virus dramatically different from any seen before. It took over Mr. Broderman's body completely. Pain management was all we could do. If it gets loose, the consequences would be incalculable."

"Jesus Christ," Clancy said. "Tell the man what you know."

"My body fought the virus off?" I said.

"The way it marshaled defenses so fast is as amazing as the virus itself. Mr. Broderman spoke of feeling disoriented at first. He became unconscious shortly after saying that. Did you . . ."

" 'Disoriented' is a good word for it," I said.

"Are we in any danger standing here talking to him?" Clancy demanded.

"Probably not, but we'd still like him in isolation."

"Not a chance," I said.

"We'd prefer it to be voluntary, but we're willing to get a court order."

Hearing "court order" refocused Clancy. His gaze shifted from me. "Hold your horses, doc. You can't do that."

"I'm told there's a Typhoid Mary precedent."

"The government's got a lot of bad lawyers and you sound like you've been listening to one."

Dr. Frankel backed off. "I said we prefer voluntary."

"You yourself said my client fought off the virus and is healthy."

"For the time being. Who knows what'll happen?"

"Who's to say it'll come back?"

I left them fencing and walked outside. Alex was with a nurse. She saw me and broke off her conversation. "I didn't realize that was you who caused that traffic jam until I read the paper a half hour ago. I came right away."

"Making news is like smoking crack. I can't help myself anymore."

"You joke too much. How did it happen?"

"I lost control of the pickup."

"The nursing supervisor said they've been doing a lot of testing."

"They tried to kill me," I said matter-of-factly.

Her eyes narrowed in that wary way she had. "The hospital?"

"Zalzathar."

"Please. Not that again." She flushed attractively. "I suppose it's my job to get you to talk about it, but I'd rather not this time."

Dr. Frankel and Clancy followed me out into the corridor.

"Dr. Epperly," I said, "meet Dr. Frankel of the Centers for Disease Control."

"Keep your voice down," Frankel said. He looked around to see if anyone was in earshot.

"Hello, Alex," Clancy boomed. You could have played night baseball by the light off his smile.

"CDC?" Alex said, ignoring him. "What brings you here?"

"It's confidential, doctor." A peevish edge was in his voice.

"I had a virus that killed another man," I said. "My immune system beat it."

"In twenty-four hours or less," Frankel said.

"What kind of virus?" Alex's eyes were wide.

"That's confidential."

"They've never seen it before," I said.

"They're threatening to lock Bogey up," Clancy said. "I was just telling the good doctor we'll sue the government for enough money to buy Rhode Island."

Frankel said if we were going to talk, could we at least go back into the hospital room. We followed him in.

He quickly sketched the situation for Alex. "You're an internist, I take it."

"No, a psychiatrist."

Frankel's eyes slid to me. "He's being treated for a mental problem?"

"You don't have to answer that question," Clancy said. He shot his cuffs.

"What connection is there between Mr. Ingersol and the man who died?" Alex asked.

"He knew him," Frankel answered.

"No, I didn't. He worked for a man I employ."

"Who's that?" Clancy asked.

"Doyle."

He gave me a look. "You been telling me everything?"

Alex opened her mouth to say something but shut it.

"No," I said.

"When will you, if you don't mind my asking?"

The old Bogey rose up, swelling like bread dough in time-lapse photography. "When I'm ready."

They fell silent at this sudden appearance of the tyrannical tycoon. Clancy nodded, as if to say, I knew you were just biding your time.

"I've wasted enough time on you," I told Frankel. "Are you coming, Alex?"

She wasn't, and I walked out alone. After a few steps, I sensed a presence at my side in the corridor. The man in the plaid shirt. I knew who he was now. Helither had told me every world had its angels.

"Hello," he said. "Let's go outside. I've never liked the air in hospitals."

We went through the automatic doors at the entrance of the hospital. Five news vans with corkscrew antennae on their roofs were in front. Reporters and photographers lounged alongside. I expected a mad rush for us, but no one seemed to notice.

"Don't worry about them," he said. "Their minds are elsewhere."

We walked out to the leafy street in front of the hospital and turned right.

"I was wondering if I was going to get any help," I said.

"We're stretched very thin." There was a note of prissy complaint in his voice. I'd been hoping for another Helither, but one look told me this angel wasn't him. I hoped he didn't see my disappointment.

"You cured that virus I had."

"Yes." He had large brown eyes and narrow shoulders. Small, neat hands and feet. Helither had been tanned and had an athletic, outdoor look. He looked like he played rugby in his spare time. This angel was the opposite. He was pale and fussy. You would peg him for insurance claims or inventory control, a detail man. Helither was blue-collar, the sort who might sell night crawlers at a bait shop or was a shop steward on a factory floor. This one found the line you forgot to fill out and pushed the application back.

"You also kept me from getting killed in that crash," I said.

"There didn't seem any point saving you from one only to lose you to the other." His tone said, was I stupid that I didn't see that?

So what happens now?"

"I wish I knew."

"Why me?" The question I'd been asking from the start.

"God puts the unlikeliest people to use." His expression said I was another example of His unfathomable ways. "Joan of Arc, for example. Shy teenager. Gandhi, obscure lawyer. Nothing to make either stand out before their time of glory. One a warrior, the other a pacifist. It would have made more sense the other way around. And for all those who have been famous, there are ten thousand people you never hear of."

"I don't care about glory."

"I doubt they did either, at least in the beginning. Maybe it went to their heads later. It's not called a martyr complex for nothing."

"I set up a foundation to give away my money."

"Very commendable."

"I'm consulting experts and considering guidelines for giving."

"Charity was simpler when it was alms for the poor, one hand to another."

"The point is I think I've done my share."

"Oh, I understand. We all think that. You're already collecting information on Mr. Soderberg."

"In self-defense. Zalzathar's here. I figured he'd use Bernie to get back at me."

He was mulling something, chewing his lip. "We've never had to deal with evil from another plane of existence. At least I haven't."

Helither had seen the struggle between good and evil as a contest. His theory was that God set up an infinite number of universes where it went on as a form of—well, entertainment for Himself wasn't fair, but that was the drift. Helither wondered if watching events unfold that He had set in motion helped God pass time. Although time was one of His creations, He was subject to it to a certain extent. Evil could triumph, as in the Total Victory Mogwert had hoped to pull off. Or good could win, as witness Gowyith. God presumably had a rooting interest in good; at least one hoped so. But He was not hands-on like Satan. He was off creating other universes, experimenting in other labs. Helither said not even angels knew why God had created evil, although it was obvious that goodness would be meaningless without it. Lots of other stuff was going on at the time, so I didn't give what he said close attention.

"He's alone there, I take it," this angel said.

"I didn't see any others."

He shook his head disapprovingly. "It's not good, alone in a backwater like that. Thinking on these questions can lead one into error. There are a hundred of us in this world, and now and then we get together. It helps when you're feeling overwhelmed and forgotten. I had a nice visit with Periflion Morateon in the, let's see, fifteenth century."

"What's your name?" I asked.

"I call myself William Tyre. I've had hundreds of names, of course. Zalzathar was a worthy foe to Helither, I take it."

"He nearly won all the marbles, that's how worthy. In all modesty, if it hadn't been for me, he would have. My advice is to call in reinforcements. They had Lucifer himself in their corner. He and Helither were actually going at it hand-to-hand at the end."

"Azimbrel-Zafieri's evil is everywhere to be seen, but it's rare for him to visit in person," Tyre said worriedly. He started to wring his hands, but stopped.

The Devil at one point in the other world had assumed the form he took in folklore—horns, hooves, cape, and all. He even carried a pitchfork. This was for my amusement. He liked his wit appreciated. "To be honest, I figured Satan would mop the floor with Helither," I said.

"He would dispute it, but he's only the first of equals. Our angelic natures are the same. Only Azimbrel-Zafieri's disobedience sets him apart. He is free to scorn the rules the rest of us must obey." There was something like envy in his voice.

"That's a big advantage." Being willing to bite and gouge when the opportunity came was the key to climbing to the top of the mountain in the corporate raider world. I had a standard speech I used to give at commencements. I told business grads only a chump didn't hit when an opponent was down. I titled it "Never Let the Bastards Up." Some faculty members got on high horses and boycotted my speech. I just laughed. I asked the new grads who had more money, me or their professors. They got the message.

"I'm worried what would happen if that virus you had spreads," Tyre fretted. "It's so new, humans have no immunities. The stories I could tell about plagues long ago. Walking across countryside with trees in leaf and flowers blooming, then seeing villages where no smoke rose from chimneys. Nothing stirring except shutters that creaked and doors that banged. Sometimes mothers and fathers had died first. The little children stayed at their sides until starvation or thirst claimed them. Their helpless cries seemed to linger in the silence. Other times the young had died in an adult's arms and it was the mourning of mothers and fathers that seemed to fill my ears. But it was only the wind, blowing down empty streets and through homes open to the elements. Rats paused in their gnawing to stare with boldness. The simple village priest fallen forward in his rectory and the miller crumpled alongside his wheel, all . . ."

"You've got the cure," I broke in. "So what's the problem?"

"Healing you alone took me close to the limits of my power," he said worriedly. "I'm afraid few would survive."

It felt like an icy finger went up my back. "That couldn't happen, could it?"

"You know this Zalzathar better than I do."

I knew he would not hesitate to turn the virus loose on the world if it suited his purpose. Or even from rage or frustration. Zalzathar did not have much emotional control. Great cities would be silent in death instead of the country villages Tyre saw. The *Homo sapiens* fling would be as over as the dinosaur experiment. What would be up to bat next, insects? Or maybe some new creation would heave dripping from the sea. Perhaps the center ring would be the oceans for a change. Whatever the case, the Great Spectator would continue to watch from afar. Maybe the next group would win the favor we and the big lizards lost.

"So God would let us go down the drain just like that," I said.

"I don't know."

"You must have an opinion."

"God is unknowable and His intent mysterious." Clearly, his manner said, I should know this by now.

"Put out the word to the others," I said. "You guys have to nip this in the bud."

"You and I are on our own," he said bleakly.

I waited for an explanation. "I didn't volunteer, either. Others did, mighty angels of great renown. They know Satan's wiles and stratagems. They would have been worthy adversaries. But no, I'm the least of the heavenly host. An unlikely choice, like you." He seemed to feel sorry for himself.

"I thought you said your natures are the same."

"Well, yes. But I'm not a warrior angel who arrives with flashing eyes, flaming sword in hand. I'm a comforter angel, one who comes in silence to be with the dying."

If I was going to be paired with someone, a warrior angel seemed better. "So how come you got picked?"

He bit at his lip again. "God knows."

A car horn gave a little shave-and-a-haircut toot behind us, and I turned to look. Alex was behind the wheel of her Grand Cherokee with a worried look. She pulled alongside, and the passenger window went down.

"Where are you going? Everyone's looking for you."

"Let them."

"Do you plan walking home? It's about ten miles."

"Okay, how about a lift?"

"Get in."

"Mind giving my friend a ride, too? I want you to hear what he has to say."

"What friend?"

Tyre was gone. "Where'd he go?" I asked.

"Who?"

"The man I was walking with."

"You were walking alone." She was crisp.

I got in the car. "You just couldn't see him."

"That usually means no one is there."

"You think I'm sounding loony again, I guess."

"What's interesting is you don't seem worried about it."

"I know I'm not nuts, that's why I'm not worried."

We pulled away from the curb. "You don't want to go back to the hospital?"

"Home, Jeeves."

We were silent for a while. She drove fast and skillfully. "So who is your invisible friend?" she asked. I could tell she was forcing herself to be light.

"He's a sort of second-rate angel." Why *did* he get picked?

"I didn't know they had a class system."

"That's just my take on it."

"What did you want me to hear from your friend?"

"It's him and me against Zalzathar and Soderberg. All the chips are on the table, winner take all."

"I'm sorry, I don't understand."

"My invisible friend and I—he's a kind of male nurse—have to figure out how to beat them."

She didn't say anything.

12

I drove the rented four-wheel Land Rover up from Missoula on the road that had run out of pavement five miles back. I was looking for a sign that pointed the way to the P-Pro Ranch. "If it's still standing, which I doubt," a rancher in a cowboy hat and a long coat with fur collar told me at the little crossroads store where I stopped for directions. "If it's not, just follow the trail of bottles."

I had not seen William Tyre since he vanished into thin air on the street by the hospital. It didn't worry me. He either was gone for long periods in the other world. Jut when I had given up on him, he would show up. One second he wasn't there, and the next he was. It always made me jump.

The weathered P-Pro Ranch sign was still standing but had a tired lean. The rutted track it pointed to made the dirt road I was on look like a superhighway. The utility vehicle bounced and lurched with twanging springs. Cows lumbered off into the brush in wide-eyed panic. Although it was afternoon, purple shadows were deep, and it was cold. I was told winter came early and stayed late. "You don't want to get snowed in up there, mister," the rancher said. "You won't get your car out before late spring, early summer."

Another half hour of travel and I made out a low ranch house in cottonwoods next to an empty log corral. The white trunks of the bare trees looked skinned. When I turned off the engine, the silence was vast. It was as if the world had just begun and there was nothing yet to create a sound. Humans must have learned to make noise to protect themselves against such annihilating silences. Then a breeze as light as a sigh rustled the few dry leaves on the trees. Some of these wafted to the ground like sad comments on the double time life does in passing by.

The ranch house was weathered and buckled like a punch-drunk fighter who had taken too many winters on the chin. I stepped on a warped front porch whose spongy planks were rising up out of their nails. A sofa that had caught the same case of sags was next to a straight-back chair with a rung missing. The sofa cushions were losing cotton stuffing from bulges like hernias. Some early settler had shown gumption, but it looked like those who came later had given up. I rapped on a door with dirty curtains. There was no answer, so I walked around to the side and looked in through smeary windows. I reached a bedroom and saw a man lying in his clothes and shoes on an unmade bed. The housekeeper gave notice years ago, judging from the rest of the room. I tapped on the window, but he was dead or passed out. I went back to the front door and tried it. It opened on dry hinges.

Eric Maye was in his early forties, but he looked much older. He smelled of gin and snored with open mouth. I couldn't rouse him even shaking his shoulders. I went into the cluttered kitchen. A trash can overflowed with empty cans and frozen food containers, and the sink was filled with dirty dishes. I hunted for a clean cup and finally washed one myself. I plugged in the coffee machine and watched as the pot warmed up. The calendar hanging on the wall by a window was a couple of months behind, unless time had stopped up here. A mountain peak with snow high up filled the kitchen window. I watched cloud shadows move on it for a while. When I turned around, Tyre sat at the kitchen table. I jumped and spilled the coffee.

"Give a man some warning." I sat down opposite. "I don't suppose you drink coffee."

"No."

"You could blacktop that dirt road outside with this." He tried to look politely interested. We heard boots on the floor in the next room. Maye came in with a look of bleary surprise, hair sticking up. He was of medium height and weight. He had bags under his eyes and two or three days' worth of salt-and-pepper stubble. "Who the fuck are you guys?"

"You see two of us?" I said in surprise.

"Two guys I'm gonna put some buckshot in." He picked up a pump-action shotgun that leaned against the wall. "How'd you get in here?"

"The front door was unlocked."

"That gives you the right to walk in?"

"I tried to wake you up."

"We mean no harm," Tyre said.

"My name's Bogey Ingersol," I said. "That's William Tyre."

His eyes came back to me, the anger fading. He lowered the shotgun. "*The* Bogey Ingersol? He's in prison."

"I've been out quite a while."

"I was surprised you spent even a day behind bars with your kind of dough. You guys want a drink? The sun's over the yardarm, as if that makes a difference."

"I'm driving," I said.

Tyre shook his head.

Maye hunted around the dirty dishes in the sink until he found a glass. He ran tap water into it. He drank that down and then another. "God, what a thirst." A half-full bottle of Tanqueray stood on a sideboard. A case was by the wood-burning stove. He poured gin into the glass with a shaking hand.

"Have a seat," he said. We sat at the kitchen table. "Sorry the place is such a mess. I'm a real pig." His voice was depressed. He took a long drink and shuddered. "To what do I owe the pleasure?"

"I want to hire you," I said.

"Me?" He laughed sourly. "For what?"

"You were the best political consultant in the country." He had run the campaigns of two presidents, twelve governors, and who knows how many senators and congressmen.

"I got out of that business two years ago."

"Mind telling me why?"

"Burnout."

"Two years is long enough to recover."

"I'd never go back."

"Why is that?" William Tyre asked. He had gone to the sink and was running water to wash the dishes.

"Your friend there could tell you."

"I'd rather hear from you."

Maye pushed the glass away. "I came into politics an idealist like everyone else. Elect the right people and the right things get done. I had a knack. At one point I had sixty-two winning campaigns in a row. I picked and chose which candidates I'd manage. I put people in office I thought would be good for the country." He looked out the window at the mountain. "And then watched them change. They stopped caring about what got them into politics in the first place. Didn't matter whether they were liberal, in the middle, or conservative. What became important was staying in office. Everything else was secondary. They cut whatever deals were necessary. Ingersol there and people like him were more than happy to pay whatever their price was to sell out. People I had taken from obscurity got tired of hearing me ream them out for betraying their ideals and stopped taking my calls until it was time for the next campaign."

I had to admit I had bought my share of politicians. I used

any number of political action committees and phony think tanks to hide campaign contributions from the watchdogs. I didn't bother with the small fry on the back benches. I only dealt with party leaders and committee chairmen, the guys with the grease. If a regulatory agency was breathing down my neck, a call to one of them took care of the problem.

"I've changed," I said.

"I have, too," Maye said. He toasted me with his empty glass. "And I'm a happier man for it."

The old me would have jeered. The new me just nodded. "Follow the news up here?" I asked. I didn't see a radio or television, and I was pretty sure a newspaper wasn't delivered to the doorstep.

"I gave that up, too. You'd be amazed how easy it was. I've been reading the Greeks." He nodded at a shelf of books. "When they get too tough, I read the Tanqueray labels. When they get blurry, I lie down."

"It wasn't just burnout," Tyre corrected. His back was to us at the sink.

Maye looked like he had been kicked in the stomach. "You know about that?"

"It's killing you," the angel said snippily. He dried his hands and sat down at the table.

Astonishment dissolved to sadness on Maye's face like new paint in rain. He began crying, wiping his eyes with a sleeve. Then he put his head down on the table and gave way completely. He sobbed like a little kid. It was hard to watch. I gave Tyre a look. Consoling people was his line of work, but it looked like he was on a break.

"His wife and infant were killed in a car accident," he explained. The comfort he gave was evidently the cold sort. "He was also married to another woman and had older children by her. Neither family knew about the other."

"I couldn't leave Geraldine and the boys," Maye said in a

choked voice. "She stood by me when I was nothing and I still loved her very much. I told her about the marriage when Gwen and Melissa were killed."

"She left him and took the children," Tyre said.

No wonder the poor bastard was drinking himself to death.

After a long time Maye lifted his head from the table. I pretended an interest in the mountain outside the window so I didn't have to see the pain in his face.

"Geraldine and the boys have forgiven you," Tyre said. "They want to see you."

Maye shook his head. "Not after what I did." He looked at Tyre. "How do you know?"

"I know." His manner said it was his business to know such things. No matter how tough things were, Helither had always been good natured.

"I didn't mean to fall in love with Gwen. I just did. She worked on a campaign for me in Michigan. One thing led to another. . . ." He shrugged helplessly. "She was in her middle thirties and worried about her biological clock. She didn't tell me until it was too late to do anything about it. I hadn't been around to notice myself. I was always on a plane to somewhere or making calls from a hotel room."

A cloud shadow covered part of the mountain in the window.

"You'll see them again," Tyre said.

"Sorry, I don't buy that," Maye said tiredly. "We're just bags of skin. When we die, the system crashes and there's no rebooting. The inability of people to accept this is what caused religion, and you know the trouble that's cost." He looked at me. "But I don't have to tell you that. I read that *Time* magazine profile a few years back. You said nobody but you deserved credit for your success. Hell, when it comes to godlessness, I'm Billy Graham compared to you."

I cleared my throat. "There's been some water under the bridge since then." The snappy phrases I tossed around on every subject under the sun, later quoted so impressively by *Time*, had been brainstormed beforehand by my PR people. I dropped them into my answers so they seemed spontaneous. "I take it you don't know that Bernard Soderberg is running for president?"

Maye ran his fingers through his hair, his mind elsewhere. "He wouldn't have a chance. What's he got besides money?"

"I found generally that's enough."

"Not in politics. You have to have a party behind you and an organization in every state. You have to be for or against something. You need the right image. You need smart people running things. You can't look like a geeky nerd with a crazy aunt in the attic. Perot proved that."

"Soderberg's changed his appearance and he's got all the other things going for him you mention. As for message, he's in favor of progress and against going back. He doesn't say back to what."

"You don't have to," Maye said, looking half interested. "People fill in the blanks themselves. When did all this happen?"

"The past few months."

"He asked you to come all the way up here to see if I'd work for him?"

"He's got all the brains and talent he needs. The best and the brightest, except for you." I gave him the names of the political consultants, ad agencies, and polling firms working for Bernie.

"It's already overkill. He doesn't need me." Maye said.

"You don't understand, I want to stop him."

"I get the drift." It seemed to make him more tired.

"He'd be bad for the country and the world. A disaster."

"He screwed you in some big business deal and you want payback."

"He's evil."

"That's not enough to keep a man out of the White House. Look at Nixon."

"This man is far worse."

"You must know him pretty well."

"I've only met him a few times."

"Then how do you know he's evil? Maybe he just needed more praise as a kid."

"Take my word for it."

"And what's 'evil' mean, anyhow? A cop will tell you one thing and a social worker another—"

Tyre interrupted. "Mr. Ingersol is right. He's an evil man under an evil influence."

"All right, he has to be stopped. I wish you luck."

A heavy gust of wind shook the house. Sudden changes in weather got my attention. I stepped to the window. It looked like a big storm was blowing in from the other side of the mountain. The sky was full of dark clouds lowering like the big top coming down at a circus.

"I'll stay," Tyre said, reading my thoughts. "Better leave before it gets here."

"The Republican dropped out, and a bunch of nobodys are scrambling for the nomination," I said. "Meanwhile, the Democrats can't agree on anyone. Soderberg looks like a winner at this point I can't stop him without you. Blowing him out of the water will take somebody who knows how to come from way behind." Clancy had told me that before he got to where he could pick and choose candidates, Maye was famous for riding long shots to victory.

"I'm not interested. Sorry."

"I'll pay whatever you say. Give me a number." That usually worked for Bogey.

"I've got enough money to last me."

"What about the country?"

"It deserves what it gets. It took me a long time to realize that."

"And the children? What about them?" I put a little throb in my voice. Another of Bogey's negotiating strategies.

He smiled faintly. "Put away the violin. I know the music backward and forward."

Maye walked me to the porch. The heat from the gin had put some color in his face. "Sorry you went to all the trouble of driving up here."

"If you change your mind, give me a call." My mind was already racing ahead. There had to be some undiscovered geniuses in his racket. The questions was whether there was time to find them before it was too late.

"You know, it could've been fun," Maye said. "I always wanted to run a campaign backed by some unscrupulous bastard with all the money in the world. Somebody who didn't give a shit about public opinion or care if he was ever in another election. I figured I could put us in the history books."

"For what?"

"The best political campaign ever."

"I'm guessing you mean dirtiest."

"Gloves off, balls-to-the-wall. No need to worry about taste or what the election reform pansies said. It would have been beautiful."

"Here's your chance. I'm that unscrupulous bastard."

He shook his head and shut the door. I guess he thought Tyre would call a cab when he was ready to go.

The wind cut like a razor. I turned the heater on full blast. How people must have dreaded winter storms there in the old days. They would have to wear everything they owned and huddle around a smoky fire, praying the wood lasted. I put on the lights to spot the deeper potholes.

I saw the first Pig Face twenty minutes later, running on all fours from the tree line across a meadow on a line to intersect the road. I must have left Maye before they were ready, and he and the others who followed were late getting into position. There were half a dozen on that side and the same number coming out of the trees on the other side of the road. All were headed for the spot in the distance where the road squeezed between a couple of rocks the size of cement trucks. It would be easy to stop the car and drag me out there. The dying light gave their purple baboon butts a kind of lavender cast. I stomped the gas pedal and the Land Rover took off like it was goosed. If it wasn't for the seat belt, my head would have gone through the roof at the first big hole I hit. The car rolled and pitched over the bumps like a boat in a gale. I was clinging to the wheel as much as steering it. The vehicle kept bottoming out and then springing up so all four wheels left the ground. I was afraid a tire was going to blow. The violent motion activated the burglar alarm, and it began caterwauling. *Eeee-aw Eeeee-aw Beep Beep Beep.*

That was what saved me. The Pig Faces on both sides came to a stop and raised up on hind legs to evaluate the threat. I gained precious yards as they were figuring out the racket was nothing to worry about. The Land Rover leaped from the crest of a knoll like a long jumper stretching for distance and slammed back to earth. *Eeeee-aw Eeeee-aw Beep Beep Beep.*

The leading Pig Face on my side of the car reached the rocks the same time as the Land Rover. I had a close-up through the window of snout, yellow tusks, and piggy eyes. They blazed with feral fury under a brutal brow. The window on the passenger side blew out and showered the inside with safety glass. The one on my side banged and filled with spidery fault lines from another blow. The boulders flashed past on both sides, and then I was in the open beyond. The Pig Faces kept up the chase in the rearview mirror. Then they were covered by the dust cloud the Land Rover kicked up.

I kept a sharp eye out but reached the highway without seeing any others. The cold wind rushing in from the broken window overwhelmed the heater, and I was chilled to the bone by the time I got to the asphalt. The alarm would not turn off. I drove through the silent, empty country sounding like an urban emergency. A highway patrolman stopped me on the outskirts of Missoula.

"What happened?" he yelled over the burglar alarm. He stood back from my window with his hand near his gun.

It was the old quandary. Tell the truth and get put in a rubber room. "I locked my keys inside," I yelled back. "I had to break the window to get in." I turned off the ignition at his signal, and the alarm fell silent.

He asked for my driver's license and the registration. "This a rental car?"

He examined the papers and looked in the back of the Land Rover. "You've got the same name as that fella out on the coast who's on the news so much. The one mixed up in that murder." He was a good-looking young officer in a parka and a Smokey the Bear hat.

"That's me, but I didn't do it."

He had me get out and stand by the front fender while he did some business on his radio. He returned to hand back the registration and my license. "Looks like you've got some busted springs the way it's riding. The muffler's got a hole in it, too. I wouldn't want to be you when you turn it in."

When I returned it, I told them to put the damages on my bank card. They were nice enough to drive me to the private airfield where the plane waited.

13

Alex poured herbal tea into china cups from a dainty English pot with yellow flowers and green leaves. She had telephoned to say she would like to see me in her office at Stanford. A gray day with a threat of rain. The Hoover Tower looked like a tent pole holding up a baggy sky.

"In the old days," I said, "it would be a single malt scotch poured this time of day."

She wore an orange blouse and black vest and a long black skirt that covered high-heel boots. Her hair was piled on her head and held with an orange comb. I told her she looked ready to spring into a saddle and ride the pampas to celebrate Halloween.

She grinned. Her eyes crinkled more than with her reassuring doctor smile. "Thank you, I guess. How much would you say you drank then?"

"I'm not your patient anymore, remember? We're just friends."

"Just curious."

"I never counted."

"I tried calling yesterday. Your housekeeper said you were away."

"I was in Montana. They tried again." I showed her a Polaroid of the Land Rover. The car rental people had taken pictures for the agency's insurance company.

"What happened to the windows?"

"They nearly headed me off at the pass. There were Pig Faces to the left of me and Pig Faces to the right of me."

"Why can't you be serious? You almost died twice."

"More than that. Lots more."

"I wasn't counting the coma."

"Neither was I."

I sipped the tea. "Gloom and doom don't work for me."

She examined the Polaroid with skepticism. "I suppose no one else witnessed this."

"Just me."

She put down her teacup with a decisive click. "There's someone I want you to see, a colleague of mine. He's just down the hall. He said give a shout and he'd look in if you didn't have any objections."

"Just as a wild guess, another shrink?"

"He's an authority on obsessional and delusional states."

"Has he helped you?"

"What do you mean?"

"You're deluding yourself if you think I'm making this up."

She brushed that off. "I told him about the Pig Faces, and now you say they're back. He says it's very rare for someone with a problem of your severity to be able to deal with reality at any level. It's far more common for them to wander the streets talking to themselves. He says it's remarkable that you set up a foundation to give away your fortune."

"Really?" I grinned again to annoy her. Something about her brought out a man's playfulness.

"It's more typical for paranoid schizophrenics to throw their money out the window. They hope their enemies will be placated and leave them alone. I told him about your invisible friend. It is a friend, right, not someone you argue with?"

"Get paranoid schizophrenic out of your head. And he's an angel, like Helither. Did you mention that fatal virus to him? How does he explain that?"

"We were asked not to speak about that. I got a registered letter from the CDC reminding me. It almost read like a threat. My point is my colleague believes it's possible the right combination of therapies might bring you back to full functioning."

"Did you tell him about Soderberg?"

"I didn't have time to go into all of your fantasies. We were interrupted."

"Well, don't."

"You don't think he's in league with the Devil anymore?" She brightened.

"I don't think it, I know it. I just don't want it to get around for the time being."

Her face fell. "I know it's almost always pointless to try to get someone to reason his way out of an obsession. But I have to try because I think you can come back. Why must this man be involved in a conspiracy? Why can't he just be someone who is very rich and has reached a time in his life when he wants to give something back to society?"

"I know the type. I used to be one of them, remember? Giving something back would never cross his mind. Soderberg wants power for its own sake. You can inflict pain and misery with it, which is what Zalzathar gets out of the deal. Suffering is like oxygen to him. He needs it to live."

"You have some very interesting insights. You stand back and analyze. I think that's a hopeful sign."

"I could talk to you until next month about all the insights I've had since I came out of my coma, but I don't have time to play around. As for letting your colleague put me under the microscope, forget it."

"He's working with new drugs that don't have the side effects of the ones you were probably leery of. He says you're an ideal candidate for an experimental program he runs for a pharmaceutical company."

"I wasn't just leery, I flat-out refused to take them. Let me make the point again: I'm not deranged. These things really happened. If you were there, you would've seen."

"If I had been there, I would have shown what you thought you saw wasn't real. You were in a kind of fugue state, and when you came out, you confused it with reality."

"I almost wish I were mentally ill," I said. "It would make you feel better."

She drew back, offended.

"I don't mean that the way it sounded."

"Then maybe you should explain."

"If I was wacko . . ."

"Please don't use words like that."

"Sorry. If I was . . . irrational . . . you could deal with that because it's familiar to you. But this is *un*rational. It can't happen according to our standards of reality, but it does. The eye can't see infrared light, but that doesn't mean it isn't there. I don't blame you for not buying my story. I wouldn't either."

Alex had a gotcha look, like a chess player who spots an opening. "We can't see infrared light, but we have instruments that do. Is there an instrument that would see what you say you have?"

"You don't need one. Eyes do nicely."

"Only yours, it seems."

"What if one time you were there and saw what I did?"

"What if I didn't?"

"Simple. You'd be right and I'd be wrong."

I looked at my watch. I had things to do. Clancy was sounding out my old Wall Street team about coming back to work and was going to call to say who was willing. When there was dirty work to be done, not many were in their league. In the meantime, I was talking to ad agency people I used to know to see which shops were currently hot. The trouble was the ones good at selling a product were greenhorns when it came to politics. I was also due in San Francisco at Wilkes Bashford's. I had given away all the Brioni suits Felicity chose to make Bogey blend in with her ultrachic crowd. Pinstripes were thrown out for silk suits that got fashionably wrinkled five minutes off the hanger. Sturdy wingtips that had trod boardroom carpets were dumped for stilettolike pumps from Rome that caused bunions and corns. There wasn't time to put back on the sixty more pounds Bogey carried, but I could dress like him. Maybe people wouldn't notice the difference so much.

"I have a proposal," I said.

"What is it?"

"It's the quarter break, and you don't have any classes to teach. Spend the time with me."

Her smile was cool. "What can we do to get you serious?"

"I'm not joking. Come with me now. This minute." I stood. "You'll see with your own eyes."

"You're serious."

"Never more serious. I haven't gotten around to counting all the bedrooms at Millwood, but you can take your pick. It's just a matter of time before they try again." Impulsiveness had been foreign to Bogey. Even marrying Felicity was part of a business plan to tap her connections to old money. He was sure he could convince some of her friends to switch their capital to his faster horse. Bogey preferred risking other people's money.

"I have a life, for one thing," Alex answered. "I have my home, my children, my friends. I'm spending the break writing a grant application."

"Your kids are in college. If they're coming home on the break, send them to Europe for a vacation. On me. They can take their friends. I'll charter a 737. Instead of youth hostels, I'll put them up in five-star hotels."

She shook her head. "They already have plans."

"They'll drop them, I bet. I would when I was their age. Tell them their mom is friends with an eccentric rich guy who enjoys blowing money. That much is true, except you'd pick a stronger word than 'eccentric.' I'll pay for somebody to house-sit your place. I'll pay for a gardener. If you think you've got termites, I'll pay to fumigate while you're gone. Bring *your* friends. Hell, there's room for everyone. Millwood's got an Olympic-size pool and tennis courts. There's a sauna and a spa. The place is like a resort, except for all the dogs. I'll have a string orchestra play in the ballroom every night. My foundation will give you your grant. I'm very influential with the board. It consists of me." A merchant with a blanket in the bazaar didn't talk any faster.

Alex looked rattled. "Wait a minute, this is too fast. I have to think about it."

"Think about it, then call and tell me when I can expect you and your friends."

Alex's Jeep Cherokee came up the drive just at sunset. The sloping lawn at Millwood was velvety with shadows. Alice and the handlers were putting the dogs back. Two kids from the community college crisscrossed the grounds with pooper-scoopers and garbage bags. The morning count of dogs stood at sixty-four. My agents were only barely finding homes fast enough to keep up. Alice said I should I expand the search into Nevada.

Alex got out from the driver's side. A tall man with sun-streaked dark hair got out the other. She stooped to rub Oliver's head. Her perfume made him sneeze. "Bogey," she said, "I'd like you to meet a friend of mine, Grant Knox." He was big, with confident good looks. His grip was an Alpha male strength test. Bogey kept V-shaped springs with pistol grips at his desk. He squeezed them three hundred times a day so he could dominate these. "How ya doin'?" Knox said jauntily. His clothes were expensive, and he had a golf tan. Of course Alex would have a partner. What had I been thinking of? She was not the sort of widow who pined away. Was there amusement in Knox's eyes? Did they talk about me?

Mildred Harris stepped from the back. She wore a bulky tan corduroy jacket and skirt the color of celery. Her square-toed shoes with heavy stitching looked stout enough to cross America. "Mr. Ingersol," she said with a cool nod. Bow-shaped glass frames made her eyebrows seem raised in surprised disapproval. Maybe they spared her the effort.

"Dr. Harris," I said.

"Where's everybody else?" I asked Alex, looking down the drive. "They coming later?"

She and Mildred exchanged looks. "I couldn't talk anyone else into coming," Alex confessed.

"She didn't have to in my case," Mildred said. "I volunteered." She made it sound like she had agreed to cross the lines with a note saying the fort was low on food and water.

"It's all the gossip and publicity," Alex said apologetically.

"People assume where there's smoke, there's fire," Mildred corrected.

"I wouldn't miss this for anything," Knox said. I was entertainment for the masses now. It was a good bet that a critic for a highbrow monthly was hard at work, hoping to be the first to make my celebrity status an ironic comment on pop culture. How long before disturbed women sent me marriage proposals? Of course Knox wouldn't miss it for anything. I had to laugh.

"What's so funny?" Alex asked me. "I told Grant you make a joke about everything." So they did talk about me.

"I wasn't kidding about a string orchestra," I said. "They begin playing at seven-thirty sharp. Thirty-two pieces, led by Mr. Adrian Smart." I showed them the printed program.

"With just the four of us as audience?" Mildred said with disbelief. Marxist theory must have something to say about the guilt the audience shares in extravagant display.

"Maybe Alice will come up from the kennels and join us," I said.

I led them up the stairs to the flagstone veranda that covered three sides of the house. The household staff was lined up in welcome on the orders of Mrs. Kable, the housekeeper. She looked to the Victorian era for her model.

A woman stepped forward to take the suitcase Mildred carried, but she refused to surrender it. "I don't need another to carry my burden."

"I thought we'd have drinks by the pool in half an hour," I said.

"Servile waiters balancing trays on fingertips, I suppose," Mildred said.

"Millie, try to be nice," Alex said. "Are the workmen finished?" she asked me.

"Not hardly. They're working now on the foundations of the east wing." Herbert Hoover and his wife had once spent the night there. "We won't hear them."

We walked inside. The decorators had finished their work and cleared out.

"How do you think it looks?" I asked.

"It's like the lobby of a really expensive hotel," Alex said after a minute. She gave me a look. "I don't mean that as a criticism."

"I'm dumb enough to take it as a compliment."

"It needs a woman's touch," Mildred said firmly.

"The decorator was a woman."

"She gave you what she thought you wanted."

"What's wrong with that?"

"I think Millie means it's somber," Alex said. "Be sure to always have plenty of flowers around. That'll lighten it up."

"Sure is big," Knox marveled.

It was nice by the pool. Steam rose off the aquamarine spar-
kle. A light breeze kept the mosquitoes down. I wondered if it
would push the fog in later.

Alex and Knox had picked adjoining bedrooms that shared
a balcony. They had fireplaces and a beautiful view of the
mountains to the west. Funny how it never crossed my mind
that she might be involved with someone. I guess I was fooled
by her sorrow over her late husband.

Mildred accepted a glass of champagne to be polite, but not
a drop passed her compressed lips. The bedroom she chose
was on the third floor under stairs. It had been a maid's room
at one time. "It's sufficient for my needs," she said.

A trio arrived in advance of the orchestra bus. It played
zippy show tunes from the poolside cabana while guards
checked the IDs of the musicians on the bus and went through
their instrument cases for weapons.

"You went to such trouble," Alex said. She wore a black
cocktail dress with a shawl for her bare shoulders. Nice
shoulders.

Knox had a good tux. He lifted his glass. "I know something
about champagne, and this isn't bad." Mildred was decked out
in an severe outfit in a durable fabric. It would also do for a
visit to the tractor works to discuss production quotas.

"The shrimp is yummy," Alex said

"There's enough for an army," Mildred said critically.

Knox had the look of someone with high expectations of
entertainment as yet unsatisfied. "I thought there'd be a lot of
media at your front gate."

"That circus has moved on."

He had been stuck in the traffic jam caused by my accident.
"I would have gone crazy without the car phone." He had seen
the demolished pickup on television. It was a miracle I survived, he said. "You don't know the half of it," I replied. He

was a commercial insurance broker, a type that flew too low to show up on Bogey's radar screen.

"There'll be a lot of leftover food," Mildred commented. "How will it be disposed of?"

"The food bank," I said.

"Crumbs from the rich man's table."

"Millie!" Alex said.

"She doesn't mean half what she says," Knox said with a chuckle. "We've had some real doozies when it comes to arguments, haven't we, Mildred?" She gave him a look of hatred.

Alice came up from the kennels in a party dress and looking nervous. I told her she looked gorgeous and introduced her. "I haven't worn this for a long time. They're finally getting settled down."

"Who, dear?" Mildred beamed. Her friendliness declared class solidarity.

"Why, the dogs."

"I hear there's a couple hundred," Knox said to me.

Alice answered. "There's a lot of dumb things dumb people are saying that're wrong."

I gazed into my champagne. I used to marvel at Felicity's levees. They were always brilliant successes. People talked for weeks afterward. Celebrated wits prepared bon mots beforehand in hopes they would be printed in the society columns. The roar of people trading aphorisms and epigrams was deafening.

All the wives in her set had pet causes. Felicity's was reviving the art of conversation. It had gone downhill since the eighteenth-century salons, where rough country sages fenced with learned aristocrats. She got a grant from the same government agency that awarded one to a performance artist who painted with her menses to make a statement about the oppression of women. It was a toss of the coin which grant outraged the right wing more.

The splendor of Millwood's great dining hall was evidence of the failure of the evening. The long, candlelit table was set for fifty, with serving staff to match. I had picked the number out of the air. They stood around with arms folded and yawning until I paid off all but a few and sent the rest home. Afterward, Knox and I danced with the women in the ballroom beneath the stuffed heads. Adrian Smart, a tiny man with a cad's mustache, laid down his baton at one point to ask Mildred to dance. His head came to her shoulder. I expected her to refuse on ideological grounds, but they glided around the floor like tugboat and ocean liner.

"The Politburo polka," I said.

"Don't be mean," Alex said.

It was what Bogey would have said. The new wardrobe wasn't enough. I would have to relearn my old attacking style. Clancy said nearly everyone on my old team was itching to come back to work. In some cases, guilt by association damaged careers when I went to prison. In others, they longed for the gunslinger swagger they had in the anything-goes culture around Bogey.

"I've never seen that smile before," Alex said.

"It's the way I always smile."

"No, it's different."

"In what way?" I had been practicing in the mirror, using a *Newsweek* photo taken when Bogey captured Ampersand Industries in a hostile takeover. Eleven thousand people lost jobs in a merger. "Wolfish" describes the *Newsweek* smile.

"I don't know," Alex said. "It's sort of cruel."

"A smile's a smile."

She looked at me critically. "Maybe it's the way you lower your head."

I changed the subject. "So you and Mr. Knox are pretty good pals?"

"He and my husband were good friends. I liked his wife, but they're divorced now."

"Just good friends. That sounds Hollywood."

"He wants to get married."

"What about you?" I might as well have all the bad news.

"It seems too soon."

"So you're going to wait a while first?"

"We don't really know each other. There, that's the way you smiled before. It's much nicer."

After the others went upstairs, Oliver and I stood on the veranda. I smoked an Esplendido, Cuba's finest. I would have to resume that vice. An expensive cigar with a quarter inch of gray ash was one of Bogey's trademarks. The moon was a minor presence, and the black sky was sprinkled with bright stars. A book I read in prison said the ancients believed they were holes in the firmament that allowed the radiance of Heaven to shine through. I turned off the lights of the grounds so we could see better.

"They're a long way off," I said.

Oliver was not interested in the stars. The only time dogs look up is if a bird catches their eye. They might wonder what sky is and how birds manage to get up there, but that is as far as it goes.

"Quite an accomplishment." I jumped as usual, dropping the cigar. William Tyre stood in the darkness.

"What is?" I asked.

"The universe," he said fussily. "Time itself swallowed by its size. But big as it is, the universe you see is only an unimaginably small part of Creation. God enjoys the work so much He makes new universes all the time. Each different from the other, as He takes delight in variety. The scientists who talk about parallel universes have an inkling. They'll never be believed, of course, anymore than the mystic who senses the divine order that lies behind appearances."

"Helither told me God is absent because He's so busy."

There was silence for a moment. "Many of us think that." Another silence. "Are there angels in his other universes? I wonder about that."

"So God's a guy?"

"Did I say that?"

"I assumed it from your use of the pronoun."

"Gender is meaningless when it comes to God. As easily say She, as some do. Both are preferable to It, in my opinion. That's so impersonal, even though no more off the mark than the other two. But words cannot describe God. Only God could describe Himself." It sounded like a pat speech he had given many times.

"I picked up my cigar. "Want one?" I asked. "Castro's own brand."

"I don't think so." Helither was warmer by far. It was the difference between one of the warm Mediterranean races and a chilly New England Yankee.

"Angels don't have vices, I guess."

"Some of us like to think so, but naturally we do. Only God is perfect." We looked at the stars for a while. I wondered if a man and an angel in some other universe were doing the same thing or would or already did. No, God was too original to repeat Himself.

"How's Maye doing?" I asked.

"We were just in time."

"For what?"

"He was going to kill himself that day."

"How do you know?"

"Trust me," he said with impatience.

"You stopped him?" An owl hooted and Oliver pricked his ears.

"We don't have that power. He changed his own mind."

"With your help?"

"We are allowed that."

"You told him you were an angel?"

"He believed he was alone. He thought I left with you."

"What made him change his mind?"

"I helped him to take his mind off himself. That's the cause of most suicides. I encouraged him to think about the effect killing himself would have on his children. He also realized he had work to do."

"Helping me, I hope."

Tyre nodded. "He comes tomorrow."

Oliver woofed softly. Lately I had been having trouble understanding what he and the kennel dogs said. It was as if they had switched to a canine dialect I didn't know. I mentioned this.

"That ability belongs to the other world. I'm surprised you've kept it as long as you have." Tyre lifted his chin toward the trees. "The dog knows they're out there."

"Who is?"

"Your enemy. They're hidden in the woods, biding their time. It's fortunate you have your guards and dogs. Zalzathar wants revenge. It's an obsession."

"Once he gets an idea in his head," I agreed, "it's hard for him to get it out." Bogey's cunning had turned that weakness to his advantage more than once.

"A very stubborn creature. But surprising powers for a wizard." There was respect in his voice.

"Do me a favor."

"If I can."

"There's a woman."

"Your friend Alex?"

"She thinks I'm crazy."

"At least they don't burn mentally disturbed people at the stake anymore. They used to think they were possessed by demons. I witnessed many of those crimes. I came to people as the flames licked around them. I wondered as I looked at the gloating faces around the fire why God showed humans so much patience. I still do. For all your proud talk of progress, this century has been among the worst. Azimbril-Zafieri and his influence have never been stronger."

"Do something to show her I'm not a nutcase. Make an appearance or something. It doesn't have to be flashy."

"Why do you want me to do that?"

"It's lonely on the point. I'd like somebody in on the secret."

"That's not all," he said accusingly.

"All right, I like her. Is that such a crime? But she's a psychiatrist. As long as she think's I'm unbalanced, she can't see me as anything other than a patient. I think it's in their code of ethics."

"We can't just make random appearances. There are rules."

"Rules are made to be broken. And somebody's doing it. Look at all the angel stuff on TV."

"Breaking rules. The old Bogey speaks."

"That's another point. I can't take these guys on with one hand tied behind my back."

"I'm not sure I understand."

"I've got to have breathing room, a little give. Some flexibility. You can't make an omelette without breaking eggs."

"I was there when that was first said," Tyre mused. "It was a Frenchman in the time of the Sun King. A very cynical and subtle counselor. The ends justify the means. Admittedly, true in extreme cases." He thought a moment. "It was a well-known conundrum long before the omelette."

I said if the present situation didn't qualify as extreme, I didn't know what did.

"What rules do you mean to break?"

"Maybe none. But I don't want to be driving for the goal line and have a penalty flag thrown."

"Like kitchen metaphors, sports analogies often justify wrong behavior."

We heard running feet. "Your guards are coming," Tyre said. I looked toward the sound. When I turned back, he was gone.

Two guards pounded up the steps and stopped when they saw me. "What happened to the lights?" one asked, panting.

"Sorry. I turned them out to look at the stars." I turned them back on. Alice had released the dogs. Like Oliver, they looked toward the woods with ears pricked.

14

Alex and Knox went off to golf the next morning, and Mildred clacked the keys on her laptop in the library. I had heard her say she was writing a paper contrasting Marx and Dickens from a deconstructionist perspective. One footnote was already twenty-two pages long. The library was a beautiful room, with books from floor to ceiling. Stained glass showed Greeks in robes discussing geometry. An early Hensen was chairman of the history department at Stanford.

"Did you buy these books by the yard?" Mildred had asked. "Or did they come with the house?" I did not rise to the bait, and Alex gave me a grateful look. She was in golf togs, shorts, and a polo shirt.

"We've been friends since we were girls. I don't agree with everything she says. She's really nice when you get to know her," Alex said later as she loaded her clubs into the car.

"So you've said."

"When she's uncomfortable in a situation, she compensates with hostility. But it's not genuine."

"Yet so amazingly like the real thing." But I smiled.

The night had been uneventful. Tyre had not returned. Oliver slept soundly at the foot of my bed, and the dogs outside were quiet except when squabbles broke out among them.

The local weekly delivered to the front gate in the morning

had an article about an outbreak of deer poaching. Butchered carcasses had been found in the woods and on the grounds of estates, many of them by children. Mothers, already guilty about the scars left when their kids saw *Bambi*, were raising hell.

After breakfast I canceled the Las Vegas lounge act I had booked for that night, Tony Martinello and his Trio. He sang and did magic tricks while riding a unicycle. The pinkie ring he wore in his photo was like a headlight. The booking agent said his humor was un-PC, and I worried how Mildred would take it. I had to walk a tightrope at this point. In bringing back the old Bogey, I did not want to turn off Alex. In the early afternoon I watched as workmen lifted the new flagpole in place. News chopper footage of the Jolly Roger flying above Millwood would say more than words that Bogey Ingersol was back in the game.

Eric Maye arrived at the front gate by taxi, and I went down to meet him. He looked pale and shaky, but his suit had a razor-sharp press. "Surprise," he said.

"This mean you've changed your mind?" I asked. He paid off the driver and we walked up toward the house.

"Are you willing to spend what it takes?"

I said I was. He nodded. "We'll put the national headquarters in Denver. I know an office tower we can lease."

"Why Denver?"

"The rest of the country hates New York and they don't like L.A., either. They'd laugh us off if we put it in San Francisco. Perot screwed up Texas for third-party politics. That leaves cities like Chicago, Atlanta, Denver. People associate Denver with the Rockies. The Rockies are the West, mountain men and trappers. The environment and so forth. It's the sort of angle the media like. It's off the beaten track politically. My hunch is Barton Thomas gets the Democratic nomination on the second, third ballot. The Republicans are talking about Wesley Harris, but that's just a sop to the liberal Rockefeller wing. He'll get the nomination but no money. We want it to look like his own kind of people are against Thomas. Christ, how many dogs do you have?"

"That's a long story. Did you say *against* Thomas?"

"Our group will be a grassroots Citizens for Soderberg."

We reached the front entrance and walked inside. Maye looked around. "You could have a political convention in here."

"Why do we want to make it look like we're for Soderberg?"

"It gives us more room for dirty tricks. Can I get something to drink? Fruit juice or something." We went to the kitchen. He swallowed a pill with the juice. "Tranquilizer. I've got the whips and jingles. I'm on the wagon until this is over."

"Mind if I ask what made you change your mind?"

"The challenge, like I said. Emptying out the bag of tricks."

"Is that all?" If his only interest was showing what fancy stuff he could do with the cuffs off, he wouldn't stick around when things got heavy.

Mayes hesitated. Drinking and his grief had lined his face. "If this guy is as bad as you say, he's got to be stopped. If even someone like you says he's evil, he must really be." He handed me a thick envelope. "It's our game plan. Everything I've ever known about politics and a few things I think are right but could never prove. I figure a hundred and twenty-five million dollars, give or take ten million." He watched my reaction.

"Whatever it takes."

"There'll be civil suits afterward, probably criminal charges."

"So be it."

"You've got a criminal record. They're tougher the second time."

"My conviction was overturned on a technicality. The government decided not to retry me. I already served as much time as I was going to."

"You're really serious, then?"

"Deadly serious."

"My fee will be five million."

"Agreed."

"Funny, I read you were a cheapskate."

I put on one of my old snarling looks and bit off the words, "No broads, caviar, or conferences at fancy resorts. I can spot padding no matter how it's hidden." Bogey watched the store pretty close or the types he hired would have robbed him blind.

"You do business with any offshore banks? We need a few to handle the money."

"Lots of them. Why offshore?"

"The first thing the press will zero in on is our money source. When they see it's coming offshore, they'll get suspicious. The feeding frenzy will begin. They'll outdo each other to dig up dirt."

"Soderberg owns half the press."

"That means the other half will be gunning for him. The first thing we need to do is buy TV time for summer and fall."

"So far in advance?"

"We'll do our buys so fast it'll make their heads swim. We'll saturate the local markets and buy all the prime time we can. They want the money up front. Broadcasters don't trust politicians for some crazy reason."

"Let me make a couple of calls and you can begin buying."

"Make the calls."

I telephoned Jared Snyder. Money was transferred offshore. Bogey had been a good customer at some of the same banks favored by drug lords. I knew I would be welcomed back.

"I need to be alone with a telephone for a long time," Maye said. I led him to the billiard room. "Make yourself comfortable."

He took off his coat and tie and picked up the phone. "Are these lines secure?"

"As secure as the Oval Office's." Doyle's crew came by every other day to sweep for bugs.

"Send me food every eight hours."

Alex and Knox returned after thirty-six holes of golf. She looked tired but happy. "I'm going to give it up, I swear. I didn't notice your flag before."

"It's the pirate flag, right?" Knox said eagerly. His prescription sunglasses slipped down. He wrinkled his nose to keep them from dropping farther. This caused his upper lip to rise. He reminded me of a squirrel who smelled groundnuts. I supposed that was jealousy.

He went off to shower and change. "Let's walk down to the dogs," Alex said. "I want to see how you relate." She gave a sidelong glance as we strolled toward their noisy welcome. "What are they saying now?"

"I don't know."

"But you said you could talk to them."

"Not anymore." The dogs flung themselves against the fences. Alice kept three and four to a run now because of overcrowding.

"That's a promising development," Alex said.

"If you say so."

"It's one fantasy put aside."

Some bully's instinct told Mildred I wanted to stay on her good side because of Alex and this emboldened her. After dinner she unlimbered a guitar and sang folk songs about revolutionary struggles in the underdeveloped world. "This is a song they wrote after Che was murdered."

"Doesn't she have a lovely voice?" Alex asked.

"Beautiful," I said. Knox made no comment. I figured he had sat through many of these solo performances. We clapped after each song. My own applause was vigorous. Mildred held up her hand as if quieting a throng at an outdoor concert. "Now I'd like to sing you a little song from Chile."

Eric Maye stayed in the billiard room, the telephone cradled on his shoulder. He mouthed something and waved me off when I looked in. I went back to the songfest. At last Mildred set aside the guitar. "Thus, the oppressed sing in their chains." Her flashing look said we remained class enemies despite my admiration for her music.

"Alex tells me you wrote a book, Mr. Ingersol."

"Everybody calls me Bogey."

"I've looked for a copy but no one seems to have one."

"They're scarce as hen's teeth for some reason."

"A man said someone came in and bought all three copies they had."

This was news to me. "Really?"

Mildred's eyes danced with malice. "I thought it was so strange, I checked with other bookstores. Collectors aren't interested in that sort of . . . book. The others had the same story."

"Mildred, you never said," Alex exclaimed.

"I did some sleuthing just out of curiosity. It was called *Top Dog*. Right, Mr. Ingersol?" I guessed she wasn't ever going to call me Bogey.

"I wrote it in prison, like the people in your songs."

"The critics were unkind, to put it mildly," she told Alex.

"Why haven't you mentioned it before? I'd love to read it," Alex said.

Knox roused himself from the stupor he had sunk into during Mildred's concert. "What's the book about?"

"It was supposedly a true story about how Mr. Ingersol was turned into a dog and transported to another universe," Mildred said. "However, it was sold as fiction in the reputable stores."

Knox laughed. "What's the joke, Bogey? C'mon, 'fess up."

"I hoped Disney would option it."

Knox was impressed. "There's real money in movies if you get a hit."

"I was hoping for tie-ins with Burger King and Mattel. Kids' meals and action figures." I gave him my easy insider's smile. "The book was secondary. I put most of my effort into marketing."

He nodded eagerly. "I've got a friend who's a writer. We go a long way back. He's poor as a church mouse. His mistake is he never thinks of action figures or the other spin-offs when he writes up his stories. I've tried to tell him."

"The plan," I said with a wink, "was to straddle both the fiction and nonfiction markets."

"There you have it," Mildred said with fury, "the cynicism of capitalism."

Someone buying up all the copies explained why they were hard to find but not why someone wanted them to disappear. I excused myself and telephoned Doyle. Clicks told me the call was being forwarded from one number to another until at last it reached him. His voice was guarded. "Doyle." I pictured him in a dark room with firearms laid out before him in the order he would use them.

"Where are you?" I asked.

"I'd rather not say."

"Sorry, I shouldn't have asked."

"What's up?"

"How's the search for Carlotta going?"

"Dead end at this point."

I waited for him to say more. When he didn't, I said: "I've got a new job for you."

"They should've swept your place for bugs today."

"They did."

"Okay, we can speak freely. What's the job?"

"Somebody's buying all the copies of a book I wrote."

He didn't say anything for a minute. "Aren't you supposed to be flattered?"

"I don't think it's because people like it."

"What's the reason, then?"

"That's what I want you to find out." I gave him the title and publisher. He said he'd check it out. "This should be easier than finding Carlotta."

We had dessert and coffee in the study. That was where Hensen the historian had written his monumental five-volume work on nineteenth-century missionary influence on South Pacific cultures. A leatherbound set was in the library. I doubted anyone had opened a volume in fifty years. Then everyone went to bed.

Bogey would have had his ear flattened to the wall separating the bedrooms. But far from wanting to eavesdrop on whatever went on between Alex and Knox, I slept in a bedroom across the house. My interior designer, Marsha Grainger, had taken the bit in her teeth with Millwood's bedrooms. Most looked like rooms in a high-class hotel, but others were definitely quirky. One had an overstuffed and cluttered Victorian look Holmes and Watson would have felt at home in. Another was Japanese, with painted paper screens and low-slung furniture. My joints cracked when I got up. There was a French Regency bedroom and one that looked like a New Orleans bordello. The one I chose this night was medieval, with a big four-poster bed and canopy just right for a romp with a bosomy serving wench. It had bearskin rugs and floor-to-ceiling tapestries. The drapes blazed with heraldic designs. There was a suit of armor for each corner of the room. It was dominated by an enormous painting of St. George fighting a dragon. The artist had led a tragic life, Marsha said. A woman had trifled with his affections and he had gone van Gogh one better by cutting off his nose.

"To spite his face?" I asked. How can you pass on an opening like that? Marsha had given me a blank look. "This was de Leon's last epic canvas before his self-mutilation in 1625. It's a style long out of fashion with the critics, but I think it has merit. The light on that wall prefigures Impressionism. Most painters showed St. George as steadfast and unflinching, but you can see that de Leon saw him as quailing before the sheer size and malignity of the beast. It's a St. George who does not believe he can win against such overwhelming odds, but fights on anyway. Instead of a splendid warrior in shining armor, you see his armor is dull and dented. The plume or his helmet is bedraggled. He looks seedy and down at the heel."

In the painting, St. George and the dragon fought at night in a small square of a medieval village. The dragon had a face like a fox and small, erect ears. Its body was huge and muscular, with black, scaly skin. Massive leathery wings were folded. It was reared back, hissing, as if it had just dodged a sword stroke. Combat had lasted quite a while, judging from how exhausted St. George looked. They had met by accident, or one had stalked the other through the narrow dirt lanes that emptied into the square. A terrified face peered from the slit of a shutter. It was the only other figure in the painting.

"The shutter is obviously closing, and St. George will be left alone to his fate, like Gary Cooper in *High Noon*. Some have seen it as de Leon's comment on the existential state of humans, their aloneness. But I think that is reading far too much into the picture."

"This doesn't seem like a very restful room," I said, looking around.

"I think it's a room where there'll be wild lovemaking. The sense of danger will release all inhibitions." There was no mistaking her look. Bogey would have been humping her on one of the animal skins in nothing flat.

"Show me the next room," I said. In that one, the bed was meant to look like a shooting blind in Southeast Asia. Lots of bamboo and ferns. The ceiling was like a starry midnight sky. Hidden speakers gave off the low growls and stealthy pad of a man-eating tiger. Insects sang, and there was the sound of rustling in dry leaves.

"What's wrong with ordinary bedrooms without a lot of extras?" I asked.

"The bedroom is a dangerous place now. AIDS and STDs have made it so. My vision reflects that."

I had been called away at that point and we never resumed the conversation. I picked the St. George room to sleep in. Oliver smelled the bearskin, and it met with his approval. He lay on his side and slept. The water in the shower—grotto was more like it—came from a Viking horn. The acoustics were perfect for singing. I sang *"My Way."* A brass band had played the song every time Bogey walked into the annual shareholders' meeting.

I sank into the feather bed. I noticed that the spread was not bearskin but a sable robe. Marsha had gone way over the edge, no question about it. But to give her her due, the bed was damned comfortable.

I slept deeply until Oliver's whine woke me. He stood looking straight ahead, hackles raised neck to tail. There was something different about the light. It flickered, and shadows swayed. I realized the light was from torches in sconces. I sat up in bed with the by-now-familiar sinking sense. The room was now part of the square, but no sign of St. George and the dragon. Oliver growled deeply, staring at the darkness where the lane left the square. The spot where the bedroom door had been was now whitewashed wall.

A dream, right? I suppose if I had been in the Tiger Room, I would be waiting for the man-eater to show himself. But when you had gone through what I had, it wasn't smart to assume a dream. I dressed quickly and stuck Cleo Basich's Glock in a pocket. It would be like blowing peas through a shooter at a dragon, but it beat stamping a foot and saying "Shoo!"

The shutter where that face had peeped was closed tight. I knocked at the door below but there was no answer. I wondered if St. George had been forced to fight because no one let him in. Oliver walked stiff-legged alongside me, still bristling. I carried one of the flaring torches to light the way. A heavy silence hung over the village. I still had enough canine instincts to share Oliver's sense that danger was somewhere close. Or maybe my right brain had become a lot sharper since all this started.

"Sorry you had to be dragged into this, Ollie," I said. He glanced at me briefly with his intelligent eyes. It was the only way we could communicate now. Then he turned his attention back to scoping out the situation. I tried every door I came to, but all were locked. They were stout, too, so I didn't waste time trying to force them. If I got out of this, that bedroom would get a makeover so it was as plain as a Motel 6 room.

Light shone against a wall ahead. It was from the open door of what I guessed was a grog shop. There were rude tables and benches inside, none occupied except for one in a corner in the shadows across the room from the fireplace.

"Come in," growled a blocky man in a dirty leather tunic and trousers like sacks. "Business isn't so good I can't squeeze another customer in." I sat at a table.

"What kind of accent is that?" I asked to make conversation. He slammed a tin pot down in front of me. He was a pug-nosed redhead with forearms like hams.

"Accent? You're the one talks queer, friend. I'll be seeing the color of yer money."

I patted my pockets.

"I don't suppose you take credit cards."

He took a step back in amazement. "You're askin' for credit, a stranger walking in from the darkness dressed like nobody anybody ever saw before?" I wore Arizona jeans and an L.L. Bean polo shirt. I would have been less conspicuous in a bearskin.

The man at the table in the corner spoke, "I'll pay." He had a woolen scarf across his face. He took a coin from a small purse and laid it on his table.

"Thank you," I said. I lifted the pot in toast and took a sip. It tasted like paint thinner. I let it dribble back into the pot. My mouth felt as dry as alkali. I thought of asking for water but thought better of it. No telling what source that came from.

He beckoned. "Join me." I went to his table and sat on the bench opposite.

"Where do you hail from, stranger?" His voice was muffled by the scarf.

"Not far from here, actually."

"I thought I knew every soul in this poor place and the sad countryside around. Bones is right, you are dressed oddly. Are you a strolling player perhaps? A jester? A tumbler?"

"This is how people dress where I come from."

"And yet you say it's close by?"

"He must be from beyond the dark wood," Bones interjected. "People are peculiar there, by all accounts."

"No one has come through the dark wood as long as I can remember," the man in the scarf answered. "And for good reason."

They looked at me in silence. "This looks like the only place open," I said.

"Aye, it's a dragon night. Seems they're more common lately."

"What's a dragon night?"

I sensed a glower on the other side of the scarf. "Your idea of fun?"

"What is?"

"Pretending to mistake my plain meaning. Or perhaps you are one of those philosophers who haggle over words."

"Can't stand them." Bogey had got a bellyful of them at Felicity's salons. They spoke an academic jargon Bogey couldn't follow until there came some sudden mention of a pop culture figure such as Rambo or Lucy, at which point everyone laughed. "What's so funny?" he would demand.

"Then why did you ask what dragon night was?"

"It means different things different places."

"Depending on what?" Bones called from where he stood with heavy arms folded.

"The dragon," I said.

"There is only one dragon," said the man in the scarf.

I didn't feel in a position to argue. Until Marsha showed me the painting, I wasn't even aware that St. George had slain a dragon. I was dumb enough to think they were mythical, and I wasn't too clear about St. George, if the truth is known. My pa and his various wives put Bogey through a series of schools for misbehaving rich kids. Little stuck that was not strictly about making money and keeping it. My only goal in life was to be richer than my father. When I succeeded with the Clampet Industries deal in the early '80s, I rubbed his nose in it.

"Any fool can do what you've done if he's willing to treat people like they're nothing." That was the old man's reply when Bogey showed him the front page article in the *Wall Street Journal*. Bogey was speechless at his monstrous hypocrisy. No one treated people worse than my father.

"You need St. George back," I told the men in the grog shop.

"He's dead, sure enough," said the red-haired man. "But when did George become a saint? I expect me own bones may be holy relics some one day if he's one."

"History books say he's a saint," I said.

"History? He was just another deluded romantic," scoffed

the man with the scarf. "He was drunk on something worse than the swill Bones there pours."

"Careful," Bones said grinningly.

"He was drunk on dreams of righting wrong and conquering evil. Chivalric poppycock. The man was as innocent as a babe in arms. It was criminal in a man his age. When at last his heroic quest was realized and he was face-to-face with evil in the form of the dragon, he was overpowered. It's the way of the world, and all know it but dreamers. He was killed after the thing had a bit of fun with him. His puny sword was useless. People who have never seen a dragon are surprised how big they are. What would you say, Bones? Bigger than three or four bulls put together?"

"Easily," the other said. "Five or six is more like it. And fast, too."

"The only dragon I've seen is in a painting I own by an artist named de Leon," I said.

The man made a strange sound behind his scarf. "My name is de Leon."

"That explains the scarf."

"What do you mean?"

"You cut your nose off because of a woman. You must have had a lot of second thoughts about that."

"Someone told you my tragic story."

"My interior designer. She likes your work."

"Interior designer? What manner of office is that? And how did she learn my story?" He paused. "You say she likes my work?"

"That's the good news."

"There is more to tell?"

I decided not to tell him that the bad news was that most critics disagreed. "This whole thing is your painting, as far as I can tell."

They stared at me in silence.

"What whole thing?" Bones asked finally.

"Your painting was on my bedroom wall," I said to de Leon. "I woke up a few minutes ago and I'm part of it." I looked around. "Where's Ollie?"

I heard him yelp outside. I rushed to the door and looked out. I was just in time to see the dragon disembowel Oliver with a swipe of talons as he held him dangling by the neck with its other claw. Oliver made a terrible scream..

"Don't go out!" de Leon said at my shoulder. "It's only a dog's life, but it'll satisfy him for now." I saw in the creature's eyes that he knew Oliver was mine and that I loved him.

I took the Glock from my pocket and walked numbly toward the dragon. It looked like it couldn't believe its good luck. It cast Oliver's limp body aside like a rag. A sour, ammonia-like stink came off the creature, as if it lay in its own filth. When I was close enough, I raised the gun and shot it in the left eye and then the right, hitting the iris both times. Blinded, the dragon threw itself around the alley with terrible cries. Its collisions with the walls shook them. It unfurled wings and rose into the darkness, its cries fading as it got farther away.

De Leon and Mr. Bones were stupefied.

"A sorcerer," Bones said, backing away. His ruddy face was pale.

"A mighty crack from that magical object in your hands and the dragon's eyes fell back into themselves," de Leon said. "Is he right? Are you a sorcerer?"

I didn't answer. I stumbled to Oliver's torn body and knelt beside him. I smoothed down his coat where the talons had pinched. He was alive for a few more seconds, and his eyes met mine one last time. They were trying to say something. Then he was still. Life was gone.

"Ollie!" I cried. Grief rose within me and scalding tears ran down my cheeks.

I staggered in the darkness back through the alley the way we had come.

"Wait," de Leon called. "How do people know of my painting?"

I became aware someone was at my side. He had a faint aura whose light showed the way. "We must hurry," William Tyre said in a jittery voice. "The others are in danger."

I followed Tyre through a doorway and we were back at Millwood in the silent corridor outside the bedroom. "This house is enchanted," he said. "I came back just in time. Everyone must leave."

"My dog was just killed."

Tyre was businesslike. "If we can hold the losses to that, we can count ourselves fortunate."

I rubbed my eyes as we hurried through inner corridors to Alex's room. The sound of her weeping reached us. I pulled myself together and opened the door. She was sitting up in bed in a satin nightgown, face buried in her hands. A balding man in corduroy trousers and a sweater near the French doors turned to us.

"Begone, demon," Tyre said. The man hesitated, as if weighing whether to obey. Then he yanked open a door and was gone.

"Oh, God, Bogey," Alex said when she dropped her hands from her face and saw me. "I'm so glad you woke me. I had the worst dream."

I felt a tug from Tyre on my sleeve. He was invisible to her. "Give me a minute," Alex said, "I need to wash my face and get something on."

He waited for me in the corridor. "Her friend," he whispered urgently. I opened Knox's bedroom door. A naked woman sat on his chest, back to us. "Begone, demon," Tyre said again. Her long, glossy black hair swung like a weighted curtain as she turned to look. Her unearthly beauty was astonishing. White skin, dark eyes, lips as ripe as fruit bursting with summer. Then her face contorted with bestial ferocity. Her long eyes narrowed and she hissed.

Tyre clapped hands sharply. She was knocked off Knox as if hit by a bolt of energy. She picked herself up off the floor with a yowl and scooted through the door with a buttocky flash. Tyre went to Knox. His chest was heaving rapidly. "She has worn him nearly to death. I'll do what I can. You see to the others." I ran downstairs to the billiard room.

Maye was asleep under the billiard table. His jacket was over him, and a pillow from the sofa cradled his head. A woman snuggling an infant stood over him. He was starting to stir.

"Leave him alone," I said.

Her sorrowing face changed like the woman in Knox's room. The infant's face did, too, and that was worse. Both shriveled into dried apples of focused malevolence. Their eyes burned with fury. They were like pinpoints of magma about to leap forth in volcanic geysers. Jesus, they were horrible.

"Begone, demon," I faltered. The words were useless unless they came from Tyre. The two advanced on me slowly. The smaller creature shifted as if getting ready to spring from the larger one's arms. Then both looked up at the ceiling as they heard something and stopped. I already had a cue stick in my hand, ready to do them whatever damage I could. With a swift look of hatred, the woman turned with her devil's spawn and fled.

15

Grant is much better," Alex said over the phone. I was in Denver and she was in Palo Alto. "They have him in rehab now. They think all that golf was too much for him."

An ambulance had taken him to the hospital. A stroke nearly killed him on the way, and it was touch-and-go for days. When he was gone, the rest of us left in cars for the Hilton by the airport. It was three in the morning.

"You must all leave Millwood," Tyre had told me fretfully. "It is infested with foul spirits, and they are growing stronger." The sound of the dogs howling in the kennels reached us. "They know."

I told the others that a dangerous gas leak forced us to evacuate. "Really?" Mildred said suspiciously. She had thrown a coat over her nightgown. "I don't smell anything."

"Pockets are spreading in the basement," I said. "It could blow any minute."

"My manuscript," she cried. She hurried off to save it for History. Maye rode with some of Doyle's security people in one car and Mildred with others in a second. Alex drove me in her Cherokee.

Alex was laughing now over the phone. Enough time had passed to allow laughter, especially since Knox was on the mend and able to speak a few words. "Mildred didn't know

what to think when you burst in on her. Between us, she feared
for her virtue."

"And you think I have fantasies."

Alex had been dreaming of her late husband when I came
into her room. He could not be happy until she joined him. "It
sounds strange, but it was almost as if he was trying to talk me
into suicide." I did not mention the man in the shadows.

She talked about Knox's improvement. "He's hard to understand, but he said something interesting about that night." Her
studied casualness made me alert. "He thought there was a cat
in his room."

I made no comment.

"Don't you think that's interesting?" she persisted. "It's like
your contractor."

I had a new game plan. She could reach her own conclu-
sions based on the evidence. I took her comment as a sign
of progress.

"They say Soderberg is going to announce for the presi-
dency tonight," Alex said after a pause to see if I picked up the
ball. We talked by telephone a couple of times a day. It was a
couple's habit we had fallen into. I was lonely without Oliver.
I missed him a thousand different times a day. He used to stick
his soft muzzle into my hand when he wanted attention, or
thought I needed it.

"So I hear," I told Alex. I hadn't told her about Oliver except
to say he was missing and had probably run off. How could I
tell her the truth?

"You were right about him running."

"I was right."

"He doesn't seem like such a bad person from what I've seen
on TV."

"A lot of people say that." Even Ted Butler had called to
praise him. "He's more interesting than anybody else in sight."

Maye had been watching Soderberg's rise in the tracking

polls. Bernie's handlers staged a media event each week that put him in a positive light. He bought a professional football team one week and promised it would win a championship within five years. He was shown roughhousing with the players. Despite skillful camera work it was clear horseplay did not come easy to Bernie.

"That's going to help with the guy vote," Maye said as we watched Bernie lifted onto shoulders in the TV spot. The gal vote remained riveted by his search for a future First Lady. "I'm just lookin' for the love of a good woman," he said in his new homespun manner.

Maye called it the Cinderella Factor. "There is no woman so plain that she can't secretly hope to be picked."

"I knew who I'd pick," I told Alex. Even I had fallen for the marketing ploy.

"Who?"

"You."

She laughed. "Flatterer."

"I'm serious."

Alex changed the subject. She always did when I talked that way. She explained how common it was for a patient to fall for the therapist.

"I fired you, remember?"

Soderberg's announcement was due to be made in Kansas City in prime time. He was on the cover of *Time* and *Newsweek* again and was the subject of all the TV panel shows the Sunday before. Maye and I watched the tube pundits do their analysis in the half hour before the announcement was scheduled. Then suddenly the networks broke in with live reports. A fast-acting food poisoning had broken out among the huge press corps in Kansas City. The buffet laid on in advance apparently was to blame. Then the plumbing in the civic auditorium began malfunctioning. Journalists kneeling over toilet bowls had to clear out when they began to back up.

I turned to Maye. "Do you know anything about this?"

"Actually, yes."

"What if somebody dies?"

"They'll only wish they could."

A queasy-looking reporter came on CNN to report that a flood of raw sewage was pouring through the building. "They don't seem to know how to stop it."

"I've got pumps tapped into the lines," Maye said. "They're forcing everything from that part of the city into the auditorium." He smiled at me. "I always wanted to spoil a candidate's announcement like this. Thank you for making it possible."

With all that, Soderberg's declaration of candidacy came across as anticlimactic. He was presidential enough in his dark blue suit and red tie, but he was rattled. His eyes left the Tele-PrompTer to scan the crowd each time someone retched. Curses came from people spattered by vomit. Bernie had trouble finding his place again in the speech.

"He doesn't do ad-lib," Maye said. "I didn't think he could."

The speech, titled "Ten Cardinal Principles," was interrupted by shots of newspeople wheeled down corridors to waiting ambulances. The network anchors spoke of the overpowering smell and held handkerchiefs to thir noses. The Q and A session scheduled afterward was canceled.

Maye stood with a satisfied look. "I'm faxing a statement to the media in your name as head of the Citizens for Soderberg." We had set up headquarters in the office tower in Atlanta and hired staff, but had kept a low profile up to now.

"What does it say?"

"It accuses the Democratic and Republican parties of conniving to prevent the American people from having a true choice."

"I'm saying they poisoned the press?"

"Just about. There's other stuff, too. The press will begin to wonder what kind of nuts are supporting Soderberg when they can keep their food down again. Bernie's announcement'll leave a bad taste more ways than one." He handed me another sheet of paper. "They'll be calling tomorrow with questions about your statement. These are the sorts to expect."

Maye was right about how the story would be played. Soderberg's announcement was second place to stories about political sabotage. "The wave of nausea hit me just as I was entering the room where Bernard Soderberg waited to make his historic announcement," one typical story began. ABC's political reporter was interviewed from his hospital bed the next day on the network's morning show. They showed him getting a cholera shot because of exposure to the sewage.

News shows showed the police tape around the abandoned diesel-powered pumps that had forced the sewage into the building. Public works department employees were being questioned. The catering people were also interrogated. Analysis of the buffet found traces of a substance used to induce vomiting in poison victims. The Republican and Democratic candidates issued statements of sympathy. They also said it was unfortunate some of Bernie's supporters had made wild and unfounded charges, meaning me. His campaign staff pointed out in background sessions that Citizens for Soderberg was not an official part of the presidential campaign. That made Maye smiled. "We're getting to them."

"He appears to disavow your support," the man from the *New York Times* said during our telephone interview the next day.

"It's a free country and he can say what he wants," I said. "But I'm backing Bernie Soderberg to the hilt. He'll put this country back on the right track."

"You think it's on the wrong track?"

"Like Bernie, I feel the country's gone in the tank, thanks to shiftless workers unwilling to do an honest day's labor even for the high wages that are pricing us out of the international markets. Between them and the damned socialists in both parties, things look pretty dark for the U.S.A. The colored races will be leading us around by our noses before we know it. Bernie knows better than I do, although he can't speak his mind as frankly. Quite a few of us business leaders share the same opinions. We get together to talk things over. You don't hear about it, of course, and maybe I'm out of line even mentioning it."

There was a stunned pause. "You're not saying that Mr. Soderberg shares these opinions?"

"He most certainly does." Then I hesitated, as if I'd had second thoughts. "But maybe it would be better if you downplayed that in your article. We don't want people to get the wrong idea. He still has to get elected, you know."

After another silence, he asked how well I knew Bernie, and I said well enough. "We don't need to be in daily communication. Our minds are pretty much in sync." The reporter pointed out that the Ten Cardinal Principles had not hinted at any of this.

"The Ten Cardinal Principles," I scoffed. "That's pap for the masses, but you can't print that."

"You say that business leaders get together to talk about things?"

"Anything wrong with that? Better that successful people decide matters than failures and bleeding hearts." The listening Maye made a circle with thumb and forefinger. I answered a couple more questions and hung up. An hour later, I called the reporter back.

"All that stuff I told you was off the record," I said. "I don't want you to use it."

I felt him bristle on the other end. "You didn't say anything about it being off the record."

"Well, I've changed my mind."

"As far as the *New York Times* is concerned, it was on the record."

I swore at him and hung up. I was pumped up, feeling more and more like the old Bogey.

The *Times* story the next day had a headline that said, "With Friends Like These." The Soderberg camp must have seen an early edition of the paper, because the campaign director, Tim Holt, flew from New York first thing in the morning and arrived in Denver without an appointment.

"He's the best political consultant in the country next to me," Maye said. We were in the office penthouse suite. Holt cooled his heels two floors below. "He's going to ask you to clear anything you have to say through him in the future. He'll want you to issue a statement saying what you told the *Times* was taken out of context or something."

"Should I?"

"Sure. Nobody will believe you."

Tim Holt was one of those sweaty pols who make a fetish of rumpled clothes and unknotted ties. He looked me directly in the eyes the way trainers do to show a dangerous animal they have no fear.

"Mr. Ingersol, we've got something in common."

"Call me Bogey." I lit my trademark Esplendido cigar and blew smoke toward the ceiling. "What is it?"

"Bogey, we both want Bernard Soderberg elected president of the United States. Am I right?"

"You said it. Bernie's a strong dose of what this country needs."

"Good. I'm glad we're in agreement on that."

"Wholeheartedly."

"If I may be entirely candid."

"I expect nothing less."

"Your remarks to the newspaper were not helpful." He leaned forward sincerely.

"I thought we were off the record."

"The media are not to be trusted. You, of all people, must realize that."

I scratched my head and put a foolish look on. "You'd think I would have learned by now, doggone it."

"I wasn't really aware of your organization until you issued your statement. You have satisfied all the legal requirements, of course."

"Of course."

"There's quite a bit of paperwork," he said doubtfully. "The reporting requirements are onerous."

"I've got it covered. Trust me."

Holt did not look like he did. "A campaign like ours depends on momentum. Even small scandals hurt. Mr. Soderberg's announcement speech was a good example. Even though the food poisoning and sewage weren't our fault, they slowed our acceleration out of the starting gate."

"I hope whoever is responsible goes to prison," I said. "I'm just sorry we don't still have flogging and dunking to go with it."

"If I may continue to speak honestly."

"Please do." I leaned forward in my seat to match his sincerity.

"Your own background as a convicted felon is causing us some concern. The unsolved murder in your neighborhood is further source of worry."

I drew back affronted "I have paid my debt to society, Mr. Holt. As for the other matter, I've not been charged with any crime."

"I know," he said apologetically, "but the media have thrown so much mud that some is bound to stick."

"I don't care what the bastards say."

"Yes, I know. As much as I might admire that in other circumstances, the fact of the matter is the association of your name with his is harmful to Mr. Soderberg's candidacy."

I put on a stricken look. "I'd never do anything to hurt Bernie's chances."

He came to the point. "It would help us if in the future your organization cleared its activities through our steering committee. Here's a better idea. Instead of operating your own Citizens for Soderberg, why not just fold it into our national committee? That would prevent future embarrassment."

I gave him Bogey's old bullfrog stare. "Are you trying to tell me what to do?"

"No, sir," Holt said hastily. "I would never do that. I know your reputation."

I subsided. "I'll run my organization how I please." I drummed fingers. "But I'll try to be more careful in the future. Let you know what's up and so forth."

He was silent a moment, calculating the best way to deal with this loose cannon. "Can I ask what you have in mind?"

"Eh?"

"What sorts of things do you plan to do for Mr. Soderberg?"

I made a stirring motion with my cigar, like a man whose ideas were as yet too vague to put into words. "Point out ways he's better than the others. A B C. Talk sense to the people. You know, blah-blah. They'll understand."

He looked apprehensive. "We want to stay on message. We have a very detailed timetable for getting it out. We're already beginning to make our media buys." Excellent, I thought. Maye's buyers had already snapped up as much TV and radio time as they would sell us. Holt's people would compete for what was left with the Democratic and Republican candidates.

"If you could appoint someone we could liaison with," Holt said wheedlingly. "I don't want to take up your valuable time whenever there's a minor question to be resolved."

"We're pretty much seat of the pants here, but I suppose I can come up with someone."

He pulled at this tie. It was loose enough now to lift over

his head. He was looking to end the meeting on an upbeat note. "Whatever differences we may have, we're agreed on one thing."

"We want Bernie as commander in chief." I smacked my knee.

When he was gone, Maye came from where he had been listening in the next room. "It's a campaign manager's worst nightmare, the well-meaning lunatic with money. I bet he has Soderberg appeal to you man-to-man to shut up and drop out of sight."

"Bernie's never appealed to anybody for anything. It's not his style."

Doyle called later that day. "The papers are full of you. So's TV." He spoke on a scrambler, and his voice sounded cartoonish.

"What are they saying?"

"You belong in the nineteenth century. That word you called the media?"

"Pinko."

"Yeah, pinko. That's got a lot of them upset."

"They can dish it out but they can't take it."

"They're rehashing the Fund for the Little Ones scandal. They're also going into that guy who had his guts ripped out."

That was good. I asked him about the bookstores.

"We've talked to quite a few owners. They all have the same story. Odd-looking men with hats pulled low bought every copy that could be had. They spoke in an accent nobody could place. One bookseller got a good look at one when his hat sailed off in the wind outside. He said he looked like an animal."

"What kind of animal?"

"He said an ape at first, but then he said a hog. He made a kind of grunting sound when he ran after his hat. He said the guy looked like he'd have been more comfortable running on all fours. Some imagination, huh? The guy ought to be writing books instead of selling them."

I had been trying to put myself in Zalzathar's mind. It wasn't easy, given how bent his was. With me dead and every copy of *Top Dog* gone, he would not have to worry about being unmasked. Not even the craziest conspiracy nut could dream up a sorcerer coming from another universe to put his man in the White House. Collecting every copy was typical Zalzathar thoroughness. Wanting Pig Faces to give me their traditional disemboweling instead of shooting me or running me down in the street also was typical. It showed how hard it was for him to change directions. Plodding straight ahead was the only style he knew.

Doyle's people secretly videotaped him in Soderberg's big entourage as it hurried from building lobbies to waiting limousines at the curb. It was conservatively cut suits instead of a ratty wizard's robe now, but there was no mistaking that obstinate, rut-bound stride. His stubbornness had helped me before, and I hoped lightning would strike twice. The advice he would be hearing from Soderberg's top strategists would be infinitely superior to what the moronic Pig Face leaders gave in the other world. Whether he followed it was another question.

"We think we might have a mole finally," Doyle said. "She won't come cheap, though. She wants half a million up front."

"What does she do for them?"

"I'd rather tell you in person. She's a hard-boiled broad but she's scared of these people."

"What if we give her the money and she splits?"

"I told her I'd find her wherever she hid."

"Like you did Carlotta Hamilton?"

"They did a Hoffa on her. That's why I can't find her, and nobody else will either. Same with those two guys we lost on the turnpike." I had set up a trust fund for their families. It had become tradition. Working for me was hazardous duty.

"Half a million's a lot of money," I said.

Doyle's silence said he didn't think so.

"Who approached who?"

"We approached her. I wouldn't bite if it was the other way around."

I told him to pay the money. We needed every edge we could get.

I fixed pizza that night. I took most of my meals in because going out was such a hassle. Cars filled with bodyguards ahead and behind. Frequent changes in direction. Running red lights. Somebody standing in the restaurant kitchen to make sure the food wasn't poisoned. You would be surprised how many places tell you to take your business elsewhere when you ask for that courtesy. At home, all I had to worry about was making sure the plastic wrapping around the frozen pizza was intact.

When I was taking it out of the oven, I became aware that Tyre was leaning against the sink on the other side of the kitchen. "Pizza," I said. "You don't know what you're missing."

In the time he had been gone he had grown a white Vandyke beard and mustache. "You look like a professor at Heidelberg in 1910." A pince-nez was all he needed to complete the picture.

"It's not vanity. Sometimes I change appearances to meet expectations. No one expects to see a white robe and furled wings anymore, except children. But people do have their ideas. This look is for a famous engineer and inventor breathing his last. He had lived his life as a materialist and atheist. He loved an uncle who wore this kind of beard. He showed him the only kindness he had known in childhood. This beard brought me close enough in appearance that he mistook me for the uncle." He sensed my irritation. "You think I should be doing more with you."

"I could use a little more help," I said. "The other side has a full-time wizard. You just make cameo appearances."

"I've been busier than you realize. Zalzathar brought a host of demons and dybbuks and other evil spirits with him. He has called forth many more from long slumber in their dark places here. Their mischief keeps us busy. And, of course, my real work is helping people make the transition from this life to the next. I can't neglect that."

"If that engineer was an atheist, why not let him die thinking that's all there is?"

"We respect that belief if it is what a person holds to right to the end," he said with a pedantic sniff. "We believe in choice, and oblivion is certainly one. In this case, the man called out for help. Pretense takes wing at that moment. I've often been with great thinkers as the last moments tick away. They spent lives developing elegant theories to explain existence, either for their own satisfaction or to gain fame. Some said life was meaningless. Others maintained that any discussion about God was pointless, as proof one way or the other was impossible. They were clever men and women proud of their accomplishments. They convinced others of the soundness of their argument. They won awards and distinctions, and their work lives on in libraries. Yet at the end, many did not prefer the vindication of proud theories at the cost of personal extinction." He smiled smugly, looking a little like the kindly druggist who sells candy to kids in a Norman Rockwell painting. "That inconsistency right to the end is all so human."

In the other world Bogey never had time to talk to Helither about the Big Questions. He was too busy dodging death and scheming to get back where he belonged.

"What's Heaven like?" I asked now.

"I couldn't begin to tell you, not if we had years. I will say that once you're there, you never want to leave. God's presence is indescribable. Language can't begin to do justice to it."

There had been a story in the paper that morning. A whole family, a man and woman and their four children, had been killed when a truck hit their car at an intersection. They were on their way to put flowers on the grave of an infant who had died. It was one of those incomprehensible tragedies. I mentioned it to Tyre. "Why do these things happen? Or wars and plagues, for that matter?"

He shook his head. "God's ways are unfathomable." I waited to see if he would say more, but that was it. So much for the Big Questions.

"Can't you get somebody to fill in for you?" It was nice that he was big on customer service, but I needed him to stop thinking like a retailer. "How about doing some hoodoo for the cause? Turning Zalzathar to stone or a pillar of salt would be a start."

"That's their game, not ours."

"A win beats a loss anytime."

He had a prissy, disappointed look. "I thought your experiences had changed you."

"Bear with me here. The richest man in the world, a guy who is also one of the most ruthless, is running for president. Add a sorcerer willing to do whatever's necessary and you have a contest no oddsmaker in his right mind would bet on."

"You underestimate yourself, Mr. Ingersol. By all accounts, you acquitted yourself very well in the other world."

"I got lucky a couple of times. If I hadn't, Zalzathar would be running the show there today." I'd be a dead dog or on the run through trackless forests and over endless plains where the sky was so vast it made you feel like a speck of dust.

"Zalzathar was denied victory then and it'll be the same this time." Tyre gave a little so-there lift of his chin.

"Helither was quite a bit more active than you've been, and there was no Bernie Soderberg." Helither actually sallied forth in battle, helmeted and sword in hand. He was an inspiration to everyone in Gowyith. Quite a contrast to Tyre's clerkish approach. "The two situations are like apples and oranges."

But Tyre seemed to think I had matters well in hand. "You call it luck," he said. "Maybe it was more than that."

I was about to say I wished I was as confident as him when

Maye walked into the kitchen. He nodded at Tyre, which eliminated the embarrassment of me asking if he saw him. "How're you? It's been a while."

"I'm glad to see you're doing better," Tyre said.

"It helps to have something to think about bigger than myself." When Tyre wasn't around, Maye didn't talk about personal stuff. The angel drew him out.

"Yes, that's so true," Tyre said. He nodded like a nurse pleased at a patient's turn for the better.

"It's an uphill battle, though," Maye said with a shake of his head. He looked at me. "The only thing we've got going for us at this point is you."

"Me?"

"The public hates your guts, even more now than before. Idi Amin and Gadhafi might have been more unpopular in their time, but you track close to their numbers in my polls. I'm starting to think you're going to be key to the campaign. The more we link your name with Bernie's, the better. We've got to figure how to keep you in the news."

16

In the weeks that followed, I saw why Eric Maye was the best in the business. He was like an acupuncturist working the pressure points. Press here and Soderberg's Ten Cardinal Principles got exposed on *Sixty Minutes* as mere slogans an ad agency strung together using focus groups. Press there and reporters dug into Bernie's arms deals and kingmaking in the Third World (*Washington Post*). Maye leaked leads about Soderberg's amazing string of corporate takeovers that had been turned up by Doyle's army of investigators. Carlotta Hamilton's disappearance was good for big headlines (*Los Angeles Times*). Maye knew all the media kingpins and had fed them juicy stories that had won Pulitzers and other prizes. "The press doesn't mind being manipulated as long as they get something out of it, too," he told me. The accumulation of negative stories gave the impression that the watchdog press had finally woken up and was finding out what lay behind the blue smoke and mirrors.

Maye himself changed from a hired gunslinger into a true believer. "The man is evil," he kept telling me.

"I told you first, remember?" I said finally.

"I thought you were just this weird rich guy with an ax to grind, but this is serious shit."

The campaign was no longer just an opportunity to show off his technique, like a figure skater doing fancy jumps on the practice ice. It had become a crusade that gave him a fresh lease on life. He sometimes put in twenty-hour days, fueled by countless little cups of espresso. When he remembered to eat, he did it standing up and talking on the telephone. He was a slave driver with the staff one minute and an inspirational motivator the next. He took on a lean, fanatical look, like a prophet who roamed the desert. His hair grew long because he wouldn't spare the time to get it cut. "The country's in danger," he told people.

Doyle made unexpected visits to tighten our security. "I'm hearing some rumbles," he explained. I already had so many thick-necked bodyguards that we seemed to use up the air in a room a short time after we walked in, but Doyle hired more. He observed Maye warily. "He's wound a little tight, isn't he?"

"He's all right."

"Looks like he's about to go postal."

"What're these rumbles you're hearing?"

"They want to shut you up permanently."

No wonder. Maye had me flying around the country, supposedly looking for companies for takeovers. He tipped the media off about my movements, and they met me at airports. I feigned surprise and anger, then let myself be baited into blustering answers. I supported him because he was the best man for the job, I said in Peoria. "And if Americans don't vote for him, they've got their heads up their ass worse than I think." The sound bite was on all the networks and was the lead story in most markets that night. Holt kept issuing statements saying I was not affiliated with the Soderberg campaign. People smiled more cynically by the day. I was not in for his calls. He must have thought my word was no good.

I arrived in Detroit in a steady rain. My bodyguards scuffled with the newspeople waiting at the airport. Jerky video footage showed me bringing my umbrella down on the shoulder blades of ducking photographers. "Maybe it's time to rethink the First

Amendment." I spoke in a calm, measured way afterward to three radio reporters invited to ride with me from the airport. "Men wore powdered wigs when they dreamed that one up. How could they forsee our problems?"

"Are those Mr. Soderberg's views?" one asked.

"No comment," I said in a way that left no doubt they were.

My eye was caught by one of the reporters. She was slinky and beautiful in a tight blue suit. "How do you think the campaign's going?" she asked teasingly. Black hair as glossy as a raven's wing, pale skin, ruby-red lips. Our knees touched.

I winked lewdly and put a bedroom purr in my voice. "We're gonna pick up all the marbles." Instead of drawing back, as so many women did from Bogey in real life, her knee pressed mine harder. Those delicious lips parted in a smile. The other reporters exchanged looks. We arrived just then at the hotel, where another pack of journalists lay in wait. The car door was snatched open by a bodyguard, and there was more pushing and shoving as I was escorted into the lobby and a waiting elevator. Photographers went flying in every direction. Enough stayed on their feet to create a strobe light storm that gave movement a psychedelic look.

Bernie had to spend the next few days insisting how much he liked the First Amendment. "Look at that," Maye said jubilantly as we watched the TV screen. "He looks like he's lying even though we've got him denying something he never said. The man's sweating through his makeup."

The possibility of more visuals like at the Detroit airport would have brought mobs of media wherever I landed, even if Maye weren't pulling strings behind the scene. In Chicago I was like a cork bobbing in the powerful current of bodyguards that forced its way through the resisting reporters and photographers. Boom mikes swayed overhead like construction cranes. Later, at the hotel, public relations people whom Maye had accompanying us ushered in a business reporter for the *Tribune*.

He was a blond young man with a cowlick and a rosy face. He looked like he belonged on a tractor, harrowing crops.

"Mind if I tape-record this?" he asked hesitantly.

I gave a weary signal of consent. "No questions about the campaign," I warned. "I'm willing to talk about where I think the economy's going, but leave Soderberg out of this."

He was obedient to a fault. He asked so many questions about the Federal Reserve's discount rate and its effect on growth, I saw I would have to grab the bull by the horns and do his work. "But all of this won't be a problem when Bernie's elected."

He hesitated at the unexpected opening, then took the plunge. "He's dropped five points in the polls in the past week. Some blame you."

"Blame me for what?"

"For bringing him down." He turned scarlet.

I slowly took an Esplendido from its tube, cut off the end, and lit it. I blew a circle of smoke that floated lazily toward the ceiling. The sound of traffic far below reached us. He watched me apprehensively as I observed the smoke ring. "You really don't get it, do you?" I said quietly.

"Get what?"

"You're doing their work."

"Whose work?"

"The people who secretly run this country."

He scoffed. "What people?"

"Hard-faced men on Wall Street. The international financiers. The Trilateral Commission. The Rockefellers. Bill Gates. The rest of them. The Jews. They own the Republican and Democratic parties lock, stock, and barrel. They own the paper you work for, and they own you."

"Nobody owns me. I write what I want."

"You're so brainwashed you can't tell the difference. Bernie Soderberg knows. That's why they're trying to keep him out of the White House."

"But you're rich and so's he. He's the richest one of all. You both made your money on Wall Street. If there is a . . . cabal . . . why wouldn't you and him be part of it?"

"Bernie can speak for himself, and maybe he will in his second term, when he can be totally honest." Another smoke ring. "As for me, I saw the light in the Fund for the Little Ones case."

His eyes grew round. His cowlick looked like it should have been attached to a cartoon bubble with a question mark in it.

"I was framed. I didn't dance to their music, so they had me put away." I gave him a crafty look. "I think they're trying to do it again with that man in California who was gutted."

That was too loony for a nuts-and-bolts business reporter. He shook his head like a boxer trying to clear his head. "To get back to the subject, some prognosticators say the Fed is going to tighten interest rates a quarter point because of inflation fears. What's your feeling? Would this be the wrong signal?"

I got rid of him fast after that. Editors listening to the tape back in his office would know what angle to go with. It wouldn't be my thoughts on the role of the central bank. Clancy telephoned later from New York to say he had been contacted by a lawyer representing the photographers I whacked with my umbrella.

"They're going to file a suit asking for five million in damages. The man thinks small. I would have asked for twenty-five. What do you want to settle for? I think twenty thousand's plenty. The lawyer'll get seven large just for making a phone call. He'll be happy."

"Whatever you say."

He asked how things were going. I could tell from his tone there was something on his mind. "You okay?" he asked.

"Sure."

"My politician friends can't figure you out."

I waited for him to explain.

"You put together this organization to help Soderberg, yet

it seems every time you turn around you hurt the guy. It's almost like it's deliberate. That powdered-wig stuff was like hitting him over the head with a baseball bat. The Constitution is sacrosanct, for crissake."

"I didn't say Bernie favored getting rid of the First Amendment. Anyhow, I merely expressed my opinion as a private citizen." I had to smile. Wait till he read what the *Chicago Tribune* published.

"Yeah, but he's taking the heat for it. People think you guys are close friends."

That impression would grow when we began running the "Two Americans Talk" TV spots that showed Bernie and me walking side by side, deep in conversation. We walked along a beach in Hawaii, in Yosemite with Half Dome in the background, and in an Iowa cornfield.

"I'm worried about the country, Bernie," I said in one of the spots.

"I am, too, Bogie."

He was put into the picture by computer imaging. I didn't tell Clancy that. A sieve was a cast-iron pot compared to Clancy. He would have called his political buddies as soon as he hung up.

"Even though he's a third-party candidate, a lot of people in Washington like what he's saying," he said.

"So do I. Look, I'm spending a fortune promoting the man."

Nothing put Clancy into a thoughtful silence than talk of big money. It was like prayer to him.

Later that night I got a call from the head of my security detail. That radio reporter from Detroit was in the lobby and wanted to see me. Bogey had a little black book he carried with the numbers of escort services in the cities he visited. The women were guaranteed to be attractive and disease-free. Those days were long gone, and I was on the straight and narrow path of virtue. But what would it hurt to look?

She was dressed to kill in a short, low-cut silk dress under a fur coat. Her dark eyes danced, and she bit her lip invitingly when I let her in.

"Hi? Remember me? Gigi?"

"Sure I do." I didn't recall having heard a name.

"Do you mind if this isn't about business?"

"Certainly not." She handed me her fur, and I made a twirling flourish with it like a bullfighter. "*Olé.*"

She laughed more than it was worth and sat down and crossed her marvelous legs. "I'd like a drink, please."

"Cocoa or Ovaltine?" The Bogey of old wouldn't have wasted time with witty banter. He would be snorting and hopping on one foot as he pulled his pants off.

"I was thinking of something a little stronger."

I went to the wet bar. "Name your poison."

She pretended to think. She gave me a twinkle like Shirley MacLaine in the Rat Pack days. "How about we go instead to a place I know?"

My convoy had grown to four cars these days. We would need a parade permit the way it was growing. "Well . . ."

"Just the two of us. We can take my car."

"What kind of place is it?" I parried.

"There's music." She recrossed her legs.

"What kind?"

"Every kind."

"Must be a big place."

"It can be very . . . intimate." Manfred stirred below. The truth was I hadn't been laid since before the coma. I came close with a she-wolf in the other world, but the pack got back early from the hunt. They chased me five miles before I swam a river to get away. You wouldn't count a she-wolf anyhow.

I told the bodyguard outside the door that we were going down to the lobby bar for a drink. He made a move to follow, but I told him to stand at ease. "I'll just be ten, fifteen minutes." The elevator doors closed on his look of doubt.

She had a zippy little sports car whose seat belts held you like a corset. Her skirt hiked up on those dancer's legs as she drove. We passed through a suburban district into an industrial area.

"Is this in a warehouse?" I asked.

"Don't worry, you're gonna like it." She patted my thigh. And left her hand there. Manfred was in a state of high alert. We pulled through the gate of what looked like a plant and drove down a dimly lit lane that separated two rows of buildings where things were assembled or manufactured. We passed well-dressed couples who had parked and walked with the quick step of people on their way to a good time.

Gigi stopped in front of a nightclub designed to look like a factory with a neon sign that said Stew's. Or maybe it really was a factory and did double duty when evening fell. Nightclub patrons liked authenticity these days. I had heard about one in a slaughterhouse where you wore heavy rubber gloves and aprons. Sawdust underfoot soaked up the blood from animals butchered during the day. Customers dancing on it felt connected to the more real world of physical work.

A thin valet with a mime's pallor and deep, dark eye sockets got behind the wheel and drove the car away. A ticket taker who could have been his twin brother waved us in with a word to Gigi I didn't hear. I didn't comment on them for fear of being thought uncool. Thus are men ruled by Manfred.

Her arm was linked through mine, guiding me through the thick crowd. Most seemed in their twenties and thirties. Many were in Halloween costume. The steel-beamed building was large, with a high ceiling hidden in darkness. It was divided into rooms of varying size, each with its own kind of music. Clusters of big machines were shrouded in plastic. As we moved through a corridor that snaked through the warehouse, we passed from one type of music to another, as if a radio dial were being turned. Cerebral jazz gave way to country and western, and that to a Glenn Miller–style orchestra playing "American Patrol." There was a rock club, a piano bar, a salon where a classical violinist in tails played.

We went back to the ballroom where the Miller band played. "Shall we go in?" she asked.

"My old man was a big fan of his." Pater thrashed me once when he saw me with one of his precious album covers. He had fond memories of the war. He was Stateside in some cushy army staff job and spent his leisure time hunting women to shag. When he was in his choleric fifties, Pop listened to his collection by the hour. Millions may have died, but he remembered the good times.

"He's cool. You should hear him talk about the crash," Gigi said. The musicians wore white dinner jackets. A Miller look-alike with a trombone led them. They segued from "American Patrol" to "Sunrise Serenade." The crowd cut a rug on the dance floor.

"Who would've thought this music would come back again?" I said. I raised my voice to be heard. "Who talks about what crash?"

"Glenn Miller." She moved to the music. "Did you know he was in a plane crash?"

We found an empty table, and a tuxedoed waiter took our order. Bourbon for me, champagne for her. Instead of a pasty-faced mime, he was made up as a clown and wore an orange wig. Rather than funny, he looked creepy. I started to feel I had made a mistake leaving my security cocoon. But it passed when Gigi pulled me out on the dance floor. Felicity made me take dance lessons when we got married. I never got good, but I had danced with enough instructors to tell when someone else was, like Gigi. We danced to "Tuxedo Junction." She glued her hard, athletic body to mine. It was not so much a promise of things to come as a guarantee. We glided on the floor to where the bandleader looked out from the stage, snapping his fingers to the beat. A spotlight on him cut through the blue tobacco smoke and made his rimless eyeglasses glint. A dead ringer for Glenn Miller.

"So he's got a routine he does?" I asked.

"Routine?" Gigi took her head from my chest to look up at me.

"Shtick, act, number."

"I don't get it."

"He pretends to be Glenn Miller."

"That's who he is, silly."

That was the point when my internal warning bells went off, joined by *ooga-ooga* Klaxons and an air raid siren. Better late than never.

"You'll hear," Gigi said. "It's almost time for him to tell."

"About the crash," I said in a flat voice.

"They never found the plane. After he tells about it, he plays the songs that were in his head, the ones he never got around to writing down or recording."

"What about we check out one of the other venues?"

"Whatever you say, sweetie. I left my purse at the table."

We threaded our way through couples on the dance floor. Gigi had a graceful, swaying walk and a seriously nice ass. A dark, handsome man with thick hair that had a patent leather shine sat at our table. A black suit and turtleneck sweater. Lots of jewelry.

"Hello," Gigi said in a scared little girl's voice. "I didn't know you were here."

He ignored her, standing and looking at me. "I was saving your table for you."

"You can have it," I said. "We're going." I was anyhow, even if I had to climb razor wire fences and thumb a ride back to the hotel.

"Before 'String of Pearls'?" the man asked. He had the bland voice of announcers on those robot radio stations that play easy-listening music. He fell in step as we left. "A pretty good crowd tonight," he said to me.

"You two know each other?"

"Gigi?" he said dismissively. "Everybody knows her."

"Why's that so bad?" she complained.

"Don't you have to visit the powder room? Stanky's my name," he told me.

"Nice to meet you."

"I'll be right back," Gigi said, pouting. We watched her disappear in the crowd. My eye was drawn to the line of people under a neon sign shaped like a palm tree.

Stanky's eye followed my look. "A terrific bill in the Palm Room tonight. Frank, Janis, Otis."

"Just as a guess, Sinatra, Joplin, and Redding?"

"You catch on fast." He lit a cigarette with a gold lighter and gave me a shrewd look through the smoke.

"Faster than I used to," I said. "Are they the genuine articles?"

"As genuine as Mr. Miller. You're not missing much leaving before he plays his new stuff. Not up to the old standard. He was burned out before his plane went into the drink. Truth is, in a way he welcomed death. But originality is left behind when you go. This is where you accomplish whatever you're going to accomplish. That's why he prefers to play the old songs over and over."

"Is this your place, Mr. Stanky?" My nose caught the faintest whiff of Pig Face. You never forget it no matter how much time passes. My heart started to hammer in my chest.

"No, I just run it for them."

"Them?"

He laughed. "The bad guys. You made a big mistake coming here."

"That's occurred to me, oddly enough."

"But who can blame you with Gigi there. She's led many here. A pretty package with all the right ribbons and bows."

He glanced around and dropped his voice, "I might be able to help you while there's time."

The Pig Face stink was coming on stronger through cigarette smoke, perfume, cologne, underarm deodorant, and the other crowd odors. I didn't have time to discover any ulterior motives through skillful interrogation. "Believe me, anything you can do is appreciated."

"Follow me." He spun on his heel and walked off. I caught up.

"Where're we going?"

"My office. They won't look there right away."

"The Pig Faces?"

"Is that what you call them?" He thought about it and laughed. "Actually, it fits."

His office had banks of TV monitors on one wall. Cameras in various parts of the building watched the crowds. Stanky locked the door behind him. "Just out of curiosity, how'd she talk you into coming?"

"She had help from Manfred."

"Who's that?"

"A close friend."

One of the monitors caught his eye. There was a disturbance in the crowd where Bob Wills and the Texas Cowboys played. A tightly packed mass of bodies moved through it like a half-submerged submarine plowing through the sea. Stanky aimed a remote at the screen, and the camera jerked in for a close-up. The ledge of brutal brow, the snoutlike nose, the heavy jaw. There was no mistaking them. Pig Faces spun men to stare into their faces, then shoved them aside. There was no sound, but judging from expressions on the screen, people were shouting and screaming.

"They're looking for you," Stanky said.

"You knew they were coming?"

"I got tipped at the last minute." He studied the screen. "Pretty rough, aren't they?"

"That's their good behavior." Stanky seemed in no hurry.

"You said you could help?" I prompted.

"We've got a little time yet."

"I wouldn't want to cut it too close." I felt sweat prickle my scalp.

He took a long drag of his cigarette and slowly let the smoke out. "You know what this place is?"

"I thought it was a nightclub. Guess I was wrong."

"What do you think it is now?"

Did we have time for this? "Dead musicians playing oldies in a big place where they used to mill machine parts or something. Is this a haunted . . . factory?"

"I'd rather call it a zone of transition. Spirits who can't sever earthly attachments after death linger a while. Why? Some can't believe what's to come can possibly beat what they've had. Others feel dread because of the lives they've led. Frank Sinatra, for example. The man had it all. Fame, fortune, the love of great beauties, the envy and admiration of other men. A singer who was one of the best of all time. Won an Academy Award. Friends with presidents and Mafia dons. Who can match that range? As his great hit song said, he did it his way. Ring-a-ding-ding. He broke a lot of rules, though."

"I see your point." I was antsy. The walls that partitioned the factory floor into rooms did not go to the ceiling. The sound of commotion reached us. "Maybe we better start moving."

The Pig Faces had left the country and western club and were on another screen, roughing up the salsa lovers. "I never saw their kind before," he said. "You brought them from another world?"

"They followed me."

"This wizard . . . ?"

"Zalzathar. He takes his orders from Satan himself."

Stanky got a sick, scared look. "I thought I'd felt his dark influence stronger since this Zalzathar arrived." He seemed already to regret his decision to help me.

"They're going to be here any minute."

"Will you tell your friends I helped you?"

"Do you want me to?"

"Yes."

"Then I will, but let's make it fast."

He stepped to a door and opened it. "In here."

A broom and dustpan were inside. "C'mon, you want me to hide in a closet?" The door didn't even have a lock.

"When the door closes, push the far wall. It opens to a tunnel."

Did he think I was a dummy? I walk into the closet and he props a door against the doorknob or something and hands me over when the Pig Faces bust in. "He's right in here," he tells them.

There was knocking at the door. My heart leaped up into my throat and stuck. "Are you there?" Gigi asked.

Stanky held his finger to his lips. She knocked a couple more times. When there was no answer, she stopped. "She'll be back," he whispered. "She'll lead them to you."

"I can still make it through the crowd and get away."

He looked at the monitors. "Look. They have the exits blocked. No one's getting in or out."

I didn't see that I had a whole lot of options.

"The tunnel drops down and meets a flood control channel on the other side of a steel door," Stanky said. He opened a drawer. "Here's a flashlight." Indecision passed like a cloud over his face again, as if he were having second thoughts. Then he seemed to firm up. "Go now or be taken."

I stepped into the closet.

17

The short brick-lined tunnel intersected with a big underground storm drain. A steel door connected the two. When it slammed shut behind me, I played the flashlight beam around. Two choices of direction, up or down. The path of least resistance seemed right. The air was stale, as if somebody else had breathed it first. I was worried by Stanky's wavering. How soon before he sold me out? My footsteps rang on the concrete floor.

I wanted out of this action-thriller. I wanted my life slowed to the pace of those European movies where they only talk. "Is that what you think?" one character asks another. Their faces fill the screen in the long, silent close-up that follows. There has been a misunderstanding, but it is hard to say over what. I saw many of these with Felicity. It is considered action when an eyebrow lifts. Or when lips purse in thought. Felicity called movies "cinemas," and the smaller the better. We never missed one that had been made in Bulgaria. As you watched the screen, your mind went to things you needed to do later. Someone sighs sadly. The camera makes a long pan of the room in a slow inventory of the objects in it. This is to show the emptiness of materialism, or perhaps to praise it. Meaning was hard to pin down. Felicity liked to discuss the movies afterward, though she never got much out of me. My mind had been elsewhere during the key scene, or I hadn't read the key subtitles. It puzzled her that I could be so stupid and yet make so much money.

I had been trucking along for ten minutes when I heard the steel door behind me slam open against the concrete wall with a sound like a gunshot. I broke into a run. The porkers would be down on all fours, making up ground in a big hurry.

Five minutes, ten minutes. I felt like I was in one of those dreams where you run like hell but don't move. The darting flashlight beam seemed to stab the inky void the same places over and over. The wind I was sucking and the slap of my shoes on concrete hid the sounds of pursuit. They would dive over one another to get at me when they caught up. My body would be reduced to bone and gristle, torn apart chunk by bloody chunk.

A swing of the flashlight picked out a steel ladder on the wall. I stopped at the bottom to pant. Grunts and squeals from up the tunnel. They were coming on fast. But behind that was another sound, like faraway surf. I climbed the ladder with the flashlight stuck in my coat pocket. There was a manhole cover at the top. I pushed but it didn't budge. The pig racket was closer and that surf sound louder, much louder. Was that panic I heard in their voices? My heart jackhammered in my chest. I shoved like a madman, and a crescent of starry sky scraped into sight. I shoved more, and it widened. Something grabbed my ankle. The sound of water was a roar. The grip on my ankle changed from "gotcha" to hanging on for dear life. I was nearly pulled off. Then it was gone, yanked loose by the tremendous force of water shooting down the storm drain like at a hydroelectric plant. I squirmed up through the manhole. I was no sooner clear than an Old Faithful geyser blew up from it.

I was on a construction site. Bare bulbs were strung overhead to guard against theft and vandalism. The geyser tumbled back as the flood below passed. The Pig Faces would flush down the drain to whatever river the channel joined, drowned like rats. I looked until I found a vehicle with keys. It was a backhoe, and it took a few minutes to figure out the gears. I donned the yellow helmet that was on the seat and drove through a locked gate, snapping chain and padlock. I stopped twice at gas stations to ask the way back to the hotel.

"You can't bring that here," a doorman yelled as I chugged up to the porte cochere.

I climbed down from the seat. "You have to speak to my supervisor." I walked into the lobby.

Doyle was already on the way, flying in by chartered business jet and sore as a boil at my disappearance. He stomped around fit to be tied when he arrived. I had to agree to hire more bodyguards or he would fire me as a client. I wouldn't be the first account to get the sack, he told me. His reputation was as much on the line as my life, and don't ask which was more important to him. I also agreed to wear shoes with tiny radio transmitters in the heels so that my location could be pinpointed at all times. "But no chips implanted in the living flesh," I said. "I draw the line there."

I joked to hide how shook up I was. "You had every reason to be," Tyre told me worriedly the next day at my suite in the office tower. The Vandyke beard and mustache were gone. "I've known Stanky since the Reformation. He could never make up his mind who to choose, us or the other side. He tries to please both. He justifies his inability to choose as being open-minded. As much as he says he believes in God's gift of free will, it's only lip service. He wants the choice made for him. His heart inclines him one way, but his head says the other side has the better cards."

"Who can blame him? It looks like no contest on its face."

"You made a choice in the other world. Finally." He gave me a veiled look. "Or so it seemed." Maybe he sensed my backsliding with Gigi.

I avoided his eye. "What was that place, anyhow?"

"The zone of transition? The enemy has a last chance to capture newly departed souls. Choice is still available even then. But it's still not easy to see which is right. It's the enemy's territory. Minds are won over by music and other seductions. Savory food, strong drink, intoxicating scents. Sex in the rear rooms. It's one last hurrah, if people so choose. The body is a temple, but it can also be a seraglio. Music, sadly, is very effective in the enemy's hands. What is plainsong compared to the bossa nova, the dance of love? Not much, and I speak as an admirer of ecclesiastical music. Whatever its contribution to piety, it's not danceable. Bodies don't touch and create heat. It reminds people of their troubles instead of taking their minds off it."

"If they're dead," I said, "how can they feel anything physical?"

"It would be a parody of choice if they couldn't."

"Where did that flood come from?"

"A small dam gave way. Its water rushed harmlessly into the storm drain."

"The timing sure was good."

"Perhaps it's the sin of pride, but I like to think it couldn't be better." He smiled in a superior way.

Clancy was on the telephone later. "I got a call from Swainhart, Hiddleby, Basher, and Pointe."

"Should they mean something to me?" I looked out the big window. A storm was moving in over the city. The mountains were already hidden.

"They're a powerhouse in New York. Two hundred partners. They represent Soderberg's campaign. They want to see the originals of those commercials you're running. The ones where you and he are walking and talking about the problems of the country."

"What about them?"

"They say they're fake. Soderberg's people claim those chats never happened."

"Stall them."

"Don't tell me they *are* fakes."

"Maybe there was a little technological enhancement."

"They got people counting how many spots were on. They claim thirty-two hundred times in forty-three media markets yesterday alone. They could ask damages for each and every one."

"There'll be even more spots today." It was market saturation to the point of overkill, no question about it.

Clancy was quiet for a minute. "That scene where you say there's too much freedom and people need more discipline. Soderberg nods his head and says, 'I agree.' Then the Hitler music comes up. That didn't really happen?" We were walking on the beach. Or I was. Soderberg came into the scene during postproduction. They'll have Marilyn Monroe and John Wayne together in a movie one day. You won't be able to tell it was all done by computers.

"We'll talk about it later," I said. "I'm coming to New York." Maye had told me it was time to journey to the capital city of media. There was not an interview show or newsmagazine that wasn't begging for me. Alex was flying in later, from San Francisco. A crew from the BBC would accompany me for a piece on the zany politics of America. Maye had given them the idea. He thought like a network executive.

That night, he and I had dinner with Elizabeth Bernaise, our mole in Soderberg's campaign. She had driven over from Salt Lake City, with Doyle's people shadowing her car to make sure she wasn't followed. She was a petite blonde, a hard-boiled egghead in a gray pinstriped suit and heels that sounded like castanets. She talked as fast as Camille Paglia. She was as much of a political animal as Maye himself. They had often been on opposing sides in campaigns. The first thing she did was shake his hand with both hers.

"Brilliant," she said. "Absolutely brilliant. What you've done would be taught in the schools if it weren't illegal." She turned to me. "Do you know how good this guy is? He's destroying us." Maye tried to look humble.

"Sure I know," I boomed. "He tells me all the time." Playing the Bogey role to the hilt, I gave out with a loud, horse laugh. "Haw, haw."

Maye asked a lot of technical questions over dinner. What the polling numbers were showing, plans for their next media campaign, organizational status in key states. They mentioned campaign professionals both knew and talked about who was up and down in Soderberg's organization. Maye took notes. "This is invaluable," he said.

"Do you have many dealings with Mr. Dark?" I asked her casually over dessert.

"He stays in the background. I think he's creepy." She gave a shudder.

I spooned sorbet. "Why?"

"I don't know, the way he looks at people. They're scum to him. We thought at first he was silent because he was shy, but that didn't last long. Say something and he ignores you, except maybe for a killing look. Do you remember Frank Hitchcock?"

Maye said sure. "He's been on my team before."

"He tried arguing with Dark when he thought he was wrong."

"Frank's a very argumentative guy."

"He vanished one night. Hasn't been seen since. Other people who cross Dark go AWOL. Their families won't tell where they're hiding. I've got a nightmare about those eyes of his. They're hard and glittery, like a cobra's. He's always whispering in Bernie's ear. He's a Rasputin type, in my opinion. He's why I decided to help you, that and the money. I just can't see him in the White House advising the president, though there have been some real doozies there. Bernie just nods his head when he gets those whispers in his ear, like those thingies people put on dashboards. Dark seemed like a total greenhorn at first. He acted dumb about the simplest things. I saw him turning a light switch on and off as if he were trying to figure out what made it work. But he learns fast, I give him that. It was his idea to have Soderberg go public with his search for a First Lady." She turned to Maye. "Which was totally blown out of the water by your ads. Nobody even talks about that anymore. Watching Bogey here chatting with Bernie made people remember how much they hated both before all this started." She looked apologetic. "I hope I didn't insult you."

"You've got to get up pretty early in the morning to offend me." I let fly with more braying laughter.

Maye asked her about morale in the campaign staff. "Good in the beginning, but now everyone's nervous. Bernie's numbers are down and his negatives way up, thanks to you guys. Things are desperate when all they can think to do is sue you." There had been a press conference to announce the lawsuit. "I thought you handled that beautifully, too."

I had gone before the cameras to say I was confused. "He wanted my help in the beginning," I faltered, "but now I guess he doesn't." I had offered to bite my lip and brush away a tear, but Maye figured that would look too phony. "But I'm going to continue to fight for him," I continued, "because Bernie Soderberg knows what's best for America." Voters tacked ingratitude onto Bernie's list of character flaws, according to our overnight polls.

Maye ran fingers through his long hair. With makeup, he could go on a Kiss revival tour. "Maybe we ought to lay low and let things build on their own." He thought a minute. "No, we'll keep jabbing to keep them off balance. Your side's got slow reactions," he told Elizabeth.

"That's because nothing is decided until Dark signs off on it."

That top-down management approach is what killed him in the other world, where Zalzathar's army was a steamroller but couldn't change directions quickly. It was like a giant with slow reflexes. You could tap-dance out of danger before the blow landed.

"Does he suspect anything?" Maye asked.

"He suspects everything and everybody. He's incapable of trust. He must've had a rotten childhood."

"So you're in the clear?"

"As much as anybody is, I suppose."

"Where'd you tell them you were going?"

She was examining her face in a compact mirror. Satisfied, she snapped it shut. "To visit my sick mother. She'll cover for me."

Maye had her promise to bail out if she had the slightest suspicion they were on to her.

"Don't worry, I'll be gone like a shot." She left the hotel in a janitorial service truck driven by one of Doyle's men.

"On to New York," Maye barked. He cracked an imaginary whip.

Our charted Citizens for Soderberg jumbo jet arrived at Kennedy International Airport at ten in the morning, the best time for the media. I came out on the ramp first and shot both arms in the air in the V-style Nixon made famous. Maye wanted that association planted. "It's great to be back in New York," I said into the bank of microphones. A hired band struck up "Roll Out the Barrel." The BBC crew was behind me, shooting as I looked out on the media horde. They looked like piranha waiting for the cow to cross the ford.

The arrival was carefully choreographed. I stood aside for the Cheerleaders for Soderberg, hard-faced women with big hair who chewed gum. They had the brazen look of pole dancers from suburban strip joints. Skimpy costumes showed a lot of tits and ass. There were actual gasps from reporters. The Hollywood casting director hired by Maye had been told we were after a trailer-trash look. "Real skanky," he ordered. The women went through a halfhearted Rah-rah for Bernie routine, shaking pompoms and smiling bitterly as the band played "Everything's Coming Up Roses."

"Waa-hoo!" I cried into the mikes when they were finished. "We're here to take back the country!" I threw my arms up in the Nixon salute again and stepped back as Citizens for Soderberg filed off the plane. They looked like a fifties propaganda film on Soviet labor heroes marching to their lathes. The liberal big-city media stared, stunned. Everything they scorned in flyover land seemed to march off that plane. Pig-eyed truck drivers with big guts and fat sideburns. Cult couples with shaved heads and burning incense sticks. Tattooed bikers wearing Harley-Davidson vests and red bandannas. Construction workers in hard hats. Farmers in mesh-top John Deere baseball caps with hatchet-faced wives. National Rifle Association activists. Small merchants in white shoes and belts. High school coaches with crew cuts and police whistles around their necks. Church deacons and Rotary Club officials. Champion bowlers and checker champions. A heavyset women whose canned fruit won blue ribbons at county fairs, and a tobacco lobbyist in a two-thousand-dollar suit. The reporters read names and occupations from the press release and then looked up at the off-loading passengers. The casting perfectly matched face to stereotype. The savings and loan executive from Arkansas looked like a swindler, for example.

Clancy shared the media's shock. "Christ, where'd you find these people?" he whispered at my side.

"They're good Americans, Bill," I said. "The salt of the earth. Like me, they see Bernie Soderberg as a beacon of light."

I was aware of his sidelong look. "His people can't seem to

get it through their heads that you're trying to help him. There's a hearing tomorrow in federal court. They're asking for an order to stop you from false and deceptive practices."

"What practices would those be, Bill?" I asked innocently.

"Saying you support him when you're really trying to sink him. And I have to admit they might have a point. Look at those reporters. Writing about these people in the abstract is one thing, but actually seeing them in the flesh is something else. They're horrified. It's the Silent Majority and the Moral Majority come to life. Every story they do from here out will be slanted against Soderberg. They'll kick him around worse than Herbert Hoover."

"I expect your usual vigorous defense in the courtroom."

"I know the judge. I helped get him appointed. Soderberg's opposition to the First Amendment will go against him." His look was suspicious. "If he really *is* opposed."

As I watched the Citizens for Soderberg come off the plane, the unworthy thought occurred about how much all this was costing. They supposedly were going to canvass New York to drum up support for Soderberg from people like themselves. They would be bused straight to other eastern seaboard cities instead. Each would get five thousand smackers and a ticket back home. Not bad for just marching off an airplane. When I came back from the parallel universe, or whatever it was, I vowed to give away my money and stay on the straight and narrow. But I had to admit to second thoughts on stray occasions, such as right then. I had outsmarted a lot of ruthless sons of bitches for that money.

Tyre had picked up on this at some point. "Some of us wondered why you, of all people, should play such a major role in all this. Your avarice epitomized the age, as did your arrogance and licentiousness. You seemed even unaware there was a difference between right and wrong, let alone care. But I realized that would just be God's point. If even you, one of the worst of the lot, could turn over a new leaf, there was hope for all others. Yet what could be more natural than someone with your background to harbor regrets and want to revert to your former ways."

When the last Citizen for Soderberg left the airplane, some megaphone voice in the media crowd from the Bronx shouted, "Mistah Ingersol! Soderberg's people claim you . . ."

I waved him off. "Sorry, no questions."

"What do you mean?" a shrewish woman screeched. "You can't do that."

"Watch me." My security people went to work clearing a way. Elbows and fists flew. I was almost beginning to enjoy these affrays, another sign of backsliding.

"I thought if you had a press conference you were supposed to answer questions," Alex said afterward. "The reporters are totally enraged." We were watching C-SPAN's replay of its live coverage. As Maye had expected, the reaction to Citizens for Soderberg was overwhelmingly negative. One picture is worth a thousand words, they say. That footage of Citizens for Soderberg marching off the plane gave New York the willies. My refusal to answer questions along with the usual scuffle between my bodyguards and the press were seen as ominous. Thanks to guilt by association, the character assassin's friend, Soderberg got most of the blame. Pundits went on camera to say his lawsuit against me was probably a smoke screen.

"This is a free country," I said to Alex. "If you don't want to answer a question, you don't have to." I lit a cigar and sent a lazy smoke ring toward the ceiling. "Oh, sorry," I said, waving away the cloud. "Do you mind?"

She was wearing a simple black sweater and slacks, probably from an outlet store. Felicity would be turned out as elegantly, but she would be wearing original Italian labels that cost a hundred times more.

"You've changed," Alex said. She gave me a cool look.

"People never mean changed for the better when they say that."

"I'm not being judgmental. Well, maybe I am."

"How am I different?"

"You're more . . . grandiose. You even walk differently."

"Hello. I have to play a role, remember? The Wall Street tiger back in his jungle. It's got to be believable, otherwise people won't buy it."

"Are you sure about the line between the role you're playing and the real you? Your confusion over that has been the problem."

"We're back to that."

"It's never been resolved. That's why it keeps coming up."

"Your husband was a big man. Six-foot-one, I'd say. Two hundred pounds. High forehead. I bet he liked casual clothes. Corduroy pants, rust-colored sweater."

Alex stared. "How did you know that?"

"The gas scare in the basement the night we left Millwood?"

"What about it?"

"We got out of there because the place was infested with evil spirits. Still is, for all I know." Alice told me on the telephone the dogs still acted spooky. They would all stand stock still and stare at the house. "Remember the cat?" I said. "You mentioned it yourself. A succubus nearly screwed your friend Knox to death. That's why he had the stroke. While that happened, you were dreaming of your husband, remember? He wanted you to kill yourself so you could be together again."

Her gaze dropped to her hands in her lap. "I think of that dream a lot." When her eyes rose again to meet mine, they were resentful. "You're saying my husband is an evil spirit now?"

"No, I'm just—"

She cut in, "He was a good husband and father. Everyone loved him. If there's a Heaven, he's there and not the other place."

"That doesn't mean some spirit can't take on his physical form to fool you. Carlotta was put in the nuthouse because one was so real."

"I'm glad no one from Stanford can hear us right now."

"They'd have to have awfully good ears."

She frowned. "Humor's sometimes a form of aggression."

"Refusal to look facts in the face isn't? Strange shit is happening and you're pretending it's not because you're afraid of what your friends at Stanford might think."

"A fact is something on which there is no dispute. That's hardly the case here."

"Here's something we can agree on," I said coldly. "You're not my doctor. You're not my girlfriend either because we've never kissed, much less slept together. So what are we? Is it my money?" I don't know why I said that. It was like the tongue of flame that leaps from a furnace when it is stoked. I wanted the words back as soon as they left my mouth. Alex looked astonished and hurt. The telephone rang suddenly. We both stared at it as if it had made a comment. It rang a second time, and I picked it up.

"Hello," I said.

"Soderberg wants to meet." It was Clancy.

I stood with my back to Alex. "What for?"

"I can't believe it. The richest man in the world, a candidate for president of the United States, wants to talk in person to the man he's threatening to sue for who knows how many millions of dollars because he suspects he's trying to screw him out of the biggest job in the world, and you ask, 'What for?' "

"Why now?"

"How do I know? I'm not a mind reader. Maybe he wants to cut a deal."

"No deals."

"How can you say 'no deals'?" Clancy was exasperated. That was what he did for a living.

"It's easy."

"Okay, you want to make sure he understands and there's no confusion?"

"I don't want a shadow of doubt in his mind."

"Then tell him to his face. I speak as your lawyer and a student of human psychology."

I considered it. There was nothing to lose. And I was starting to feel curious. What could he possibly offer that he thought I might accept? I felt that old Bogey excitement when he had someone on the run and smelled victory. "All right, set it up. But take your time. I'm in no hurry."

"Thank you." There was relief in his voice.

I hung up and turned back to Alex to tell her. She was gone.

18

New York assigned a police detail to the hotel. This was to hold back the crowds when I came and went with my bodyguards. The mob was bigger than usual outside the hotel one morning. People pointed and shouted when Clancy and I got into my limo. A skull-and-crossbones flag fluttered on the aerial so people knew who ran the red lights and blared horns in traffic tie-ups. That stuff gets around.

"Who are all these people?" I asked. Police and protesters were pushing and shoving.

"They're from some union in Ohio," Clancy answered. "They were thrown out of work years ago in one of your mergers." The car roof was too low for the V salute, so I gave them the middle finger. Camera flashes went off.

"What'd you do that for?" Clancy protested. "Look at them now."

Bottles and other objects rained on the car, and it was smacked by the flat side of placards. Spittle ran down the windows as we pulled away.

"Bastard!" a man shouted.

"You took our jobs!" another yelled.

"My kids . . ."

"Shove it up . . ."

The cars moved away from the curb, and I gave one or two

waves like Prince Philip in the royal carriage before settling back in my seat.

"What's the point of making them so mad?" Clancy asked.

I was playing to the cameras, but I didn't tell him that. It was one media availability after another, ranging from sit-down interviews to that upraised finger in the window. Only New York could give a person that kind of spotlight. My fame grew on the foundation of my previous notoriety so that my name was on everyone's lips and my face nearly as well known as Soderberg's. I was a mother lode for the controversy the media feed on. The public loved to hate me. The poll numbers showed I had topped many historical figures in the most-loathed category. "A lot of people don't remember Pol Pot," Maye explained when I left Mr. Pot behind. I guess he didn't want me to get a swelled head. There were a number of movies based on me in development. Clancy saw a source of potential litigation there. We each wore dark blue pinstripes. His tie was red and mine was purple. The sirens of our police escort howled in the downtown canyons.

"Global warming is a lie promoted by socialism," I had told the *Wall Street Journal.* "And don't tell me about so-called scientific studies. They're crap."

"Canada," I said with a sneer to the *Toronto Star* reporter. "You birds are a pain in the ass. I wouldn't be surprised if you aren't pretty high up on Bernie Soderberg's list of problems to fix after the election."

"People ought to be glad they have jobs," I told *Newsweek.* "You don't see Chinese workers asking for more. They know it's a global market."

"Don't quote me on this, but we trust the Russians as far as we can throw them." The *New York Times* naturally quoted me. Its editorial page demanded to know if my remark reflected the candidate's thinking. Soderberg's camp said it did not. Elizabeth Bernaise passed word that they were going crazy there.

Dark's control-freak methods meant they swung the bat after the ball was already in the catcher's mitt.

We bought time on a local station for a telethon, supposedly to let John Q. Citizen show support for Bernie. The "volunteers" answering the phones looked like they had served time. They stared challengingly at the camera. An 800 number was at the bottom of the screen, but lines were rigged so calls came through only every five minutes or so. The second-rate comic picked for emcee, Bucky Hofferman, was in the dark about this. None of the guest celebrities advertised showed up. An accordionist and a prissy man with a trap drum played musical selections from the disco era. It was painful to watch Bucky panic as he struggled to fill the dead air. Outbursts of strange laughter came from the phone volunteers. Bucky mopped sweat with his handkerchief. "Boy, it's hot in here." There was a sob in his voice. The media gloated the next day, calling the telethon a flop. Soderberg's people said it had not been authorized. Commentators scoffed at this as attempted spin control.

"We can't talk about it, of course," I told *Time* magazine, "but, yes, I expect to play a major role in the Soderberg administration." The news programs began showing split screens with me saying something and Bernie denying it. Maye laughed until he cried.

He had me talk to reporters until we were down to small fry and foreigners. "The French are cowards," I told *Le Monde*. "Both wars proved that." The prime minister denounced me in Paris. I told the Omaha newspaper that Bernie would explain his farm policy when he was good and ready. I shook my head gravely. "But I'll tell you this, we've been living high on the hog too long." Big black headlines scared the heartland the next day. The governor of Nebraska wanted to know why some ex-con was allowed to shoot off his mouth on national TV. Maye was nearly rolling on the floor.

The press got bored at last. One part of me was glad it was time to pack up and go. Alex had returned to California on the red-eye that same night I insulted her. She was icy when I reached her on the telephone. "Do you really think I'm after your money?"

"I don't know why I said that."

"What makes you think we're going to sleep together?"

"I don't know why I said that, either. You're a shrink. You know what stress does to people."

She had sent back the consulting fee I had paid her for Carlotta. If things were to be patched up, and I was beginning to wonder if it was possible, it would have to be in person. The funny thing was that I was enjoying being back in New York. It brings out the best of the worst of you. Climb to the top there and you have licked some of the toughest bastards in the world. When I was married to Felicity, we had been at the top of the B-list, almost A-listers. We didn't hang with the Sulzbergers, but I knew Mort Zuckerman to nod at. Our names were in the society columns, and one of our parties was featured in *People* magazine. We moved in a swirl of excitement and publicity. When I looked back, it wasn't all that bad. In fact, it was pretty good at times.

Clancy and I were on our way to see Soderberg. "He almost refused the meeting because you've taken so long," Clancy said. "His campaign manager, a guy named Holt, says you've done about all the damage you can." Maye's daily polling confirmed this. Soderberg was reeling but could still stage a comeback. "We need a knockout punch," Maye told me.

As we drove through Manhattan, paparazzi on motorbikes buzzed alongside like gnats. I rolled down the window. "You bastards killed Princess Di." The Soderberg Tower dominated a downtown block of Manhattan. It looked sterile enough for surgery. A huge map in the marble lobby whose vastness was meant to cow visitors showed the global reach of his empire. Each floor was occupied by the world headquarters of one of his companies. Clancy and I were met by a Swiss executive in a monocle and escorted to the cherrywood-paneled elevator that went directly to Soderberg's lair on the sixty-third floor. Some of the most powerful men in the corporate world had cowered as they rose in that elevator to meet the great man.

The Swiss and Clancy exchanged polite chitchat while I maintained a magnate's aloof silence. When we reached the top, we passed through outer chambers populated by respectful staff in dark suits. If this were not America, I bet they would have bowed. We were shown into an office big enough for church services. Tall windows on three sides gazed out on stupendous views. The Swiss seated us in leather chairs and left noiselessly. "He used to be chairman of the World Bank," Clancy whispered.

I clipped and lit an Esplendido. It would stink up the place in nothing flat. "I don't think I could throw a baseball to that far wall," Clancy said, looking around. He noticed the smoke. "I read that Soderberg is allergic to cigars and cigarettes."

"Good," I said.

Soderberg kept us waiting long enough to establish his colossal importance before entering the room, with Holt a step behind. Soderberg gave the impression of a dynamo who had enough juice to light a whole city himself. He came toward us with brisk strides. He was in a white tropical suit and string tie, like Colonel Sanders. He wore lifts but was still short. When I stood to shake his hand, I looked down on the surgical stitching for his hair plugs.

"Howdy," he drawled. His strange pale eyes had large, dark pupils. If the computer that beat the Russian chess champ had eyes, that's what they would look like. His grip was surprisingly strong as he pulled me closer, like a planet exerting gravitational pull. It was one of those intimidation tactics Bogey knew forward and backward. We released each other's hands like strange dogs who had finished circling one another warily.

"Take a load off, ma friend." His biscuits-and-gravy accent

seemed unforced by now. All sat except Holt, wrinkled and disheveled as before. He stood at Soderberg's side like a vassal with his lord and sovereign.

"You've been much in the news lately, Mistah Ingersol," Bernie said dryly. "I declare, you been keepin' us busy."

"Call me Bogey." I drew on my cigar. "The accent's nice."

Holt interpreted his boss's frown. "Mr. Soderberg doesn't like smoke."

I looked around. "Guess that's why I don't see an ashtray."

"Please take Mistah Ingersol's cigar for him," Bernie said pleasantly. I surrendered it, and Holt walked it to the door like a dead rat and handed it to someone outside.

It was not in Clancy's nature to be totally ignored. "The name's Bill Clancy." He tried to sound hearty but was too awe-struck by Soderberg to bring it off.

Soderberg's eyes flicked to the lawyer. "I know about you, Mistah Clancy." Clancy seemed to shrink. Like most fixers, he had things in the closet he did not want out. Something in Soderberg's voice said he knew all about them.

Those eyes returned to me. "How kin we resolve this sit'a'shun?"

I gave him a cool look back. "Drop out of the race."

He leaned back in his chair and took me in as if I were a number that had turned up wrong in an equation. "Why'd I wanna do that now?"

"You don't want to be president."

He folded his small, flabby hands in his lap. "I reckon I'm a more qualified jedge of that there 'n ya'll are."

"Did the idea ever occur to you before you met Dark?"

He blinked. "You know Mistah Dark?"

"He didn't tell you?"

"Tell me whut?"

"That we'd met before."

"Cain't say he did."

"His real name is Zalzathar. He's an evil wizard." Clancy's head spun toward me as his jaw dropped.

Soderberg leaned back in his chair. "A whut?" He dragged the word out lazily: "Whuuuuut?"

"From another world. That's where I met him. He's evil."

"Ah-*huh*."

Clancy tried to change the subject. "About the lawsuit your lawyers have filed in federal court—"

Soderberg waved him off as he continued to look at me. "I was tryin' all this time to figger why you'd go to all this trouble and expense to damage me. It didn't seem reasonable. Hell, now I see it wasn't even rational."

"Remember the first time you ever met Dark?"

"But maybe you're pullin' my leg. I cain't tempt you with worldly goods, I 'spect, but maybe I can with pow-ah. Even an irrational person can respeck that. I'm gonna need someone smart to step in 'n' run my affairs when I'm elected." He gave me a shrewd look. "Mebbe you're jes' the man. Sixty-seven companies in fifty-four countries, North Sea oil to banana plantations in the tropics. Hollywood movies to biotech outfits. Man's gotta be damn good to keep track of the whole ball of wax. You might be that man."

"Or does it seem like you've always known him?"

Soderberg decided to consider my question. "When did I first meet him?" He seemed surprised when he couldn't pinpoint it.

"Wasn't that long ago," I said. "Not even two years. Seem odd you can't remember when you met?"

His frown said he was searching his mainframe harder.

I interrupted the search. "He's using you."

He scoffed. "Fer whut?"

"His own purposes."

Clancy was pale. He was picturing what Soderberg's lawyers would do to me on the witness stand.

"You're a fine one to talk about evil," Soderberg drawled. "You did prison time and now you're a suspect in a murder." I watched his hands. The psychological profile Doyle commissioned said Soderberg unconsciously rubbed forefinger and thumb together when his mind arrived at a new possibility. This came out from interviews with former employees and the manuscripts of two tell-all books suppressed when Soderberg bought their publishing houses.

"I can't let you be president," I said. "Because then Dark could do whatever he wanted through you. He'd have you start wars."

"You think he's got some kinda control over me?" Soderberg chuckled.

"You just don't realize it yet."

Soderberg glanced at Holt. The conversation had taken a turn he couldn't have guessed at in his wildest dreams. Clancy hung his head.

Holt cleared his throat. "This has gotten a little off track. You've put our campaign in a tailspin, but we can still pull out if you stop hammering us. We'd like it to be voluntary, but our lawyers say we can get a court order to stop your smears."

"They're blowing smoke," Clancy said weakly. "This is a free-speech issue."

"He'd have you start wars," I told Soderberg again.

"I cain't believe we're having this conversation," he answered. "Mistah Dark is a . . . " He stopped.

"Is what?" I prompted. "You can't remember when you met him. Tell me what you know about him."

"I know he's . . . " Soderberg stopped. That steel-trap mind went blank.

"He's your closest adviser. You two are always talking. What do you know about the man? Where'd he come from? You must have seen a résumé."

Clancy rallied. "Did you do any kind of background check?"

He looked at Holt. "What about you? What do you know about this man?"

"He's Mr. Soderberg's friend," Holt said.

"Friend?" I said to Bernie. "You've got a friend you don't know anything about?" Soderberg's forefinger and thumb began to slowly rub together. "People who run for president grow up from kids thinking they'll do that," I continued. "Was that the case with you?"

"No," he admitted. "I never once thought I'd do that. Like ya'll, I jes' wanted to be rich and run people. That was plenty good 'nuf." He seemed to give himself a mental shake. "That's plumb crazy. There's no such things as wizards. This here's the twenty-first goddamn century. Let's get real, pee-pul."

"I bet you first realized you wanted to be president after you met Dark. Did he give any arguments why you should, or did you just wake up one day and that was what you wanted to be?"

"I'd climbed all the mountains. I wanted to give something back." Campaign boilerplate. Soderberg looked puzzled, as if he had never really thought about those words before. There was enough friction from the rubbing thumb and forefinger now to start a campfire.

"We've found the future First Lady," Holt said suddenly. "Somebody you know."

I looked at him. "Who is it?"

"Your former wife, Felicity."

"A lovely woman," Soderberg said. "Cain't understand why you divorced her."

I was too astonished to say anything.

"I see what you're doing," Clancy said. It was finally something he could get his mind around.

"It gives motive," Holt said. "Ex-husband maddened by jealousy seeks revenge. The American people will say, 'Aha.'"

"How much did you pay her?" I asked.

"I won't have a lady's honor impugned." Soderberg gave a

slow chuckle. "But she drives a hard bargain, as I'm sure you know."

"You'd be her fourth marriage. This country won't buy that."

"The elderly Italian count died of natural causes," Holt said. "The English earl was killed riding to the hounds. You're a jailbird. Her run of bad luck ends with Mr. Soderberg. We've got all the story points down. She'll be a voice for the suffering children."

"She doesn't like kids."

He was making a big mistake letting Felicity get her nose under his tent, but I wasn't about to point that out. "Who's idea is this—Dark's?"

Their surprise told me it was. "It's his revenge for how I screwed things up for him in the other world. He was all set to rule until I threw a monkey wrench into the works." Zalzathar would think it was twisting the knife in the wound to put Felicity in Soderberg's bed.

"Where'd ya'll say this other world is?" Soderberg asked casually.

"I don't know."

Clancy let out a deep sigh.

"How'd ya'll get there?"

"He transported me somehow. It was a mistake."

"A mistake?"

"He really wanted you. Bad as I was, you were worse. I was a penny-ante asshole to your major-league bad guy. I stepped on people to get ahead. You did it because you liked hurting them. The damage I did was on the side. Yours was intentional."

"Uh-huh." He steepled his fingers and looked at me over them. "And what was this other world like?"

"Good and evil are clear. There's no ambiguity, unlike here."

"The wizard was bad and you were good? Then why'd he want you there to gum up the works?"

"To advise him on strategy. And I wasn't good. I looked for a deal to cut. My choice was Dark—Zalzathar—or Helither."

"And who might Helither be?"

"An angel."

"My, my. A wizard, an angel, and you."

"There were others. Humans and Pig Faces."

"Humans with pig faces?" Soderberg glanced at Holt and Clancy as if to say, "I hope you're getting all this."

"No," I answered, "humans and creatures with pig faces. They were opposite sides in a war to decide who survived. The angel and the humans won, but they couldn't have done it without me."

"You made a choice then?"

"I was forced to finally. You'd have made a different one, and the other side would've won."

"How'd this wizard know which side I'd pick?"

"He knew you then and knows you now."

"This here angel in the other world—did he follow you here, or are you on your own?" His amused glance went to Holt and Clancy again. "Seems unfair to have only you against me and Mistah Dark."

"No, but there's another one helping."

Soderberg looked around brightly. "Is he here in the room now? Can you make him visible? He's got wings, I 'spect. Or maybe it's a she-angel?"

"We better go, Bogey," Clancy said in a defeated voice.

"Whatever for?" Soderberg said. "We're jes' gettin' warmed up." His smile faded. "Mistah Holt here had the bright idea we could deal with your client. 'Course, he couldn't know he was nuttier than a fruitcake. Tell ya what I'm gonna do. Y'all call him off—get a trustee appointed to manage his affairs or sumpin'—and I won't sue him and you for every nickel you both got. A lawyer with an insane client cain't go around helpin' him ruin lives. I know that much about the law."

"We have to talk," Clancy said to me. "Thank you for your time," he told Soderberg humbly.

"There's more," I said.

"Gracious sakes, more?"

"The wizard worked for Mogwert."

"And who is that?"

"An evil presence without form."

"More evil. I shudda known."

"And beyond them was the ultimate source of it all."

Soderberg blinked. "Yes?"

"The Prince of Darkness himself, Lucifer."

He made a tut-tutting sound. "What a poor, sad case you are, Mr. Ingersol. You sound like some barefoot desert theologian, and here it's the twenty-first century." He had dropped the cornpone accent. "Evil is not an inherent quality, much less a being with tail and cloven hooves. It is correctable behavior. When genome mapping has been completed, we'll see that evil is the outcome of the interplay of errant genes and inadequate nurturing. When they've been identified, they can be removed through breeding or perhaps surgical intervention at the cell level. What you call evil will disappear. What you say is goodness and I call socially approved behavior will be triumphant. Man is his own god."

"You forgot the horns."

"I beg your pardon?"

I smiled. "The Devil's also got horns."

"I'm sure you believe that."

"So where did Dark come from?"

This was the only thing that did not compute. "I . . . he's a valued member of my organization."

"Is he a lawyer?" I pressed. "A Harvard M.B.A.? An organizational theorist or a motivational expert? What is he, Bernie? A numbers cruncher? A strategist or conceptualizer?"

Holt broke in. "Bottom line, are you going to stop your distortions?"

"Oh, no," I told him. "You ain't seen nothing yet."

Holt gave Soderberg a look. He knew they could not win unless I agreed to lay off. I took out another Esplendido. "Got a light?" I asked Bernie.

"Why do you have to deliberately antagonize people?" Clancy was gloomy afterward. We were in the limo headed back to the hotel. "What was all that shit about wizards and devils?"

When we got back, Maye was missing.

19

I flew back to San Francisco the next day. The night had brought no trace of Maye. "It doesn't look good," Doyle admitted in the morning. He rubbed his crew cut worriedly. Every hour that passed without Maye turning up reduced the chance we would ever see him alive. Doyle said studies by the FBI showed this. He was glad I was leaving New York. His state-of-the-art security bubble had developed a leak. He wanted me where he could control access better than in a hotel.

"It's been real quiet for days," Alice told me when I arrived at Millwood. "The dogs aren't nervous or anything."

They gave me the usual rousing welcome. I took half a dozen with me on an inspection tour of the house, and Alice was right. They grinned and pranced at my side and didn't show the least worry. There were no evil spirits in residence. I kept expecting Oliver to round a corner, eyes shining, ears back, and tail whirling like a propeller. He would have been shocked at seeing this rabble from the kennels inside. I telephoned Alex but she wasn't home. I left a message saying I hoped to see her soon.

Zalzathar had finally learned who was drawing up the plays to keep his man out of the White House. If I had been honest with Maye about who Dark really was, maybe he would have seen the danger coming and dodged the bullet. He disappeared after telling one of the security people he was going out for a Polish sausage from a street vendor. But if I had told him about the wizard, he would have split. *Adiós* and *hasta la vista,* baby. I played hardball with people's lives without their knowledge, let alone permission. Telling myself that the end justified the means didn't make me feel any better.

I wanted to talk to Tyre about this. Maybe he had some argument to ease my guilt. The greatest good for the greatest number, say. Any flimsy rationalization would help. But there was no sign of the angel. Maye had been close to suicide when I met him and went down fighting the good fight instead. That was something. He had even been happy, also something. But neither was good enough to make me feel better.

I went out to the winter vegetable garden with the dogs trailing to see if any green young shoots had poked up yet. A deep silence hung over the estate, and shadows were deep. Fog streamed over the coastal mountains, a lurid red in the last rays of the sun. The adrenaline I ran on in New York was depleted, and I felt tired and draggy. I went back inside and turned on the TV. The spots that showed Soderberg and me chatting on our walks were everywhere, but I had dropped out of the news. Even the tabloids had given up hanging around the front gate and were off looking for fresh game. I heated up a frozen lasagne dinner in the microwave. After I ate, I sat in an easy chair before a fire in the library. If I found out how much money Soderberg offered Felicity, I could make a better offer. Felicity always went with the highest bid. But they would foresee that and keep her on ice until she was presented to the public. "My former husband? Oh, mad. Completely insane." She would be believable. Felicity was never so convincing as when she lied.

The dogs and I dozed in the warmth from the fire as Millwood was stealthily enveloped by fog. When a shifting log awoke me, they had become wolves lying on their bellies. They watched

me intently, slanted eyes reflecting the firelight. Instinct told me
if I moved, they would attack. I tried to swallow and couldn't.

"You're beginning to sweat," a deep voice said. "Excellent."
Zalzathar moved into my line of vision and stood with back to
the fireplace.

I didn't ask how he got in, but he knew what I was thinking.
"I waved my magic wand," he said sarcastically.

"What took you so long?"

"You had protection. A lesser angel."

"What happened to him?"

Zalzathar ignored the question. He was dapper in hounds-
tooth, dark trousers, and a green silk tie. His eyebrows didn't
meet in the middle anymore. He would never be handsome,
but he would pass muster in any merchant bank. Some of those
guys are pretty evil-looking.

"What a lot of trouble you've given me," he said.

"If only you'd said something."

"Soderberg's contempt led me to underestimate you."

"I think I'm going to cry."

A cold smile. His teeth had been cleaned and straightened.
I wondered if they had been able to do anything about his
breath. It was a yard long in the other place. "Mockery, another
trait that seemed to qualify you. Dishonesty, greed, arrogance,
selfishness, lust, cruelty—there were so many."

"That qualified me to work for you?" It was strange. I had
been terrified of him in the other world, but contempt is all I
felt at that moment.

"This campaign against Soderberg showed what you're capable of. A sense of shame would have stopped the ordinary
person."

"I'll get a big head if you keep this up." I shifted in the chair,
and the wolves tensed for the spring. The light from the fireplace gleamed on their bared teeth.

"Easy, my friends," Zalzathar said soothingly.

"Are those my dogs?"

"Dogs are such worthless things. So grateful for the smallest things." He looked around. "What a tasteless place you have here."

"You're a funny one to be talking about taste."

"You'd be surprised how fast I've learned. In a strange way, I suppose I owe you thanks. Your world is so much more interesting than mine. I hadn't realized how cramped I was. The palette there was so limiting—black or white. No ambiguity to cloud the issues. Here there's a whole range of grays to put to one's use. It's possible to be so much more original. Opportunities are everywhere." His smile made me think of the executioner testing the sharpness of the blade and finding it satisfactory. "On a scale of ten, how frightened are you? Eight? Nine? Be honest with me. There's no reason to hide your feelings at this point. I enjoyed your terror so in the other place."

"Before you lost everything?" It was the kind of thrust Zalzathar himself would be proud of. His eyes showed the pain. "You came so close," I taunted.

His voice was cold, "But for you."

"You must still be pretty upset. A whole world could've been under your control. Let me make my sad face."

"More of your mockery." He made a little motion with his hand, and a crushing pressure gripped my chest like a massive coronary. When I began to pass out, he did it again, and the pressure stopped. "Did that hurt?" he asked in an innocent voice.

"Is that the worst you can do, asshole?" Defiance was better than cringing with Zalzathar. It only encouraged him when victims crawled and begged for mercy.

"No, I can do far worse. But you'd like it over quickly, wouldn't you? What could be more natural? That would be nice for you, but where's the fun for me? Pain is something to be savored."

"You must have gotten in big trouble with Azimbrel-Zafieri for blowing it in the other world." Lucifer did not like that name for him any more than Zalzathar liked hearing it now. He moved his spellmaking hand, and I felt like shrieking from the pain. This time it felt like an air hose held to a rotting tooth.

"Owwww." I held my jaw. The motion made the wolves rise halfway. Zalzathar looked at me thoughtfully.

"What wonderful magic your dentists have. What worse pain is there than a toothache? Even a wizard is powerless against it, as I know from experience. I can't begin to count how many Pig Faces died when I was in the throes of toothaches. They ran with squeals to escape my anger, but I cut them down as they fled. The dentist here was very shocked when he looked into my mouth. Such neglect, he said. He scraped and drilled and polished. Where teeth were missing, his clever artifice crafted replacements. I bet you can't even tell." He opened his mouth and bent for me to inspect. I made a strangled sound. He motioned with his hand again, and the pain was gone.

"Yes," he said, "my master was very . . . disappointed. He was going to make things warm for me, very warm indeed. Forgiveness isn't one of his strengths. I surprised him when I asked to follow you to this world. He moves freely himself through the barriers separating the universes, but it never occurred to him that I could conjure a spell that would allow me as well. He believed it was impossible, a violation of the laws The One decreed in the Beginning. This, of course, became its appeal to him. His aim is the destruction of all trace of The One's original design. Let no moral or physical law be left standing. In chaos he reigns."

I didn't say anything. Zalzathar always preferred monologues anyhow.

"He saw my audacity as a challenge to his own authority at first, and it angered him. But I reminded him that he was the source of my cunning and power, and he was pleased. He consented to letting me follow you to gain my revenge." He spread his arms as if in benediction. "And I found all of this waiting. My revenge had to be put aside at first for these abundant opportunities. But forgotten? No, never."

"What happens when you blow this one? Soderberg's not going to be elected president. He goes back to being just another rich guy."

"Nothing's certain, as my master has decreed. All is relative. That is our hope and belief. But I like our chances with you out of the way." He rubbed his hands briskly, a gourmand before the feast. "What prodigious work awaits."

"You can't beat God."

"In the long run, I suppose you're right. He'll take one of His famous sabbaticals from creating and return His attention to this world to see how it fared. But His idea of time is different from ours. Maybe even my master's existence will seem no longer than a firefly's hours when The One returns. And doesn't the prevalence of evil tell us that it's at least as natural as goodness in the ecology of the universes?" His smile was crafty. "That being the case, perhaps I'm doing The One's will as much as any angel. I see Him as the general contractor who lays the foundation and then goes on to the next job while others complete the finish work. This is a big universe you have here, far bigger than where I come from. But they're only two in an infinite stack of them, and The One's creating more all the time! How else to account for his absence. Or perhaps you think of Him as a voyeur who sits with arms folded, the lone spectator in the stands. That makes Him more malignant than even my master, wouldn't you say, both author and witness of monstrous cruelties. Think of just this century alone. Say what you will about Satan, at least he shows interest. He gets his hands dirty. Not for him the grandeur of God's silence. He's one of us."

The simpleminded Pig Faces were suckers for his gift of gab. They believed everything he said. But I had to admit he was a persuasive bastard. It was clear he had spent a lot of time thinking about the subject. I gave him another zinger. "That was stupid bringing those Pig Faces with you."

He was not the sort to be generous in victory, but he probably felt he was enough in control to admit a mistake. "They've been useless. They make people suspicious. Maybe it's their vibes." He was proud of the slang.

"Try their rotten smell. Where'd yours go, by the way?"

"I brought them for that instant of terror when you realized I had followed you here for my revenge. What was it like?"

"Blow it out your ass."

He moved his hand, and I was looking up at him from way below. "Dog you were and dog you are." He laughed like a stage villain and reached down to pick me up. "But not the powerful beast you were in my world." He dangled me before a mirror on the wall. I was a hairless Chihuahua with the bulging eyes of that ridiculous breed. My legs churned in midair like a cartoon character that had run off a cliff and didn't know it yet. I *ki-yiied* in terror.

"That's more like it," Zalzathar said with satisfaction. He set me back down on the floor. The astonished wolves drew near to smell. They bumped me with their noses from one to another. I ricocheted like a cue ball off the cushions.

"You're barely a mouthful for the smallest of them," Zalzathar said with amusement. "Amazing the difference in size among dogs."

"You've had your fun," I piped in a shrill yap. "Switch me back."

"Back? Oh, I'm afraid not. Get used to your new shape for the brief time left to you."

"Wha . . . what do you mean?"

"You began this adventure running, and you will end it that way. I'm going to give you a head start. A minute or two. We'll see how long it takes the pack to run you down." He picked me up by the scruff of the neck and walked through the big house. The nails of the wolves clicked on the floor alongside as I swung in his hand. The fog outside had that Holmesian thickness again. He shut the door on the wolves and put me down on the flagstones. "A pity it's so wet. Your scent will hang in the air and make it easier for them to find you."

"Look, let's talk." I literally whined. "We can do a deal."

"You have nothing more I want or need, except the entertainment your last moments give me." He shut the door, and I tore off across the flagstones. It took a long time to reach the steps that led out to the great lawn, thanks to my absurdly short legs. I descended the steps in trembly little hops. I tried to remember what Chihuahuas were bred for. Some useless luxury of the Mayans? I scampered through the wet fog. Suddenly a figure loomed dimly. I yelped and skidded to a halt on the wet grass. It was a German shepherd.

"What's this, a rat?" he growled.

"N-n-no."

He gave me a thorough inspection as I stood rigid. This satisfied him that I told the truth. I was lucky at that. One of the terrier breeds would have snapped my neck with one shake without asking any questions. A collie and some kind of hound drifted up through the fog and gave me their own nuzzling once-over. That meant Alice had released the dogs for a run. Zalzathar must not have realized.

"Wolves are after me," I said with a gasp. They snorted skeptically. "I'm telling the truth. Any minute now."

"There're no wolves been smelled around here," a Scotty who arrived scoffed. "Never has been. Some say there's no such thing." As he spoke, the wizard released the wolves. They howled as they came after me. The dogs threw up their heads.

"This squirt's telling the truth," the hound said.

I spurted off into the fog, making for the front gate. A minute later, the wolf pack collided with the dogs. A terrific fight began at once. I reached the gate, where two guards looked in the direction of the fighting.

"Suppose we ought to go see what that is?" one asked.

"And get bit? No, thanks. They've got animal handlers up there for that."

I passed between the vertical iron bars of the gate. I was so small it was easy. I skittered like a wind-up toy across the asphalt where the media had parked its RVs and cars during their stakeout. Zalzathar would realize something had gone wrong and would be coming to see. In addition to being slow, I soon saw that Chihuahuas had no stamina. I was exhausted after running a couple of hundred yards to the Chad Warner estate. He was a big plastics manufacturer who spent most of the time in Asia. His wife had come to the Cleo Basich's welcoming party for me. Adele Warner was his third or fourth wife, a blond bimbo learning to put on society airs, one of which was to look down on a jailbird like me. When we were introduced, she seemed surprised that I didn't wear a do-rag.

She stood on her terrace with a black maid. Both wore heavy coats. "They've got those bright lights on at Millwood," Adele was saying as I trotted up, panting. "I know the zoning doesn't allow them."

"Sounds like dogs fightin'," the maid said.

"Oh, and those dogs! All the neighbors are suing."

"Some folks don't care if they bother other folks."

"Look," Adele said, spotting me, "isn't he darling? He must be cold. Look how he's shivering." Another shortcoming of that breed—no insulation against the cold. She bent and scooped me up. I rose in a cloud of perfume and juniper berry. A gin drinker. I licked her face.

"What a love," she squealed.

"Maybe he's runnin' from them dogs. Little fella like that wouldn't have no chance." The sounds of snarling and yelping were clear even at this distance.

"I'm taking him inside. Look how he's panting. He must have run a long way."

She carried me inside, and the maid closed the door. The big, heavy furniture and the tapestries of medieval scenes on the walls said this was the home of a man who saw himself as a warrior. A lot of CEOs suffer from that delusion. The business schools encourage it.

She plumped down in an overstuffed sofa with me. I stared up past her knockers to her face. "He looks so frightened." She hugged me to her bosom to warm me. My head swam from her perfume. I gave a tiny sneeze.

"Oh, baby's got a cold," Adele said. "Poor little baby." She hugged me closer. My flimsy rib cage made a cracking sound. These women who exercise with personal trainers and play tennis all day don't know their own strength. I gave off a feeble peep and she raised me to her face and planted a kiss on the end of my nose.

Knocking at the door. "Get the gun, Roseanne," Adele commanded.

"I got the piece right here, don't you worry none." The memory of Winston Byron's murder was still fresh, and the neighborhood had reached a high level of armed vigilance. Adele set me down, and I scampered under the sofa.

Zalzathar stood in the fog smiling insincerely when Roseanne opened up, the automatic in her hand. "I'm Mr. Dark from up the road. I'm looking for a small dog that got away, a Chihuahua."

"We haven't seen it," Adele said briskly. "Good night."

Zalzathar was opening his mouth to speak when Roseanne slammed the door in his face.

"Call the police and report there's a stranger going door to door," Adele said in a too-loud voice.

"Yes, ma'am," Roseanne answered as loudly, "I've got them on the phone right now." The two stared hard at the door. When it was clear Zalzathar was gone, they relaxed. "Don't like his looks," the maid whispered. "My first husband had them eyes. He was a crackhead that'd soon kill you as look at you when he needed a fix."

"I suppose that man Ingersol and he were in prison together. Chad says he's a terrible person who cheated a children's organization out of money."

She got down on her hands and knees and scooped me from under the sofa. "Come along, my little snookums."

20

He's so cute," Mimi Drinkwater cooed. "Look at the way he looks at the TV. You'd think he knew what they were saying." She was Adele Warner's best friend. They got together a couple of times a week to have lunch and tear apart the reputations of friends and enemies. Mostly friends. Ignoring them, I stood in front of the set, head cocked like the RCA dog. I was sinking deeper into Chihuahuaness, and it took more concentration to understand what was said. There was no sugarcoating the horror of that. How long before my human identity was gone for good? When I went to Guatemala to try to talk my old partner Barnes Drake into selling me his remaining share of the company, he gave me a long lecture about afterlife. A heart attack had nearly finished him and he had seen the white light in the tunnel and the family and friends waiting to welcome him. When I died, would I be greeted by those who had gone before? Or would it be frisking canines? Maybe dogs didn't even go down the tunnel to the white light. Some say God must have a bent sense of humor. I thought about that. What if I was the butt of a divine leg pull, some incomprehensible joke? Luckily, dogs sleep a lot. Without that escape, I might have begun frothing at the mouth and got put down.

Now that I was a dog again, I was aware once more of a tremendous number of smells. The house teemed with odors:

the fresh flowers delivered daily, food smells in the kitchen, furniture, carpets, cleaners used by the housekeeper, the dust they missed in corners, brass, plastics, wood, the people who worked there, Adele herself. I often stood with my nose working, sorting out the scents. Her menses were a ripeness one day. It reminded me that Felicity had often claimed her body's biological state as an excuse not to make love. "I'm not in estrus," she would say coldly.

The only course that made sense was to find Alex. I didn't know what she could do, but at least I could count on her sympathy once she understood it was I trapped in this dog's body . . . assuming I could somehow make the point. Maybe she would know just by looking into my big brown eyes. Or perhaps I could scratch a message with a pencil gripped in my teeth.

"He likes the news programs the most," Adele said. "Sometimes it even looks like he's reading the newspaper. He stands on it and I see his head moving back and forth. Do you like his new ribbon?"

"Why's it pink? He's a male."

"Oh, I don't know. It's my favorite color. Anyhow, I'm going to have him neutered."

I was stunned.

"Poor thing. You'd think he knew what you were saying from that look."

"They say it mellows them out," Adele continued. "When he's not sleeping, he paces all the time and whines and growls. He's always trying to get out."

"He probably wants back to where he came from. Dogs have a homing instinct."

"That's pigeons."

"Dogs, too."

"You're wrong. Dogs get lost all the time."

"I read it somewhere." Mimi had dyed red hair and long

crimson nails. She was older than Adele and married to a manufacturer. Plastic surgery had given Mimi's face a molded look,
as if to cut down on wind resistance. "Maybe he's got worms
and that makes him restless. You can find out by looking at
his stool."

"No, thanks."

Adele told other friends on the telephone she bet Mimi's
face scared little kids. Adele feared cosmetic surgery herself but
felt it was inevitable if she was to hold her man. She told me
all her secrets. We lay on the bed piled with the magazines
she leafed through, looking at the pictures and ads. She wore
a silk gown (pink) and clasped me between her mountainous
breasts. She suspected that Chad had a mistress in Asia, probably more than one. He had kinky tastes in sex that she put up
with but didn't like. She liked the looks of the man who
cleaned the swimming pool, but thought one of the gardeners
was even hunkier. She wondered if her hair needed highlights.
She had put on a pound and a half, and would Chad notice? I
heard dozens of these confidences. Scores. The heat from her
voluptuous body was arousing despite everything on my mind.
Once she flung me from her. "Filthy thing." That must have
been when she decided to neuter me.

"Where's he going now?" Mimi said.

"I le goes off on his own a lot. I think he's still looking for
a way out."

There was a way out, but it lay past the striped house cat
named Matty. Corpulent and sinister, she dozed on her fat
belly by the hot-water heater in the passageway back of the
kitchen. She came and went by the cat door. But every time I
hoped to escape through it, she was there.

"Go away or I'll claw and bite you," Matty hissed. She
weighed twice what I did, and her teeth were big enough to do
serious damage. I was an interloper who threatened her cushy
position in the household. I had felt her jealous eyes on me

when Adele carried me around the house. "You're an ugly thing," she spat.

I had retreated a safe distance and yapped at her until Adele came and got me. "Ba-a-d! This is Matty's place. You stay away from her."

I trotted in my perky way now down the long hall spaced every few yards with tables that towered overhead with lamps and cut flowers. I passed through rooms with heavy leather furniture, gun cases, and antlered heads. I wondered if his victims had sensed Warner before he squeezed off the shot that brought them down. Some rifles had telescopes, so maybe they never knew what hit them. Not a bad way to go. I was having a lot of gloomy thoughts like that. Photographs on the wall showed him standing with a foot planted on their bodies, a big man with cold eyes. The clubs Bogey belonged to before he was drummed out were full of that type. We understood that the world was a jungle and only the fittest got to join clubs like ours. The fittest didn't have any problem with cutting legal corners, so the indictment had not taken away any of the wary respect they had for Bogey. But the conviction did. I got dumped in the loser category and was crossed off lists. My old mates wanted Soderberg elected president, so that changed overnight when it looked like we were tight. They assumed Soderberg's denials about my role in the campaign were part of the game plan to fool the suckers. I had received feelers from my old clubs asking whether I wanted to be a member again. The Hazelwood Country Club said it was willing to suspend the clause in its charter forbidding membership to felons. I could even have my old locker back. I wrote back to tell them where they could stick the locker.

A fat cook with a droopy mustache sat on a stool in the kitchen in his starched whites. He peeled potatoes as he watched CNN. The political analyst was talking to the anchorman.

Anchorman: "Well, Barry, the polls show Bernard Soderberg's candidacy is perking up again."

Analyst: "That's thanks to how the Republicans and Democrats are cat-fighting, Charles. They feel they have to weaken each other before they turn on Soderberg. He's making hay in the meantime."

Anchorman: "It helps that those TV spots that the ailing tycoon W. B. Ingersol was bankrolling have stopped."

Analyst: "The latest word is he remains in a coma. It's a sad relapse for him, but you're right, Charles. A definite plus for Soderberg. He's buying up every minute of that time for his own spots and they're paying off big time." The cook changed the channel and sneered at a celebrity chef dicing vegetables. "Like a big shot like that's gonna do his own chopping. Ri-i-ght."

So my human form was back in slumberland. That figured. I continued through the kitchen to the back where Matty was. One of these days she would be outdoors or scratching in the cat box and I could bust out. But not this time either. She stopped purring when she saw me. "Come closer and I'll chew the ears off your head." I backed off.

That night Chad Warner came back from his Asian factories and mistresses. We heard tires crunch outside, and then he walked through the doorway, scowling. Adele jumped up from a chair and simpered. "Hello, darling, where'd you come from?" Warner gazed around challengingly, as if he expected to find a man. He had thick, dark hair low on his forehead and a suspicious face. "What's that?" he demanded when he caught sight of me.

"My new doggie. Isn't he cute?"

"That's not a dog."

"Yes it is, sweetheart."

"Hell, he belongs in a cage with an exercise wheel."

"This is such a surprise. I didn't expect you until next week. How long will you be home?"

"Not long. I'm hungry. Let's go out to eat."

She hurried off to dress. He picked me up and held me at arm's length. His upper lip lifted in a sneer, showing big, square teeth. "What a pitiful excuse for a dog." I wagged my tail. He set me down roughly. "You're going to the pound tomorrow, pal." When Adele was dressed, she followed him out the door, running to keep up.

I scampered to the kitchen, where the cook watched out the window as their car left. "What am I supposed to do with this dinner?" he said with disgust. When he turned around, I sat up and begged. It's harder than it looks. "Well, why not? It's gonna go to waste anyhow. Better let it cool." He took a fat bratwurst from a saucepan—I saw why Adele had to watch her weight—and put it in my food dish. He opened a beer for himself and turned the TV on.

When the bratwurst cooled enough, I dragged it behind me to the passage where Matty sat in a purring trance, eyes nearly closed.

"That's mine," she hissed, instantly alert.

"Be my guest." I dropped the sausage.

Matty had a choice of hooking me with a claw as I skittered past or going for the sausage. Greed ruled, and she lumbered for the meal as I shot to freedom. A symphony of outdoor smells greeted my wet nose, but I didn't have time to enjoy them. I knew from watching out from the windowseat when delivery vans came that the rolling gate was on a timer and would shut any second. A clunk and whirring sound and it started to move. I just did manage to squeeze out before it closed on me like a jaw. I turned right and headed for El Camino Real, the main thoroughfare down the peninsula. I guessed Palo Alto was ten or twelve miles away. With my tiny limbs that was like a hundred miles.

When you are a Chihuahua, everything qualifies as a potential threat. Cars, small boys, stray toms, raccoons and skunks, owls on silent wings at night, you name it, all are menaces. I trotted until exhaustion overcame me and then holed up under some stairs. The slap of the morning paper woke me, and I continued on to El Camino. I was famished by then and begged outside a doughnut shop ("Isn't he cute?" a woman said) until somebody tossed me one with sprinkles. I wolfed that down and continued south. Crossing each side street was an adventure. Small as I was, drivers couldn't see me very well. I tried to time my tottery gallops across for when traffic lightened, but still I had several narrow escapes. It seemed just a matter of time before I was roadkill.

I got a brilliant idea when I saw a tramp with a prophet's beard pushing a shopping cart heaped high with his stuff. Why walk if you can ride? His face creased in a smile with several teeth missing when I capered up. I made a show of running after my tail and then walked on my hind legs. "Why, where'd you come from, pardner?" He lifted me to the top of the heap on his cart and we set off. His name was Emil, and he wore three layers of clothes and an army fatigue jacket. The cuffs of his raggedy jeans hung over mismatched running shoes. His hair was dirty and tangled, and it was possible he had bathed within the past year, though I wouldn't bet on it. Dogs like powerful odors, so it was more interesting than offensive.

Garbage bags hung like saddlebags on either side of the shopping cart filled with bottles and aluminum cans. He talked to himself nonstop in a speedy, jerky voice. "Wonder if that trash can ahead's got something for Emil. What's that fella in that fancy car lookin' at? Maybe I'll eat them raisins in a while. Wonder what I should call the dog. Bet he ran away from somewhere. Mack's got a pit bull mean as the devil. This one'd be just a biteful for him. Better tell Mack st-a-ay a-a-way. This is San Mateo, I believe. Maybe I'll spend the night in the storm drain less'n there's somebody there. Well, here I am at the trash can. Guess I'll look." His commentary parched him, and he stopped to pull at a water bottle every few blocks. When it was empty, he refilled it at gas stations. He urinated behind buildings. "Man told me to piss somewhere's else. He yelled mean-like at Emil. Like where'm supposed to go?"

He was tall and had wide, bony shoulders like a scarecrow. His big hands looked like they belonged to someone competent with tools. I began to get some idea of his background over the next few days as he jabbered away nonstop. When he was a kid, "bad people" had hurt him. He remembered his mother and talked to her from time to time. "You there, Momma?" he turned his head looking for her. He had spent time in mental hospitals but was thrown out on the streets when they were closed. There were bad people on the streets, and he tried to avoid them. He was a gentle guy who should have been on medication. Every now and then, some biochemical jolt brought back a flicker of sanity. "What am I doing here?" he would ask in a normal voice. "What happened to me?"

He parked the shopping cart outside the entrance of a day-old bread outlet and came out with Ding Dongs and frosted cupcakes. All that sugar had to be bad for him. The people in the store had given him some cardboard. He threw away the sign on the front of the shopping cart that said "Help a Vetnam Vetren." With a Magic Marker he slowly wrote "Sparki and me Is Hugry."

"Sparky's you. Emil and Sparky's partners now." His smile was beatific. He gave me a whole Ding Dong for myself. "Eat that down and get strong." I paid for it later and I grazed on grass and weeds to unblock the plumbing. "Sparky's like a cow," Emil said with a laugh.

We panhandled outside supermarkets. I did the walking-on-hind-legs trick and sat up to beg. Emil was surprised how well we did. Coins rained into the can until we were ordered to move on. "That's all you, Sparky," he said when he counted it up. "Emil never got this much from people." I felt a warm gush of pride and happiness. That night I got thinking what a bad sign that was. I was sinking ever deeper into doghood. I would be licking his hand next. I threw my head back and howled.

"Why's Sparky howlin'?" Emil asked. "Sounds like your heart's broke." We were camped in a culvert near the freeway with half a dozen other bums, each with his own shopping cart. One prosperous individual had two. Traffic whooshed above us.

"Shut that dog up," a surly voice said.

Emil picked me up and held me protectively. His breath was a powerful blend of junk food, Tokay, and the chewing tobacco that blackened what teeth he had left. "Emil says you shut up," he fired back.

Peacemakers restored calm, and after a while they all fell into drunken, snorting sleep. Emil had made a tent by stretching a tarp over the shopping cart, and I stood looking out from the foot. Cold stars were scattered across the black sky. What had Zalzathar done to Tyre? The powers of the greatest wizard were inferior to those of the least angel. Helither had assured Bogey of this in the other world.

I had kept the thought buried because I had enough terror to deal with, but now I had to consider it. Was Lucifer himself in the mix now? Tyre wouldn't have a chance against that famed schemer. That would be like matching a bantamweight against a heavyweight. I stifled a whimper. As slowly as Emil traveled and despite all the stops to scrounge for bottles and cans, Alex's home was not far now. It was time to leave him.

I trotted from the camp into the night and made it nearly to her neighborhood before dawn broke and people let dogs out for morning runs. I had to find a hiding spot from them. I crept under a hedge too thick for bigger dogs to penetrate. I gave a persistent, blue tick hound a nip on the nose when he tried to wiggle through to where I was holed up. He backed out with a yelp and was gone. At midmorning I scratched at Alex's front door.

"Well, look who's here." Alex bent down from her impossible height and scooped me into her arms as I yapped shrilly. "Where'd you come from?" She stood, and it was like taking an express elevator ride.

She wore a chic warm-up outfit from a shoe company—so much human memory had seeped away that I could not put a name to its famous logo—and her hair was pinned back. I caught the smell of papery flower bulbs on her hands and the soil she had been planting them in. Alex studied me, her eyes amused and sympathetic. "Are you lost, little doggie?" I moaned and wriggled. "I bet you're hungry and thirsty." Lapdogs bring out the maternal feeling in women. We are small and needy, like babies. I played it to the hilt, looking at her with beseeching eyes. She carried me inside. Bread was baking, and its aroma filled the house. Morning light flooded through her windows. The calm and order of her tasteful home could not have been a greater contrast to the hobo jungle. The telephone rang as she stroked my laid-back ears. She carried me to a desk where books were open.

"Hello? Oh, hi. Guess what? I heard scratching at the door just now and when I opened it, there was the cutest little dog wanting in. I'm holding him right now." A voice spoke on the other end. "No," Alex replied, "There's no collar or license." She sat in a chair, and I gazed up at her face from her lap. The caller asked a question. "Chihuahua. My aunt used to have one. It must be a neighbor's. He has the deepest eyes. They're almost human."

She talked for a while—I assumed it was a Stanford colleague, from what Alex said on her end—and then said she had to go. She carried me into the kitchen and gave me water in a bowl. I lapped thirstily. She cut up a leftover chicken breast and put it on a plate. I finished that off in a hurry. Dogs do not tarry over food, so subtle flavors are wasted on them. Food is coal to stoke the furnace and is put away as fast as possible. Pause to savor and another dog might snatch it from under your nose. This is canine wisdom handed down who knows how many generations. When Alex walked back into the living room, I trotted after her as smartly as a *magna cum laude* grad of obedience school.

"I'll take you around the neighborhood a little later and see where you belong," Alex said. She sat back at her desk and put on glasses. She was soon lost in her work. A yellow legal pad lay on the floor by her feet with a pencil nearby. Picking it up with my teeth and turning my head, I was just able to make point touch paper. I dragged it up and down, sideways and back. It would not win any penmanship awards, but it was clear enough.

ME.

Alex looked at her watch and picked up the phone. she dialed a number and waited for an answer. "Hello, it's Dr. Epperly. Is this Angelica? Hi. How's our patient this morning? Any change at all?" She asked several questions and listened intently to the answers. She did not like what she was hearing. It dawned that she was talking to a nurse about me. She put the phone down and looked off in space, a sad look on her face. I barked and spun about like a fool on the yellow pad. When she looked down, I withdrew so she could see the word.

"You wrote 'me'," Alex said with astonishment. "What a cute trick. That must've been hard to teach."

I shook my head and growled. I picked up the pencil with my teeth again and dragged it over the pad. The curves of the letter B were hardest, with G a close second.

BOGIE.

Alex gasped. "Oh, my God!" Then the rational left brain rebelled. "No, it can't be." I wondered if I would have to write out my Social Security number on the pad to convince her. A knock came at the front door. I cringed and looked around wildly. But before I could move, Alex picked me up and walked to the door.

The man there had sandy hair and smile lines in a rugged face weathered by sun and rain. He wore jeans and a woolen shirt. His hands were in his pockets. It was Helither, the angel from the other world.

"There he is," he said in a gentle, friendly voice.

"Is he yours?" Alex asked. "How did you teach him those tricks?" she asked desperately.

Helither chuckled, and the lines in his face deepened. "No, he's not mine." He moved his hand, and Alex was holding a naked man. Me. She jumped back, fists to her mouth in fright. Helither moved his hand again, and I stood in what looked like a cassock. Alex swayed, and I just did manage to get my arms around her before she sank to the floor.

21

I carried her to a sofa and laid her down gently. "She's fainted," I said. I thought it only happened in Victorian novels. The coarse cassock rasped against my bare skin. A hair shirt would not be much worse.

"She'll be all right," Helither said.

I looked at him. "You haven't changed." He still reminded me of someone who worked outside, a farmer or landscape gardener. He had a crinkly pattern of lines around his eyes that said he smiled a lot.

"Only God can change us. What about you?" He gave me the slow smile I remembered from before. "Did I get all the pieces back together right?"

I felt my various parts. They seemed okay. I looked into a mirror on the wall. Same story there. I half expected a tonsure to go with the cassock. I was not all that surprised to see him. I somehow knew he would show up when things looked about as bad as they could.

"Zalzathar's been at work, I see," Helither said.

"He's called Dark here. It shows real imagination, right? He's close to a man with a chance to be elected president." I didn't know how much he knew about this time and place. Judging from the cassock, not much. "That's what we call the leader of the country."

Helither was impressed. "Fast work."

"It makes me think he's been getting help."

"From the Father of Lies?" Helither wasn't what you would call handsome, but he had a radiance. "That's a perfect name you have for him here. Shaitan, Eblis, Apollyon, Ahriman, Angra Mainyu, Clootie. Many are your names for him. A good sign. It shows you think a lot about him. That's how to avoid Lucifer's snares. His prey is the unvigilant."

"I've got news for you. I never heard those names you said, except Lucifer." I gave him a cool look. "And nobody thinks about the Devil, as far as I can tell. He went out of style long ago, like Studebakers and Lifebuoy. It couldn't be more different than where you come from, where all people do is think about good and evil."

His smile faded. "Then his power here must be great indeed."

"It'll be a lot greater if Soderberg's elected. There was an angel who was trying to help me, but he's AWOL."

"He isn't the first to be fooled by Satan. Many were duped by his promise in the beginning. Others fall victim from time to time. She's coming around."

I knelt beside Alex and rubbed her hand. Her long lashes fluttered open. "What happened?"

"You fainted."

"You were a dog. I was holding you."

"I tried to tell you but you wouldn't believe me."

She attempted to sit up but lay back again. "Dizzy."

"I know what you're going through. Nobody had more trouble with it than me."

"Where's that man who was at the door?"

Helither stepped forward. "Here."

"So it's all true, everything he said." Her eyes were huge.

"I know how hard it must be for you."

"You're an angel?" Her voice was small and shy.

Helither nodded, smiling. No one seeing him would doubt

it. His radiance seemed to brighten, and the outline of his body got fuzzy. It was easy to see how painters got their idea of halos. A pleasant warmth came from him as well. "Will you help us?" he asked.

She nodded slowly. "I'll do whatever I can." Alex looked at me. "All those things that happened, I began to think they were connected. And then when you fell back into your coma sitting in a chair, for no reason that anyone could see—"

The telephone rang. Helither looked at it with curiosity. I took it to Alex. "Hello?" She listened for a moment. "I'm sure he'll turn up." She hung up and turned to me. "The nurse left the room for a few seconds. When she came back, you were gone. A little dog was on your bed, barking. A Chihuahua."

"The doctors will think I'm running down the street in a hospital gown with my butt hanging out." I explained hospital gowns to Helither. He smiled politely. "I expected you'd show up at some point," I continued. "I just hope you're not too late."

"When the angel you knew as Tyre went over to the Deceiver's side, it was felt my past experience with you and Zalzathar would be useful."

"I'm worried that Satan himself is involved now."

"There appears little doubt." When the battle for Gowyith was at its height, Helither fought hand to hand with the Devil. Up to that point, I had figured he would be no match for Beelzebub. It was a close battle, as I later learned, and I guess only God could say who won. I realized long afterward when I did research on the subject that Helither was not just an ordinary angel, but an archangel.

Alex drove us to Millwood. She kept stealing peeks at Helither in the rearview mirror as he looked around, taking everything in. Ox-drawn carts swaying down rutted tracks were as high tech as it got back in the other world. The freeway, the cars, and all the buildings we passed had to be mind-blowing. Or would have been if he were human. "It must be hard to remember God when you are surrounded by so many glories that cry out the genius of man," he mused.

"Don't forget women," Alex said with a smile.

"In many ways," he answered seriously, "the greatest of His creations."

"If you think what you see from the car is something, wait'll you get a load of cloning and the biotech industry," I said. "We're really cooking in those areas." Bogey had been an early investor. "Who needs God?" he had told *Time*.

"And yet," Helither continued, not seeming to hear me, "every good achievement gratifies God. He wants you to succeed and be happy."

"So why is there evil?" Alex said suddenly. Talk about throwing the high, hard one when someone has just stepped into the batter's box. "Everybody wonders at some point in their life." We were on Highway 280, nearing the turnoff to Portola Valley.

"God's mind is unknowable, even to an angel. Do you want my opinion?"

"Sure."

"If there was no evil, what merit would there be in goodness?"

"I see," Alex said. She was not impressed, and who could blame her? A neat bit of logic is thin comfort for the victims of the latest massacre, to give just one example. TV shows bulldozers pushing them into mass graves. Somebody else chose the path of evil, but they are the ones who got it in the back of the neck. Or to choose another example, the tornado that drops the roof on people in a church, praying. There is at least one of those stories every year. What's that all about?

Helither said, "It's easy for us to see now, but what generosity it required of a Being of perfect goodness to conceive of its absolute opposite and decide that the greatest gift to humans would be autonomy and the freedom to choose."

"Maybe I'm just being a mom, but I'm thinking of all the hate in the world. As a psychiatrist, I see what it does to people."

"But there must also be a lot of kindness."

"Yes, but more wouldn't hurt."

I stayed out of it. In the other world, Bogey had told Helither he thought the kind of freedom he praised so highly was overrated. The chance of screwing up was too great, given how much rode on the outcome. If it wasn't easy to go wrong, so many people wouldn't be doing it. How many got the chance to clean up their act that I did? Despite my philanthropy, there was no undoing the harm Bogey had done. Newspapers had stories about the aftermath of his takeovers. One photograph showed a middle-class family that one of Bogey's downsizings had thrown into destitution. They were living in a car about to be repossessed. The desperation in their faces had given even Bogey a pang. Then he remembered those were the breaks of the game. He didn't make the rules, goddamnit. Life had its winners and losers. Why hadn't they saved for a rainy day? Doyle had been looking for that family, but nothing I gave them now would make up for what they had gone through. And then there were all the thousands of other families I didn't know about. They had just been ciphers, numbers in a column.

The guards at the gates of Millwood were dumbfounded to see me in the car alongside Alex. Not only was I out of the coma, I also had somehow managed to get beyond the tightly guarded perimeter without their knowledge. It would mean a grilling from Doyle when he found out. Alex drove to the steps that led up to the big house. Dogs barked in the kennels down the slope and Alice came out and peered up at us, hand shielding her eyes from the sun. Helither got out, looking toward the coastal mountains.

"That fog," he said quietly. "I don't like it."

It poured over the mountains like a tidal wave over a sea-wall. Usually the fog lingered at the ridgeline, as if making up its mind whether to keep coming. Now it seemed like it was on a timetable. It hid the setting sun and sent long shadows hurrying toward us.

"It seems different," I admitted.

"It's the wizard's work," Helither said after a moment's study. He stood with hands casually in his back pockets, watching the fog. He glanced at me. "They're coming after you."

"Who is?" Alex asked in a scared voice.

"Zalzathar and all the terrible creatures he brought from my world." He gave her a gentle look. "This will be no place for a nice person like you."

"What's going to happen?" she asked.

Helither looked back at the fog. "Zalzathar has lost patience. Bigger game's afoot, and he wants to finish with our friend here once and for all. What hatred he feels for you, Bogey."

"Tell me about it."

"You asked me to help you," Alex said. "I'm not going to run away now."

"A great testing approaches." Helither looked grim. "When I asked you to help, that's not what I had in mind."

"Can we call the police?"

Helither shook his head.

A great testing. He was not one for exaggeration. I had the hollowed-out feeling fear brings. As many times as I had felt it, you would think I would be used to it. "Is it necessary that I be here," I asked. "I mean absolutely necessary? I've been through enough." That was the old Bogey again, and I sensed Alex's surprise. I didn't look at her. One minute at my desk in the middle of Manhattan, humming capital of world commerce. An eye blink later, a dog running through an enchanted forest hung with monstrous cobwebs. And I had gone through sheer hell ever since. At a certain point, your dues card ought to be handed back stamped paid in full. "Why can't I hit the road with Alex?" If Helither wanted to stay, that was his business. Alex and I could drive to the airport and wing off in the Gulfstream before that evil fog got to Millwood. One phone call and the engine would be turning over and the plane ready to taxi when we got there.

Helither gave me an easy look. "It would be nice if it were that easy, but they'd just follow wherever you went. Isn't it better to finish it now?"

Easy for him to say. He would survive anything, even defeat. He would go on to the next showdown and the one after that and so on to the end of time, or until Gabriel blew the horn. At that point, maybe the universe collapses back into the unimaginably dense pinpoint of matter it had been before the Big Bang. And what then? Another Big Bang to see if we got it right this time? How many times had it gone on before, and how many more to come? Smart people had been thinking about this forever, and nobody had an answer.

"If you're an angel, we can't lose no matter what's coming," Alex insisted. "Isn't that true?"

He had an apologetic look, as if sorry to let her down. "The deck isn't stacked." An oddly modern way of putting it. "The other side wins sometimes."

"Sometimes?" I scoffed.

"Often," he admitted.

"I thought God was all-powerful," Alex said.

Helither looked at the fog as if taking its measure. "Yes, God is all-powerful."

"And all-knowing."

"Yes, that, too."

"So He knows what's going to happen because He's making it happen?"

Helither looked at her. "My opinion again?"

"Yes."

"In giving you freedom, God put limits on Himself. He chose not to know how things will turn out for you. The big picture remains clear for Him, but the details are yours to decide. In His mercy, however, we are authorized to intercede in the affairs of humans." He looked at me. "I think you better send everyone away. Your guards and the others. They could be hurt. What is that noisy flying machine?"

A helicopter approached looking like it was going to land on the lawn. "It's probably a news chopper," I said. "All the TV stations have them." Alex was still looking at me as if she wondered how much old Bogey was left.

"TV?" Helither asked. They still used town criers and dispatch riders in his world.

"I'll explain later," I said.

The helicopter landed long enough for Doyle's squatty figure to jump down. A wooden chest was thrown off behind him. Head ducked, he hurried toward us, dragging it on wheels. The helicopter lifted off again with a roar and a backwash that flattened the grass.

"Who is he?" Helither asked.

"His name is Doyle. He's my head of security."

Doyle left the chest at the foot of the stairs and climbed them up to where we stood. "Nice robe," he said to me. "You get it from a monk or something?" He nodded to Alex. "Nice to see you again." He gave Helither a curious look.

"What are you doing here?" I asked.

"I could ask you the same question. You're supposed to be dead to the world as doctors scratch their heads in puzzlement."

"As long as you're here, tell your guys to pack up and clear out."

"They should do it quickly," Helither said.

"Make it five minutes," I said.

"Okay, you're the boss. But I'm staying. I got a feeling I'm supposed to be here."

"Something's going to happen, but you can't help," I said.

"Where did your feeling come from?" Helither asked. He was smiling at Doyle.

"A dream," he said with embarrassment. "You were in trouble," he said to me, "and needed my help. Bad things were about to happen, and just then I woke up. I go with hunches, so I came running."

"He can stay," Helither said simply. "He's meant to be here with us."

I went inside to put something on that didn't flap against bare calves while Doyle got rid of the guards. Alex stood with her back turned while I dressed in moccasins, chinos, and sweatshirt. Whatever came, at least I'd be comfortable. "You still have time to change your mind," I said. We heard the security team driving off in their vans.

"So do you."

"He's right. Zalzathar would just keep after me until he found me. If Soderberg's elected, it would be all that much easier, with the FBI working for him."

"Maybe I'm meant to be here, too. I wonder if I should call my children." She thought a minute. "No," she said decisively, "it would just worry them."

I went back outside and helped Doyle drag the heavy trunk up the stairs. The domestic staff left in a holiday mood, happy for the time off. Helither was still watching the fog.

"What's in here?" I asked Doyle.

"Armament."

"That won't do us any good."

"You don't know what I've got. Assault weapons, grenade launchers, automatics, a shotgun, even my Javanese throwing knives. I'm loaded for bear, man. You're waiting for the same guys who were chasing us on the East Coast, right? I'm betting they're contract killers. Correct?"

"More like foreign terrorists," I said dryly.

"His weapons might be helpful," Helither said thoughtfully.

"How's that possible?" I asked.

"Hello," Doyle said. "Earth to Bogey. Guns and bullets and bombs that go boom-boom make bad boys go away chop-chop."

I ignored him for Helither's answer. "The wizard's powers have been strengthened. That fog tells me so."

"Wizard's the code name?" Doyle interrupted. "We know who's running them from behind that handle?"

"I'm uncertain what my powers are in this world," Helither continued. "It might be that ours nullify each other a little or a lot, all the time or some of the time. In that case, the physical laws here are in force."

Doyle looked from Helither to me. "What are you guys talking about? Powers? You talking about legal powers? Are you a cop? Federal?"

"Leave your trunk behind," I said. "There are cars in the garage and keys on the board just after you walk in. Take your pick. Come back when it's all over. That's an order."

"Look, you know what would happen to my business if I did that? Doyle walks away when the situation heats up, that's the word that would get around. I'd be back doing plant security in bad neighborhoods. I've got elite clients who expect elite service. What's he doing?"

Helither held one arm out straight and his other hand up like a traffic cop. The far-off fogbank suddenly shot higher, as if it had hit a glass wall and the weight of the mass pushing from behind left nowhere to go but up. Then Helither's hand began to shake from the opposing pressure. He dropped it suddenly, and the fog came toward us again. "Very much stronger" he said, half to himself.

Alex let out a deep breath she had been holding, but I doubted Doyle saw any connection between Helither and the fogbank. It was too far away, for one thing. He must have thought Helither was doing some martial arts toning exercise. "Anyhow," Doyle said, "that dream gave me the same feeling I had that time I was driving and the bad guys chased us. Remember how I knew every turn to take even though I'd never been in that area before?"

"I remember," Alex said.

"It was the same deal as then. Maybe I'm getting psychic in my old age." He dragged the trunk inside.

"Are you going to tell him?" Alex asked.

"You tell him. You know the story."

"I'll tell him that . . . " She got a mixed-up expression.

It was wrong of me to smile. I did it anyhow. "See what I've had to put up with?"

"He'd think I was crazy."

"He'd think we were all nuts. He'd hole up in the house with those guns and tell us to come and get him."

"What are contract killers?" Helither asked. He was probably visualizing some monster with teeth and claws.

"Paid assassins," I said. "They're so common these days you can get them cheap."

His eyes went back to the fogbank. "It will be a long night."

We went inside, and Alex fixed omelettes. I telephoned Alice at the kennels. "Take the rest of the day off."

"What about the dogs?"

"Let them run loose. I'll put them away later."

"Is there anything wrong?"

"Not a thing." I hung up and sat down at a table in the kitchen with Doyle. He smiled as Alex heaped his plate. "Now, there's a lady knows how to make an omelette. Cheese and green peppers and all the other good stuff."

Alex sat down, and we ate. "What about the other guy, Helither? Isn't he going to eat?" Doyle asked.

"He doesn't have much of an appetite," I said.

Doyle chowed down. "So you figure whatever's going to happen will be tonight?"

"It looks that way."

"Did you get a tip from Bernaise?" Elizabeth Bernaise, our mole in Soderberg's campaign. I had all but forgotten about her. I didn't reply, and Doyle nodded knowingly. "I knew she'd be worth it."

He finished what was on his plate and mopped it with bread. "We let them take the first shot. We're just defending ourselves after that point. It doesn't really matter, though. They'll drop all kinds of shell casings out there, and nobody'll be able to say who fired first. They're intruders anyhow, illegal trespassers. Self-defense. It won't take long for the cops to get here once the fireworks start. They'll take care of whatever's left." He paused, as if a thought had occurred to him. "You know how to use a weapon?" he asked Alex.

"I've gone duck hunting. That was years ago. I didn't mind clay pigeons, but I didn't like shooting at real ones."

"So you know how to use a shotgun?"

"Yes."

"Great. How about the other guy?"

"He's not much for guns," I said.

"We can use him as a spotter. Set him up in a window on one side of this big place and have him shout if he sees something."

"It'll be too foggy to see anything," I said.

"I don't see any fog."

"You will."

It reached Millwood forty-five minutes later, thick as cotton

wool and freezing cold. It deadened noise, soaking up sound.
I called the dogs into the house. It sounded like I was yelling
into a small closet. Their breath hung in the air as they loped
up. They crowded in and set out to investigate every nook and
cranny. There must have been fifty dogs. I hoped all were
housebroken.

"Damn it all," Doyle called from the top of the stairs, "you
ought to keep those dogs outside so they can't sneak up." He
wore a strange getup like a leather overcoat. Guns and ammo
belts hung from loops. It had to weigh a ton.

"They'll be worth more to us inside," I said. I didn't like
the thought of them outside. Millwood might not be much
protection compared to the walls of Gowyith, but being inside
was better than nothing.

Doyle, Alex, and I were at windows on different sides of the
house when darkness fell. We each had a flashlight. Helither
drifted around the house in his relaxed way, a knot of tail-
wagging dogs at his heels. His air of quiet confidence had
bucked up weary defenders at Gowyith and had the same effect
with us. But as soon as he glided off again in his soundless way,
my jumpiness came back. I stood with the Glock automatic in
my hand at the window of the Victorian bedroom, which had
a good view of the grounds. All I saw was impenetrable fog.
When the moon rose, shapes seemed to move in it, but they
could have been eddies from a breeze that picked up and then
died away. I felt the piercing cold on the other side of the
window. I wondered if it would kill my winter vegetables. The
hours dragged past.

Then the lights of Millwood dimmed, as if a brownout was
draining the power. The telephone on the nightstand next to
the bed rang. It was Alex. "Do you smell that terrible smell?"
Just then, Doyle let fly with a burst of semiautomatic fire. Her
receiver clattered down. A few seconds later, her shotgun
boomed once and then again. Still nothing visible from my

window. The dogs made a huge racket throughout the house. Then they fell silent, as if on command.

"What the hell's going on?" My father stood at the door, slit-eyed and pink-faced with anger. He'd had only one other expression, a sour, knowing smile when mankind lived down to his expectations. He was in his golfing duds, including the lucky maroon shirt worn when he'd made a hole in one. "What place is this?" he demanded. I raised the Glock and shot him in the chest. He slumped into something as dark and glistening as a huge slug. Saliva-like fluid pumped from its fat body as it slid back out the door with a sucking sound. I followed it to the hall outside and put in a couple more rounds. I recognized it from the other world. It was a swamp creature with a name that sounds like someone hawking phlegm. Zalzathar liked them because they were plastic enough to mimic whatever he wanted them to. When they got close enough, they enveloped prey before it could dodge clear. He must have counted on me gaping open-mouthed as pater approached, fatally paralyzed by the taboo against parricide.

The shotgun boomed again, and I ran across the house to where Alex was. She stood at the open window of the room called the Captain's Quarters. Its nautical decor featured hardwood floors, hooked rugs, and polished brass. There was even a binnacle and a ship's wheel. She looked over her shoulder at me. "There are pigs out there, only they're standing up." I reached her side. The room smelled like naval broadsides had been fired.

"How can you see anything?" I asked. Not that you needed to with that smell telling you something foul was out there. It even cut through the cordite.

"A light picks them up. It cuts right through the fog." A beam suddenly stabbed down from the roof to show a Pig Face slinking toward the house. Alex winged it with a blast, and it squealed and limped out of the light. As she ejected the spent shell, the beam went out.

"Is there a spotlight on your roof?" Alex asked. "This is like shooting fish in a barrel."

"It must be Helither." We heard more semiautomatic fire, from Doyle. The noise was blotted up by the fog. It would not be heard even as far as the front gate. He fired long bursts, the *pop-pop-popping* changing voices like soloists in a choir as he switched guns. He was a one-man weapons company. Then silence again.

The power went out.

"I'm scared of the dark," Alex whispered.

"You're a psychiatrist."

"I don't care."

"They're in the house," I said.

"Oh, God, how do you know?"

"I shot one a minute ago. Not a Pig Face, something else. They can change shapes. This one looked like my father. If you see something that looks like your late husband, drill it. Same with your kids."

She was silent a moment. "I won't shoot at anything that looks like my children." Her flat voice told me to skip the arguments. The yammering of the dogs downstairs said something was cornered.

"I'll go look," I said. "Lock the door behind me."

My flashlight beam picked out a cyclonic whirl of leaping and flying bodies in the billiard room. Four Pig Faces were defending themselves. The dogs leaped snarling and were tossed aside like rag dolls. But there were too many to kill. The creatures were barely able to fling one aside before two more were on them. A brave little Boston bull terrier had sunk his teeth into the purple backside of one Pig Face and hung on. When it had a free hand, the Pig Face tried to swipe him off, but it was going to take undivided attention to free itself from that terrier. The snarls and yelps, squeals and grunts were deafening. Furniture was knocked over and lamps broken. The place stunk like a Porta Potti at a weekend rock concert. Some gland that went into action when they fought made the Pig Faces smell even worse than usual. I rested the flashlight on the billiard table. I was apart from the fighting but close enough so no great feat of marksmanship was required, even with my shaking hands. Four carefully aimed shots and four Pig Eyes were down and kicking under the pack of dogs. They didn't struggle long. The Boston bull let loose and bristled with indignation. He looked like he felt the others were taking credit for his work.

Doyle resumed firing upstairs in the far wing, and Alex's shotgun boomed overhead. It was like Fort Apache. Through a window, I saw one of Helither's beams cut through the fog as Alex fired another blast. Given her accuracy and Doyle's, it must look like Custer's Last Stand out there.

I moved from the billiard room toward the ballroom. As I passed through its space, the flashlight made it seem as if the mounted heads on the walls followed me with their glass eyes. In a study where gentlemen had withdrawn during the Grover Cleveland administration for brandy and cigars, a shadow stood by a window. It turned in surprise but did not move as I came close.

It was the incubus who was always trying to kick me when I was a dog in the other world. Unless Zalzathar had brought another with him, this was the one who had made Carlotta his sex slave. As was typical, he was standing on the sidelines while others did the fighting. Despite their mutual animosity, Bogey had admired his talent for this.

"Who are you?" he asked. An elegant hand was raised against the flashlight's beam. An incubus is always handsome and well turned out. In this case, a dark suit and open-necked shirt with a gold chain. Dark hair pomaded and combed straight back. Sensual lips now stretched back in a false smile that showed even, white teeth.

"Shouldn't I ask you that?"

"I'm here for the woman." His voice was low and intimate, a perfect instrument for seduction. I wondered if he thought I was a fellow demon he had not met. "I've heard a lot of fighting. Zalzathar said it would be easy. The light is in my eyes."

"Where is Zalzathar?"

"I wish I knew." The incubus seemed fretful. "He said it would be easy."

"Things are going fine," I said.

"Oh, do you really think so? Those loud noises worry me."

"Everything's going as planned."

"What is the plan? Nobody's told me anything." He sounded sulky. "Zalzathar is in one of his high-and-mighty moods. Revenge is fine, but don't you think he's gone overboard? If things are so promising here, why not leave revenge until later? That big dog can wait."

"He's not a dog anymore," I said.

"Nobody tells me anything. If I didn't eavesdrop, I would know even less. I can't see what you look like with that light in my eye." I kept the beam in his face.

"He's a human now," I said.

"Whether dog or human, I wouldn't want to be in his shoes when he's in Zalzathar's hands. I hope it isn't long now. He said he would be easy." He shot his cuffs and patted his hair. "Do you know anything about the woman?"

"She's a nice woman."

"Nice?" He was surprised. "Did you say *nice*?"

"Yes."

"What did you say you do for Zalzathar?" There was uncertainty in his voice.

"What happened to Carlotta?"

"Dead. Weren't you told?"

"Was it you?"

"Of course. Zalzathar promised."

"I'm not surprised you don't recognize me."

"There are so many of us." Another insincere smile.

"I was a dog before."

A long silence. "You're him?"

"Yes."

The illusion dissolved into true demon's form, scaly and lizzardlike. A forked tongue flickered. Its eyes were a lacquered black. It hissed as I shot between those reptilian eyes. It sank to the floor with a sound like air escaping from a tire. I was aware of a sudden silence.

Footsteps approached. Helither was with Alex.

"We must go." His voice was calm, but it was obvious things had taken a bad turn.

"Where's Doyle?" I asked.

"In a better place," Helither said. "His heroism earned him that."

22

Helither's angelic radiance had enough candlepower to light the way as we hurried through Millwood's large rooms. The dogs fell in silently around us, bristling. We went through the passage to the big garage. I snatched the first set of keys my hands found on the board and we got in the Jaguar. The leather seats were as cold as graveyard marble. "I don't think there's enough juice to open the garage door," I said. Helither pointed, and the door rose. The car lights were almost useless in the fog. I kept a feather touch on the accelerator, navigating the drive mostly by memory. The windshield wipers swept back and forth hypnotically. After a few minutes, the dogs peeled off into the fog.

"It's so cold," Alex said with a shiver.

"It'll take a while for the heater to warm up," I said. Helither was in the backseat. I saw in the rearview mirror that he peered intently into the fog.

"We're leaving in time," he said.

The fog was right up against the windshield. Helither's door opened and closed and he walked alongside the car on the driver's side. He moved out in front of the Jaguar, the aura seeming to burn off the fog around him.

"What's he afraid of? Why are we leaving?" Alex asked.

"I don't even want to think about it."

We ghosted through the fog like a gleam of consciousness

until we reached the front gate. Helither gestured, and it opened. He beckoned us through. I rolled the window down when we reached him.

"Keep going," he said, looking in the direction we had come. "Don't stop." The dogs rushed out the gate like fans charging from a stadium for their cars. It would be hell for Rita Rutaway and the animal control people tomorrow.

The farther we drove, the more the fog thinned. It was like depression lifting. By the time we reached El Camino Real, the sky was clear. "Those things were hideous," Alex said with a shudder.

"March through the woods with them weeks on end and you'll know what hideous is." I learned what "laying waste" to countryside meant. Pig Faces didn't so much move through land as mug it.

"I'm beginning to see how strong you had to be," Alex said.

"Bogey or me?"

"Both of you. It was just like a fable before. Is Doyle dead? Is that what the angel meant?"

"He must have taken a lot of the bastards with him." At least Doyle didn't leave family behind to grieve. I didn't need more of that guilt.

"Why didn't the police come? There was so much shooting."

"That fog sucked sound up. Nobody heard a thing."

We turned right on El Camino and reached Highway 101. We headed toward San Francisco. It was nearly four, and traffic was light. I turned on the radio. The news said the three candidates for president were getting ready to debate in Los Angeles. The anchor said it was expected to push the great numbers of undecided voters into a decision. "Political analysts are saying any of the three can win at this point." Alex saw me checking the rearview mirror.

"Is someone following us?"

"Not so far. The election's that close?" I was stunned. Soderberg had made good use of my time as a Chihuahua.

"He started doing better as soon as your ads went off the air. Thomas and Harris attacked each other so much, he looked good in comparison."

I used the car phone to reach Clancy at his place in Georgetown. He picked up the receiver on the second ring. "Huh?" I heard a woman complain sleepily in the background.

"Who's running the campaign?" I said.

There was a thunderstruck silence. "Bogey?"

"You heard me, who's running the show in Denver?"

Clancy took a deep breath through his nose to collect his thoughts. "Some guy named Purvis." He was a bright young man Maye had been high on.

"Why'd he take the TV ads off?"

"With you unconscious and out of it, there didn't seem any point in wasting the money."

"Who made the decision?"

"Well, I did," he blustered. "They were declining in effectiveness. The average American had seen each spot six point seven times. They're sick of you and Soderberg walking on the beach. Where are you?"

"San Francisco, but I'm flying to Denver. Meet me there." I hung up. Fifteen minutes later, the Gulfstream was taxiing onto the runway. Alex worried about missing work at Stanford. "I'm giving them a new wing," I said. "I'll write you an excuse."

Once in the air, I had second thoughts. We could change flight plans. Go anywhere we wanted. Once I was out of their hair, maybe they would forget about us. I could buy a resort in the nicest part of the world, and the days and nights would pass pleasantly. I mentioned this to Alex.

"You're not serious," she said. "That's the old Bogey talking."

"I'm just brainstorming possible options."

"That's not one." Her face was hard. Then it softened. "You're just kidding, right?"

"Right."

Purvis had been alerted and waited to pick us up in Denver. "Glad you're feeling better, sir." I introduced him to Alex. She had a blanket around her and the dazed look of someone who had been through the invasion of Iwo Jima. "I must look a fright." She started fooling with her hair.

"You look mighty fine to me, ma'am." Purvis was tall, blond, and clear-eyed. He had just gotten back from two years as a Mormon missionary when Maye hired him.

"Are you in touch with Elizabeth Bernaise?" I asked. I needed the inside view from Soderberg's campaign.

"No, sir. Mr. Maye's orders were to keep contact to a minimum. Soderberg is in L.A. with the other candidates. We assume she's with him."

It was time to pull her out of harm's way. I had enough blood on my hands. "Signal her to meet us here tonight."

"Yes, sir." A van of bodyguards led and another followed as he pulled out of the airport and headed for the city. We rented all the rooms of a motel on the outskirts. The bodyguards took up stations that gave them good lines of fire. Alex and I took separate rooms and slept most of the day. I had fog-haunted dreams. Toward evening, Clancy flew in from Washington.

"You're looking good," he said. Clancy would tell you that on your deathbed. He nodded at Purvis. "Good to see you."

I asked what people were thinking in the capital.

"Thomas and Harris have been punching each other so long they're arm-weary. Soderberg wins if he doesn't make a big mistake in the debate. So what happens now?"

"Let's wait until Ms. Bernaise joins us."

Purvis looked at his watch. "That should be in less than an hour."

"Who's she?" Clancy asked.

"Our mole in the Soderberg campaign."

"Whose idea was that?"

"Maye's."

"The man was a genius, I always said so. Pity how he disappeared into thin air. What do the docs say about your comas? If they're going to come and go, we better have a conservatorship arrangement that kicks in so we don't have to scramble next time."

"I've got a feeling one way or another that was the last one."

Elizabeth Bernaise walked through the door right on time. Her bottle-blond hair was windblown. She wore a pink warm-up suit. "I left everything behind," she said. "I didn't dare walk out with even a briefcase."

"You won't be going back," I said.

She let out a big breath. "I can't tell you how happy that makes me. It's getting so creepy. I'm seeing more and more strange types. They whisper among themselves and clam up if you come close."

"What do you mean, 'strange'?" I asked.

"It's hard to put into words. Weird."

"Soderberg's confident?"

"We—they—think there's a real good shot at winning, depending on the debate. Your former wife's been a real plus. Beauty plus brains."

Purvis had shown me videotapes of the interviews the major networks did with the candidates' wives. Felicity outshone the others. She was poised and utterly charming. She and Soderberg planned to marry in the White House the day he was inaugurated.

"We want to make the White House a family place again," she told the interviewer. She was a half foot taller than Soderberg, but you would not know this because of the way they were photographed. When she was asked about me, a shadow passed over her porcelain features. "It was terrible watching how he deteriorated mentally. I kept the marriage together as long as I could."

"Did she ever take acting lessons?" Clancy asked.

"Born liars don't need them," I answered. Elizabeth laughed too loudly, and I saw the strain in her face. She had earned her money. "What about all that mud we threw?" I asked her.

"He rode out the storm. People expect political scandal these days."

"How are we going to stop him?"

She bit her lower lip. "I've been giving it a lot of thought. I tried it out on Maye before he . . . and he agreed it had possibilities."

"I'm all ears."

"Soderberg is Teflon by now. Everything's been said that can be. Go after someone around him instead. Go after Dark."

"The adviser? What can we say about him?" Clancy asked.

"Make something up. I got a feeling whatever we said would be nothing compared to the truth."

"We can't just make stuff up," Clancy protested.

"Because it wouldn't be right?" I asked.

"Because we'd be found out."

"Not if we do it right. Or, if we were, maybe it would be too late."

"Maybe you don't have any reputation left to lose, but some of us do."

"I don't care what they say about me. I'm getting out of politics," Elizabeth said. "After what I've seen."

"What could we make up?" Clancy asked.

"Let's say he's a child molester," she said with a cool look.

"Where's the evidence?"

"We make that up, too."

"Doyle could swing that," Clancy mused.

"Doyle's not with us anymore," I said.

He gave me a sharp look. "What happened?"

I didn't want to spook Elizabeth. "I'll tell you later. Who's his number two?"

"A guy name of Hirschorn."

"Get him on it. Build me the record of a child molester. Dates, arrests, the rest of it. It's got to look legit." I wasn't exactly in unknown territory here. Bogey had fabricated evidence before to blackmail rivals. The enormity of his lies and the difficulty of denial had left them speechless.

"All right," Clancy said, "it's your funeral."

"It always has been. How do we leak this?" I asked Elizabeth. More lip-biting. "We give it to Harris," she said. "Thomas is too principled. Or too afraid it might backfire."

"Do you think Harris would agree to see me if he needs convincing?"

"Are you kidding? You're poison."

"You know him?" I asked Clancy.

"I've played golf with him a few times. I know his chief of staff, Dave Maynard, better."

"Can you plant it with him?"

Clancy considered. "I could say someone in the FBI passed it on to me to do with whatever I wanted."

"No," Elizabeth said firmly, "you're too identified with Mr. Ingersol. I'll pass it on. I'll say I'm a defector."

"You've already earned your money," I said.

"This is on the house. I don't want Dark pulling strings in the White House. There's something about him . . . " She stopped.

"Something evil?" I suggested.

"Yes," she said with relief. "That's just the word for it."

Clancy snorted. "Evil." He was going to bring up Nixon, but I cut him off. "Okay," I said to Elizabeth. "When can you pass it on to this Maynard guy?"

"I'll see him when everyone gets together in a couple of days to go over the final arrangements for the debate. I'll slip it to him then." She got a determined look on her face and picked up her purse. "If that's the plan, I'd better get back before I'm missed." She returned to L.A. in the Gulfstream.

"The woman's got balls," Clancy said.

That night Alex and I made love for the first time. "It took you a while to get around to that," she said afterward as we nestled in one another's arms. Her body was long and white.

"I was your patient, remember? And you thought I was off my rocker for a long time after that. That cramps a man's style."

"I would still think you were crazy if I hadn't seen what I've seen."

"I thought you didn't say 'crazy.' "

"It's the only word I can think of that does justice to all this."

A few nights before the big debate, we went to a chic French restaurant in Los Angeles. My bodyguards sat at a separate table glowering at the Hollywood crowd that gave the place its cachet. "It's awful having to travel everywhere with them," Alex said. "I'd hate to be famous. Look how people are watching us. Not us, I guess, but you. Isn't that Oliver Stone waving?"

"Bogey loved fame. It's like a drug after a while. You need maintenance doses." A mention in the society column, a story on the business page, a word or two on the business roundup on TV. "He didn't like it nearly so much when it changed to notoriety." The photographers who had been welcomed and given hundred-dollar bills for prints became enemy paparazzi. They were bowled over like ten pins by Bogey's security people. I supposed he was mocking me, but I waved back at Stone.

"You folks enjoying yourselves?" An elegant, smiling man bronzed to perfection by a tanning salon stood beside us. A plate on his tuxedo lapel said Manager. "Anything you need?"

"No, thanks," I said.

"You're a beautiful lady," he told Alex. He pulled out a chair and sat down. "Do you mind? We get a lot of industry people in here, but we don't often see Wall Street big shots." He was as slim as a stiletto and had thick, dark hair combed straight back. Small, neat ears and thick eyebrows with sardonic peaks.

"We were just talking about celebrity," Alex said. "How unpleasant it is."

"I totally disagree. Fame is wonderful." He gave a little laugh. "You might get a few to disagree, the odd misanthrope or religious fanatic who rejects the world. But everyone else welcomes fame. It gives the illusion of mass. That's preferable to the sense of nothingness most people feel." A slight accent, unplaceable.

"Is nothingness what most people feel?" I asked. Bogey would have been on his feet crimson-faced by now, outraged by the insolence. But there was something familiar about this man.

"If they're intelligent," he announced.

Alex gave me an oh-brother look and excused herself to go to the ladies' room.

"A very beautiful woman," he said, watching her go. "Are you fucking her? I would if I were you. Take your pleasures while you may. The time comes when you can't enjoy them anymore. That's when you'll regret every single one you let pass by." His eyes were coal black and seemed to burn. "You know by now that life is as insubstantial as a wisp of smoke. Wave your hand and it's gone. *Poof.*"

I felt the blood drain from my face. We had met once before, in Gowyith.

It was the Prince of Deception himself, Satan.

"I see you know me," he said.

I felt like a snail shriveling on a hot plate. My mouth was too dry to speak. My joints seemed frozen and I could not move.

"First there and now here. You seem to always be in my way, Mr. Ingersol."

Short, blunt fingers drummed on the table. He tilted his

head to one side, his expression amused yet scornful. "Come, come. Cat got your tongue?"

"I don't want any trouble," I got out hoarsely. "I've got no quarrel with you."

"Liar. I don't believe you. All that is necessary for the triumph of evil is for good men to do nothing. A crude proposition, but it has a kernel of truth. Not that you're a good man— there is much I find to admire in you even now. But you're apparently unwilling to just do nothing. Instead, you meddle in what's none of your business."

"None of my business? They've tried to kill me more times than I can count."

"It was all a mistake." He spread his hands and smiled. Rings with large stones glinted on his fingers. "I'm not ashamed to own up to it. I don't claim to be perfect, unlike a certain party. Helither interfered with Zalzathar at the last minute and you got picked instead of another. Because of that, a world was lost to me. So who's the real victim? Yours truly, that's who. But that's history. What's done is done, and nothing can change it. I'm willing to forgive and forget. Well, I'm willing to forget. Because what we have here is a new chance, a golden opportunity. Victory has eluded me by the smallest margin so many times." He held thumb and forefinger nearly touching to show how small. "Hitler's rashness and Stalin's stupidity, just to name two examples." He slapped his forehead. "What pains I went to to prepare the way, only to see one cancel out the other. How often does a chance like that come along? Not often, I can tell you from long and bitter experience. Or take thermonuclear weapons. They should have poisoned the Earth by now. Deserts should burn where cities are and millions of mothers be despairing over the horrible mutants they gave birth to. But not one warhead has been fired in anger. I've been forced to adopt slower methods to achieve the same goal. It's frustrating, enough to make one wonder if the unseen hand of God truly

does guide events. But we know better, don't we? The old Far-
ceur doesn't linger at the scene of the crime. New glories await
Him elsewhere with choirs of brownnosing angels perpetually
singing His praises. No, blind luck explains it much better. Into
each life good and bad fall, like rain. Some people seem to get
all the luck, some can't get a break. You've seen it yourself. It's
completely arbitrary, with no rhyme or reason. Who knows
better than I? I was God's favorite. Well, one of them, anyhow.
And look what happened. Cast from Heaven and reviled ever
since." He had taken out a cigar and now lit it.

"Do you mind?" The broad nasal vowels of a New Yorker
came from the adjoining table. "There's no smoking in restaurants, dummy." She was a middle-aged woman, expensively
dressed and with what looked in that light like a good face-
lift. I guessed she was a hard-bitten studio executive, used to
getting her way. Four depressed men sat at the table. Writers,
probably. She and the Devil locked gazes, neither yielding.
Without warning, he seemed to erupt, swelling horribly. His
clothes split as the body beneath burst through them. He was
the repulsive red demon, befanged and eyes abulge, who pitch-
forked sinners into the flames in Medieval paintings.

"Eeeeeeeee," the woman cried, falling back in her chair. Her
scream was still hanging in the air when Satan was back in his
tuxedo. It had been no more than a split second and no one
had seen the transformation but the woman and me. She began
to sob.

"She's befouled herself," he said. "Look at the disgust of the
men with her. The story'll be in the trades. She won't survive
the humiliation. Shit her pants at Le Cirque. Look, it's all over
the back of her dress. I know her work and she has qualities I
like, but nobody fucks with me."

His snapping eyes returned to me, and I felt my own sphinc-
ter loosen. I willed it tight again. He took a long pull on the
cigar. "Yes, reviled ever since for my so-called rebellion, which

in reality was only an attempt to help the Big Guy, to take some of the load off of His shoulders. An act of charity, totally misconstrued. You heard differently, I suppose. So many damnable lies are put around about me, and I'm the one called the Great Deceiver."

The shattered woman tottered toward the rest room, weeping hysterically. A waitress followed with a towel held to hide her stained hindquarters. The restaurant buzzed.

"Speaking of lies," he continued, "yours have killed us. Soderberg should be up five to ten points in the polls. Instead, it's a dead heat among all three. The man makes a bargain with us and I don't come through on my end. It looks bad."

I was recovered from my first shock, but I wasn't sure what approach to take. Deny everything? He would see through that. I knew from the first time we met in Gowyith that he was razor sharp but a long way from all-knowing. He could guess what you were thinking a lot but couldn't read minds or what was in hearts. I gambled and went on the offensive. "Zalzathar follows me to my world and tries to kill me. I'm supposed to take that lying down?"

"That was my fault," he said smoothly. "He wanted revenge, so I said okay. It's not my style to encourage turning the other cheek. If somebody wants revenge, fine. Who am I to say no to payback? In some parts of the world, it keeps me in business." He kissed his fingers. "People don't even remember why they should hate one another, they just do. Momentum keeps it going from one generation to the next. But I'm prepared to say in your case that I made a mistake in green-lighting Zalzathar. It complicated matters unnecessarily. I didn't need you as an enemy. In fact, I always thought of you as my kind of guy." His smile was brilliant. He was loaded with personality, no doubt about it. He could charm the birds from the trees. "And I still think you are. It's not your nature to weep over the poor and downtrodden. You're an achiever. You made things happen on Wall Street. You were just scratching the surface of your potential."

"I've got to admit life was more interesting before."

"Exactly! Competition is where a man tests his mettle. The blade is sharpened against the whetstone. Imposing one's will on others, reaching the finish line first. That's what it's all about. The competition skunked and hanging their heads as you do the victory dance in the end zone—how sweet it is."

I looked off, as if in wistful agreement. Beelzebub can be conned. He is blinded by his need to believe people are corruptible. "I'm just a dirt-gardener with a lot of dogs now," I said with self-pity.

"You made a mistake choosing the other side," he said grandly. "I'm willing to let bygones be bygones."

"But I thought that wasn't your style."

"I'm flexible. Always have been."

"What about Helither?" I asked casually.

His face darkened. "What about him?"

"He's in the picture now. Can you take care of him the way you did Tyre?"

"Tyre," he said with contempt, "a small-timer trying to punch above his weight. He was like one of those planes that go down from metal fatigue. One minute flying fine and the next a hole in the ground. But Helither's a different story. I underestimated him before." He gnawed a fingernail. They were all bitten down to the quick. It looked like behind that big front, insecurity seethed.

"What do you want from me?" I asked.

"Just what I said, keep out of it. Soderberg wins if you stay on the sidelines." He shot a look from under his brows. "I'll make it worth your while. Money, power, women. Or men, if you'd rather. You've got your price. Everyone does."

I pretended to think. "Okay, dump Soderberg and make me president."

He looked pleased and annoyed. He liked it that I was pig enough to ask for the whole pie. Greed was good, but my price was too steep.

"There was a time when I could've agreed just like that," he said with a snap of his fingers. "Kings were poisoned by princes, who were murdered by rivals. Poison or the dagger and, presto, you had the fate of an empire decided. I can't tell you how many times the scenario played itself out. But that kind of simplicity is not possible nowadays. Even I have to work within limits and with the tools available to me. You can't believe how democracy and the media have complicated things for me. Try to ignore public opinion today and see what happens. The most you can hope to do is manipulate it. But I don't have to tell you about that. You've been killing us."

I decided to play to the vengeance thing. "The wizard's got to suffer like I have. That bastard's made my life miserable. And I want suitable compensation for my pain and suffering." I took an Esplendido from a tube and lit up.

"Compensation's no problem. Whatever you want. You want your own oil field? I know one with a guaranteed half-billion barrels begging to be discovered. I can fix it for you. But I owe Zalzathar. He's been loyal through thick and thin. The prize is nearly mine, thanks to him." But betrayal came easy to him. He smiled slowly. "Martyrdom is foreign to those who follow me, but they understand cruel necessity. As a matter of fact, I've been thinking that he might have outlived his usefulness. His style is all wrong for this world."

I blew a ring of smoke. His answering ring came across the table and slowly enveloped mine, as if taking a piece in a board game. "I want him to hear it from my own lips," I said.

"You want to savor the moment. I can understand that."

"After the debate."

His eyes narrowed in suspicion. "Why wait?" Alex was making her way back across the restaurant toward us.

"I guess I'm just sadistic. I want victory to be so close he can taste it before the rug is yanked out from under him."

He could appreciate that, too. The cigar was gripped lightly in his white teeth. "Very well."

"One other thing."

"Yes?"

"This isn't one of those Faustian bargains where you get my soul. Understood?"

"A ridiculous folk tale. One long joke, basically. When I see the opera, I have to laugh. Why would I want your soul? I have more than I can count as it is. Even *my* greed on that score was satisfied long ago."

"In that case, good-bye. I want to finish dinner with my lady friend."

His eyebrows rose in amusement. It was rare that he was told to beat it. "You're dismissing me?"

"That's about the size of it. *Sayonara.*"

He stood and bowed with a smile. By the time Alex reached the table, he had melted into the crowd.

"Sorry I took so long," she said, sitting down. "There was a hysterical woman in the rest room. I tried to help. She'd had the most awful accident. I saw that strange man leaving. What did you two talk about?"

I didn't want her to know she had been sitting at the same table as the Devil. No telling how people will react to that. "The big debate," I said. "What else?"

23

Alex flew back to Stanford the next day. "The department chair wants to talk to me. I think it's my promotion to full professor." It was something she had been working toward for a long time, and she was as bubbly as champagne. The old Bogey would have pointed out that if any promotion was coming, it was thanks to him. I just smiled encouragingly. "I want to get back to the real world," she said. "But if you need me, I'll stay."

Because of all the media and fat cats from both parties in town for the debate, I couldn't take an entire hotel floor. So I settled for the penthouse suite in the Beverly Wilshire Hotel with the bodyguards sitting in the hall outside. That afternoon a call came from the lobby.

"I'm Fred Price of the Secret Service. I'm with Felicity Ingersol's security detail. She'll be arriving in five minutes and wants to see you." My first thought was no way. She had me warehoused in a cut-rate convalescent hospital in Florida and gone off to live it up with her beach-boy lover (he lasted two months) and her Eurotrash pals. Now she was engaged to Soderberg. I guessed she had been assigned to pump me about my intentions. Still, I had loved her at one time and she wasn't all bad. No more than 75 percent. I bet she didn't have a clue who and what she had gotten herself involved with.

"Mr. Ingersol?" the voice on the phone prompted.

"All right, I'll see her."

Six minutes later one of my bodyguards knocked on the door. "Your former wife," he said. The corridor was full of men in dark suits with wires in their ears. As drop-dead gorgeous as ever, Felicity wore a pale green Versace original. She was as vivid against their dark mass as a tropical bird.

"Darling!" She pressed a cool cheek to mine when she walked through the doorway in a cloud of expensive fragrance, trailing a scarf behind her. She reminded me of a star expecting an ovation at her entrance in a Broadway play. "You've been very naughty about returning my calls."

I closed the door and watched as she moved around the suite. She whirled toward me artfully. "How do I look?"

"Beautiful." She never tired of hearing it.

"You're almost gaunt, but it's attractive. You used to be so big."

"You mean fat," I said curtly. "What can I do for you?"

"Don't be surly, darling. We *were* married."

"And the wedding bells are going to ring again. Congratulations."

"Isn't it funny?" She wrinkled her nose in the cute way she did to get around people. "He's such a dorky little man."

"How much is he paying you?"

"You haven't changed. Money's all you think about."

"Well?"

"He told me you asked him. Let's just say it's a nice amount. You won't have to every worry about me nagging you again." She fluttered her long eyelashes. "And you, how have you been? I hope you're feeling better."

"I've had my ups and downs."

"More ups than downs, I hope."

"I haven't done the math yet."

She flounced down on a chair. "It won't be a real marriage, darling. It's just for appearances. Presidents can't be bachelors.

It's an unwritten law, apparently. But there won't be anything physical. That's agreed. In fact, it's all right with Sodie if you and I have an affair. We have to be very discreet, of course. "

"*Sodie?* Is that what you call him?"

She laughed. "He doesn't like it, but I think he's getting used to it." She put on a pouty look. "You do want to have an affair with me, don't you?"

"I'm all fixed up in that department, thanks."

"You have a girlfriend? Really? Who is it?"

"None of your business. Look, if you're smart, you'll drop Sodie before you get in too deep."

"Why do you say that?" Her expression was coy now. "If I didn't know better, I'd say you were jealous."

"He's mixed up with some pretty bad elements."

"At least he's never been in prison. Not everyone these days can make that claim." She laughed.

"I'm serious."

"You're not going to start talking about evil wizards and such things are you, darling? Sodie said you might."

"What if I did?"

"Go ahead, if you really need to. Everyone thinks you're crazy, anyhow."

"Do you?"

She looked at me critically. "You look all right, but there's probably brain damage from the comas. Nothing else can explain the fantastic amount of money you've been spending to stop Sodie. They say it's over a hundred million dollars. The Bogey I married was so tight he squeaked when he walked. You'd stop to pick up a dime off the street."

"What's in it for you?"

"What woman wouldn't want to be First Lady?"

"There's never a minute's privacy in the White House. Everybody's always watching you. You have to make conversation with some of the world's great bores."

"How would that be any different from the people you brought home?"

"You blew off most of those dinners. Or you retired upstairs with a headache. You can't do that in the White House. You have to sit there and take it. Otherwise, there's a diplomatic incident."

"You're not going to do anything more to try to keep Sodie from being elected, are you?" Felicity could change direction on a dime. "All his political consultants and those men who do polls say you're the only one who can stop him now."

"Is that what they sent you to find out? Go back and tell them no, I won't do any more to stop him."

"They didn't send me to find out anything." She pretended to be hurt. "I was worried about you. What made you change your mind?"

"I guess I just wised up."

She gave me a shrewd look. "I know you well enough to know you're not telling me everything."

"I never did."

Her famous temper flared. "You mean those whores you had?"

I didn't feel like defending Bogey. "I'm a new man," I said.

Her anger faded. "I'd almost say you were. It's not just your looks. There's more. It's not unattractive."

"Thanks."

"I said 'not unattractive,' not 'attractive.' There's a difference." She laughed gaily. "My guards are bigger than your guards, and they have badges, too."

"I guess that means you win."

"I admit I like all the excitement. Just driving across town, we have police escorts with sirens. It's so thrilling. When Sodie and I go into a building, they stop people from entering or leaving."

"That won't always give you the kick it does now."

"You always were a spoilsport."

"Speaking of that, how are you and Mr. Dark getting on?"

"See what I mean?" Her expression changed, though. "I don't talk to him very much. I don't like his eyes. They're cold and mean. Do you know him?"

"We've met."

"Sodie listens to him a lot. They're always whispering."

She stayed a few minutes more, but she had got what she came for. She kissed me on the cheek on her way out. "You'll come to the inauguration, won't you? We'll be married after he's sworn in."

I gave her a big phony smile. "Wild horses couldn't keep me away."

"You can even bring your girlfriend," she said archly. One reason I had been avoiding her was I was half afraid of her old magic. It was nice to discover it didn't work anymore. The difference was Alex.

When I closed the door and turned, Helither was sitting in an easy chair. It gave me the usual start.

"Sorry," he said. He was rumpled as usual, looking as if he had just come in from planting corn.

"I saw Satan last night," I said.

"I know. I was there."

"I didn't see you."

"He did. That's why you are still alive. That poor woman. I couldn't do anything about that."

"I made a deal with him." I explained it. I also told him about the bogus record for molesting children to frame Zalzathar. Copies would be handed out to the media the minute Harris dropped the bomb. "Bearing false witness is wrong, right? But it's the only thing I could come up with."

"Sometimes one evil is necessary to prevent a greater evil," Helither admitted. "And it's not as if the wizard is innocent. He's been responsible for many evils." He rumpled his hair and some stayed stuck up. You would take him for a country bump-kin. "Satan's anger will be terrible to see if his plans fail."

"Will he come looking for me?" My stomach began doing funny things.

"There's a good chance," Helither said. "If not right away, later. Vengeance is dear to him."

"You're not going to leave me twisting in the wind alone?"

"Of course not. But he's a wily adversary. He has outwitted us many times before."

"You should have told me that sooner." It was not too late to cancel this whole operation. Getting that resort in some far corner of the world sounded better all the time. And then there was the promised oil field. I could sink into hedonism and let the rest of the world go hang. Helither seemed aware of the way my thoughts were drifting.

"You have to have faith."

"I'd rather have a guarantee, thanks."

"The only guarantee is you'll die one day and go to your reward." He hesitated and with a look of compassion said, "If reward it is."

There it was, the stick that alternated with the carrot, not that I ever saw much carrot. Nobody talked about the old fire-and-brimstone Hell anymore, except barefoot preachers bel-lowing in the backwoods. It was an outmoded concept that embarrassed educated people. But didn't something bad have to happen if you screwed up enough? Wasn't there some ac-counting? What about bloodthirsty tyrants who slaughtered whole populations, or serial killers who tortured and murdered on the retail basis—did they just slip into oblivion when they died? I read in prison that oblivion was the desirable state Bud-dhists call Nirvana. It's what comes after a virtuous life, or maybe many virtuous lives—I'm sketchy on the details. You see my point. Oblivion is reward or punishment, not both. But which is it, and how do you know?

• • • •

The Republican, Wesley Harris, was from Virginia. The Democrat, Barton Thomas, was from Ohio. Both had impressive heads of thick hair. Both were middle height, middle-aged. They had nice voices in the middle range and chopped the air like JFK when they talked. It was hard to tell them apart in other ways, too. Dark, pinstriped suits, red ties, shiny shoes. The political parties had become so alike they turned out nearly identical candidates who said the same things in nearly the same words. At least Soderberg's platitudes were different. They came off sounding fresh. Phony as it was, his molasses accent made him seem less prepackaged. Under the rules of the debate he got to stand on a box behind his lectern so he seemed as tall as the others. Each talked about defense, education, medical care, foreign trade, and a dozen other issues. Nobody uttered a single sentence that had not been subjected to focus-group research. The debate was dull as a result.

Or was until the end, when the candidates got the opportunity to talk about whatever they wanted. Soderberg spoke about how he wanted everyone to have equal opportunity in this great land of ours. Thomas said we had to go boldly into the future. Harris said it was regrettable that Bernie had a close adviser with an extensive record of pedophilia, and would he care to explain?

The camera came in tight on Soderberg's dumbfounded face as he blustered. "I . . . Who do you . . . There's no one . . . "

"I refer to Mr. Dark," Harris said grimly. He held up a sheet of paper. "Here's his rap sheet."

"Rap sheet . . . " Bernie began to sweat. He patted his forehead with a handkerchief. Maye had been right. He wasn't good at ad-libbing.

"Twenty-three arrests," Harris said. "Two convictions."

The NBC camera found Zalzathar in the crowd in the auditorium. Others in Soderberg's entourage had taken a step away from him, as if to distance themselves from his pollution. The wizard was bewildered. His eyes darted around.

"I'd like to see what's in your hand," Bernie said to Harris, beginning to rally. "It's a lie, and I protest this outrageous smear at the last minute . . ."

He fell silent as Harris walked from his lectern toward him. "There you are," he said, handing the sheet to Soderberg. "Copies are being given to the press." Rattled, Bernie began to read it. Cries came from the audience, and the cameras returned to Zalzathar. He was gripping his chest with both hands, eyes wide and mouth opening and closing. He slumped to his knees and fell face forward. There were shouts, and a woman screamed.

"My God," Alex said. "He's had a heart attack." At Helither's suggestion, I had gotten out of L.A. and we were watching the debate on four TV sets at Millwood.

"I guess he won't be available for denials," I said.

Talking heads began to fill the screens to analyze the shocking development. I muted the sets. "Who'd have guessed Bernie would have a pervert giving him advice," I said. "What will the mothers of America think?"

"They won't like it," Alex said. "He's through."

A doctor in the crowd pronounced Zalzathar dead as he lay on the floor. The instant he became a liability, Satan got rid of him. You need a long spoon to sup with the Devil, and Mr. Dark's had suddenly gotten too short. Purvis proved Maye's faith in him hadn't been misplaced by bribing a medical attendant to slip a couple of snapshots of young boys into his wallet on the ride to the morgue. Very cute, very explicit. There was no way Soderberg's people could put a spin on that. He fell 10 percent overnight and kept dropping. Most voters switched to Harris for showing them the filthy corruption at the heart of Bernie's campaign, and he won going away. Bernie finished a badly beaten third.

I telephoned Felicity two weeks later. "I hope you got your money up front."

"I learned a thing or two dealing with you, darling." She was getting ready to fly the Concorde back to Europe. "Sodie's very grumpy. Raging, actually. He's saying very hard things about you. You better be careful."

Clancy told me the civil lawsuit Bernie filed for fraud, defamation, and a bunch of other charges because of my vile conduct in the campaign looks like a leadpipe cinch. The damages a jury can expect to reward him would clean me out of every cent I had, if I hadn't already shipped my money to the shady offshore banks Bogey did business with. There is no way it can be traced. Millwood belongs to the charitable foundation, so he won't get his hooks into that, either. With luck, he might collect the totaled pickup I keep around to remind me how close I came to cashing in. Other than my clothes, it's about the only possession I have in my own name. The election-fraud charges the federal government is drawing up are a more serious matter. Given my past and the flagrance of the violations, Clancy is afraid I might have to serve more time. So be it. If I'm sent to the same prison, it will sort of be like rejoining a contemplative order. Alex has promised to wait. Larry King wanted me on his show, but I said no. *Unsolved Mysteries* is doing a special on Winston Byron's murder. They offered me a chance to clear the air. I turned them down, too. As long as they are in the area, they plan a segment on the strange, fugitive creatures spotted in the forests of the watershed toward the ocean. They are believed responsible for the deer carcasses found from time to time. A ranger who got a close look said they were half-pigs and half-humans. He was put on a medical leave and later said, on second thought, he believed they were homeless people. I doubt they can last long without Zalzathar doing their thinking for them.

I strolled out to the veranda at sunset, followed by the Chihuahua whose body I once inhabited. He goes everywhere I go. He's no Oliver, but I'll get another yellow Lab someday. The kennel dogs are back, bailed out of the pound. Emil works there. I see that he takes his medication every day and, like me, he's a new man. Some might say he's the saner of the two. Rita Rutaway still issues me citations, jerking them from her pad.

Suddenly, Helither was at my side. "Azimbrel-Zafieri is gone from this world for now, off to make mischief someplace else," he said easily. "So I guess I'll go back where I belong."

"It turned out all right," I said.

"Sometimes it does."

I looked toward the coastal mountains. Not a hint of fog. I turned back to thank him, but he was gone. An outline like gold dust seemed to hang where he had been, then it slowly dissolved.

Alex came over later with some ideas for decorating Millwood. She was sorry to have missed the archangel. She still has a lot of questions for him.